REWRITE

REWRITE

A Novel

TEMENUGA TRIFONOVA

I N₁ I O₂ I N₁
CANADA

*Publisher's note: This book is a work of fiction. Names, characters, places and
incidents are either the product of the author's imagination or are used
fictitiously, and any resemblance to actual persons living or dead
is entirely coincidental.*

Library and Archives Canada Cataloguing in Publication

Trifonova, Temenuga, author
Rewrite / Temenuga Trifonova.

ISBN 978–1–926942–74–2 (pbk.)

I. Title.

PS8639.R534R49 2014   C813'.6   C2014–904748–7

Printed and bound in Canada on 100% recycled paper.

Now Or Never Publishing
#313, 1255 Seymour Street
Vancouver, British Columbia
Canada V6B 0H1

nonpublishing.com
Fighting Words.

We acknowledge the support of the Canada Council
for the Arts for our publishing program.

For my mother

Prologue

Bruno had never suffered from short or long term amnesia, unless, that is, he had suffered from amnesia of suffering. Suffering presupposed that one took it seriously. Since Bruno found this presupposition difficult to take seriously his only hope was that he had, at some point, suffered but forgotten about it. Yet even the doubt that he had ever suffered, the feeling that his amnesia of suffering was a well-constructed self-delusion, like everything else in his life, was not enough to make him suffer. Sometimes, when he couldn't bear it any more—but of course he could, otherwise he wouldn't claim he was incapable of suffering—he took a cab to the nearest hospital. The best time to go was around lunchtime when the corridors were alive with bleeding bodies, putrid smells, and creaking wheelchairs. He would wander about, pretending to look for a particular specialist so he could get a general idea of the range of human suffering available that day. He would choose a spot, sit down—ideally, in one of the hospital wheelchairs lined up against the wall—and gorge his eyes on the puss oozing from the open wounds around him. Most people would probably dismiss him as a vulture feeding on other people's pain, but their analogy would be faulty: he got his kicks out of flesh that was still alive. He kept to himself, he didn't talk, and he didn't smile politely at the coquettish blood-splattered nurses passing by. He felt safe and cozy amidst all that malodorous flesh hanging from hospital beds and wheelchairs. The hypnotic sound of intravenous glucose trickling into the varicose veins of the repulsive old man sitting next to him would make him doze off, just as he used to do on the school bus when he was a kid. No one asked him what he was doing there. Why should they? They were busy suffering. They simply assumed he was one of them.

Occasionally, they would glance at him with that familiar look of disinterested curiosity: 'I wonder what he's got.'

One day one of them—an old woman with a dilated stomach—looked at him with something reminiscent of sympathy. He felt a hot flush come over him, as though he were poised on the threshold of the most incredible orgasm. It was the familiar shame of the impostor, but it didn't make him look away in embarrassment. Just the opposite: he felt a perverse sort of satisfaction in feeling exposed by her unsolicited look. He looked back straight into her eyes: 'Yes, that's me. The great pretender!' He hovered in that moment of bliss, enveloped in the warm cocoon of his absolute self-hatred, twisting and turning inside it, thoroughly enjoying the self-laceration normally associated with tragic Dostoevsky characters.

Then he crashed. As the woman looked away from him, returning to her own pain, quietly moaning and shaking, he realized how lucky she was, how privileged they all were. The woman pressing her dilated stomach with both hands while secretly peeing under her seat, the pimpled teenager awkwardly trying to hide her mangled wrists behind her back, the half-arthritic-half-asthmatic old man: they each had their own—*real*—pain, which no one could take away from them, and they sat around it like a little campfire, warming themselves up, their twisted faces aglow in its painful but familiar light. They certainly didn't want to share their pain with anyone, even though that would have made it more bearable, or precisely because of that.

He felt a sudden urge to spit in the old woman's face. He imagined his saliva running down her face, wrapping it up like a translucent membrane. He saw her old face cracking up, her mouth opening wide, her cavity-ridden yellow teeth pointing at him. He saw her get up in the morning, walk unsteadily to the kitchen, and boil some water in her rusty kettle to clean her teeth prosthesis from all the slime her sedated, pornographic dreams had secreted overnight. She stumbles into her undergarments, colorless after years of being hand-washed with a cheap soap. She walks down the street, with an empty look on her miniature face, holes running down her wrinkled beige tights. There she is now, sitting across from him, like an obedient little sheep, staring at the door to the doctor's office with a vague anticipation in her empty eyes. Her life is a series of errands she invents for herself every morning. What else would she do if she didn't have that rotten stomach of hers to think about? Her reason for living is to do whatever is necessary to simply continue living. She has devoted herself to the task with all the strength she has left in her decomposing body. The more her body gives up on her, the more reason she has to go on. To try to talk to her would be like talking to a Christian: no matter how convincing you may sound when you try to make them face the pathetic pyramid of self-justifications propping up their faith, they still look at you with those bovine eyes and keep reassuring you that they are going to pray for you, yes they will, as if *you* are the one living a life of self-delusion and despair.

Bruno threw the blanket aside and sat up in bed, pressing his stomach with both hands. He felt bloated. The feeling was not limited to his stomach but evenly distributed throughout his body. Even his eyeballs were bloated. He walked his fingers tentatively from his upper to his lower abdomen, his facial muscles ready to contract in response to the pain. There was no pain. The dream he had that night floated into his free-of-pain consciousness. In the dream he is walking around his apartment. It feels like a space station but in fact it is a room in a dingy motel with no room service. He is worried because he can't remember when his return flight departs. He opens his fridge: there is someone else's food inside. Suddenly he feels lost. Why? Did he suddenly forget who he was just because someone replaced a few pieces of stinky cheese with pork chops and egg salad? Had the Italian salami and the slice of Roquefort now missing from the fridge provided the exact coordinates of his existence so far, keeping him grounded?

In *The Philosophy of Sleep* (1830)[1] the Scottish physician and writer Robert Macnish insists on a strong analogy between insanity and dreaming. "A dream may be considered as a transient paroxysm of delirium and delirium as a permanent dream," he writes. "In health we rarely dream. In disease, especially of the brain, liver or stomach, dreams are both common and of a very distressing kind. Dreams are uniformly resuscitation or re-embodiment of thoughts which have formerly, in some shape or other, occupied the mind." Of course, it all made perfect sense, Bruno reasoned. The empty fridge was a reference to *her* leaving him. Or perhaps it was just a reminder that he had to go grocery shopping.

The short walk to the kitchen proved an unprecedented ordeal: the hallway seemed to have shrunk overnight and the floor under his bare feet felt rubbery. A brisk shower would help him get rid of this oppressive feeling. The cold water threw his body into a shock and for a minute he felt light, almost transparent. As soon as he got out of the shower, however, the feeling returned. He instinctively opened his mouth, hoping to release the extra air filling his guts; instead, he felt more air infiltrating his insides and stretching them in all directions. This is what an inflatable doll must feel like when they first blow it up and all the air rushes through its previously wrinkled, neatly folded body. Good God, it's come to this: one minute you are fine, occasionally over-identifying with fictional characters, but still within the accepted norms, and before you know it you are imagining what inflatable dolls 'feel like' or writing Facebook messages to garden gnomes. Fuck. Where did *they* come from? They had never been part of his frame of reference yet suddenly they were popping up in his stream of consciousness like . . . garden gnomes.

Standing barefoot on the cold kitchen floor, stirring his yogurt, he found himself observing the energetic movement of his right hand with a curious detachment, surprised to see it perform the repetitive movement with such inexplicable determination, as if driven by a will of its own. He was so wrapped up in watching his hand's performance that he was surprised to see, out of the corner of his eye, something else suddenly move. It was his left hand, which he must have raised, he now reasoned, to put the piece of bread in the toaster.

Yes, he had reasoned correctly. Moving away from the toaster his left hand picked up the bowl of yogurt while the right one continued to perform the same circular movement he had observed previously. The kettle's insistent whistle pierced the air, shaking him out of the stupor he had fallen into in the course of observing his hands' breakfast ritual. The hot coffee brought tears into his eyes. He stared at the food through his tears while his stomach expanded further and his limbs grew heavier. His head was drooping lower and lower. An overfamiliar image of melting human heads and clocks propped up by long sticks came into gradual focus at the back of his mind. He would have to consider getting a stick like that if his head continued to droop further. And if the present overwhelming feeling of heaviness spreading throughout his body was any indication he might have to consider getting several sticks to prop up the parts where the muscles beneath his hanging flesh proved most unresponsive. He lifted his right arm to check the degree to which the flesh above the elbow had gotten loose, but he had forgotten that his right hand was still holding the bowl of yogurt, which now formed an unpleasant off-white puddle on the floor.

Suddenly, a wave of determination surged through his loose flesh, tightening every muscle on its way. He stood up, picked up the plastic garbage can and with one decisive movement swept his breakfast into it. He proceeded to evacuate methodically every food item he found in the fridge. Feeling slightly more in control—of what, he wondered—he resolved to think of this as the beginning of a cleansing procedure that was long overdue. Yes, it was time to scrape up all the extra fat from his daily routine, reduce the clutter in his mind. Deflate. Tighten. Tune up.

On the bus to the university he sat up straight, trying not to look at the two dead whitish fish in his lap. He supposed the other passengers would insist they were his hands. *His* hands. His *hands*. His hands *were*. What people refer to as 'things'—e.g. 'fire' or 'earth' or 'hands'—are not substances but only qualities perpetually recurring in the cycle of becoming without ever attaining being: therefore, using the verb "to be" to refer to them is entirely inappropriate. The intelligible is that which is *eternal*; the sensible is that which *comes to be*. The *real* does not *become* real, and that which is always *becoming* is *not real*. On his left was sitting a young man in an expensive suit, calculating something on a paper napkin, entering the result in the corresponding Excel table slot, growing older. He looked grounded. Excel tables are known to have that effect on people. Ok, on *some* people. Now and then Excel man mumbled something to himself. *67.4%. 46.9%. 21%.* What magical number would he say next, Bruno wondered, staring at the electric poles running past the dirty window. The other passengers were engaged in aggressively animated conversations in complete disregard for Bruno's (granted, minor) ontological panic attack. There was nothing unfamiliar about their unintelligible exchanges, the sort of meaningless morning chatter he usually managed to ignore with almost no mental effort on his part. This morning, however, there was something crudely real about their voices. The warm, plump bodies pressing against his, the incessant muttering, the irritating laughter over nothing in particular, formed a smothering cocoon from which he tried to escape—unsuccessfully—by pretending to assume an anthropological stance and studying the passengers' gestures and facial expressions as though he were studying an African tribe on the verge of extinction. His cultural-anthropologist persona was overwhelmed by the seemingly inexhaustible variety of body language his 'subjects' were using to communicate the most banal feelings and thoughts.

He was struck by the devastating inefficiency of all this posturing and pontificating: a single barely formulated, trivial thought was propped up by an entire series of minute grimaces, flicks of the hand or rolling of the eyes, which were then repeated over and over again, with the order now scrambled, despite the fact that the particular insignificant thought being expressed had already been made perfectly clear and did not require any further elaboration. As he tried in vain to lift himself above the surrounding cacophony of flesh Bruno became acutely aware that his own body, no less plump and ripe, occupied a particular part of the uncomfortable bus seat, just as his face, despite its seemingly neutral expression, played a (silent) part in the banal series of exchanges around him.

I

The university courtyard was empty: empty of students (the Fall term was just ending) but still full of the spirit of learnedness. The spirit of learnedness depended on a variety of factors, Bruno had discovered, not least of which was the careful distribution of middle-sized squirrels on college lawns. Although at first glance squirrels seemed to detract from the spirit of learnedness, in reality they unobtrusively added to it: it was in this *calculated unobtrusiveness* that the true spirit of learnedness was to be found. When one saw so many squirrels scurrying between century old stone buildings and archways, you could not doubt that a whole lot of learning was taking place behind the thick, forbidding walls. The spirit of learnedness increased exponentially if each squirrel on the freshly cut lawn happened to be matched, serendipitously of course, by a heinous gargoyle on a conspicuous corner of a weathered stone building or archway.

Up in his office he checked his eyes in the small mirror on the wall. Under the puffy eyelids his eyeballs were plump and colorless, like a pair of over-ripe lychees. In the back of his desk drawer he found a box of pain-relievers. He popped two, three, ok . . . four in his mouth. He had no recollection of what he did the rest of the day. In a fit of academic despair, brought about by his reluctant perusal of an unfortunate batch of term papers, he had been foolish enough to schedule mandatory end-of-term conferences with all students enrolled in his upper-level undergraduate course *Fin-de siècle Paris: A Cultural and Social History*. Throughout the rest of the day students came and went, fiddled apathetically with their essays, yawned in response to his critical comments, some cried, others took it all in stride. His last appointment was at 6PM. Sophie Calles. He took out her essay from the filing cabinet and stared at his comments in the margins:

"Missing thesis statement!" "Acknowledge your sources!" "Redundant!" "Awkward!" "What would Foucault say about this?!" There was a knock on the door. Squeezing the pen between his fingers he said stoically:

"Come in."

The bare willow trees outside the window swayed in the wind. Was it winter already? The tiny hands of the clock on the table in front of him moved forward relentlessly. Sophie Calles, a scrawny girl with a big mouth, was staring at one of his comments: "Awkward and unnecessary!" Bruno tapped the paper with his red pen and underlined his comment several times, as if he really meant it to be taken seriously. She reached for a paper tissue. The mascara running down her cheeks made her look like a heroin chic model from a women's fashion magazine. Maybe *Elle. She* used to buy them religiously. He felt a sudden urge to be cruel to Sophie, instantly resented himself for feeling this way, and then felt an even stronger resentment towards her for provoking such urges in him and for making him resent himself for them.

"I see you're taking this class for the second time," he said with just the right amount of indifference.

"Third," Sophie corrected him, blushing.

He looked up at her and was suddenly overwhelmed by the thought that one day she would die. This happened to him often. He would look at a colleague sitting across from him during a department meeting, or at the cashier in the drugstore scanning his rolls of toilet paper, and he would see them lying, dressed up in their best clothes, inside a beautifully-crafted coffin. Or he would imagine these mundane moments of their lives as snapshots that would later appear in somebody's photo album and, eventually, on a flea market table in another city, mixed in with other anonymous snapshots of people both dead and alive. He was not sad that this or that person was as good as dead (the only thing keeping them alive was time, which was also the thing that would kill them). He was simply puzzled by his morbid obsession with other people's death.

Sophie kept folding and unfolding her soiled paper tissue. Bruno observed her nervous movements with overstated detachment that seemed to embarrass her even more. Suddenly everything he was supposed to tell her about her term paper vanished from his mind. The thought of saying another word struck him as not merely superfluous but repulsive. He saw himself lying at the bottom of a gigantic tank full of verbiage, densely packed. He tried to move his legs and arms but they, too, were made of verbiage. 6:20PM.

Ten minutes to go.

He stood up, picked up his coat in slow motion and glided, past the look of incomprehension in her eyes, towards the mahogany door that was meant to preserve the confidentiality of professor-student conferences. The electric poles in the street cast deep shadows in the hallway, cutting the wall-to-wall carpet into straight lines. A perfect chiaroscuro night. He stood in front of the Faculty of Fine Arts building, not quite sure what to do with himself. A single ray of light shot through the impending darkness and was reflected back from a shiny metal plaque on the front of the building. There was something familiar about the letters engraved on the plaque. He formed the corresponding sounds with his lips: "Professor Bruno Leblon." He repeated the combination of letters and sounds several times. These engraved signs were supposed to refer to him in some unfathomable way. Bruno Leblon. Bruno Leblon. Leblon . . .

"Excuse me."

A graduate student in a tight leather jacket and hipster skinny jeans casually rolled up to reveal a pair of checkered socks.

"Is the History Department in this building?" he asked. "I'm looking for Professor Leblon's office."

Bruno heard a voice that sounded vaguely familiar. He could only assume it was his own.

"Sorry, I don't know him," the voice said.

The shop windows downtown had been decorated for Christmas since October. Vulgarly cute dwarfs, dolls and gnomes grinned at him from behind fake plastic trees covered with dazzling fake snow while a meticulously designed toy train moved relentlessly up and down a loop, past tiny plastic fir trees covered with artificial snow, causing the children glued to the shop windows to burst out in hysterical laughter. Something big and white gleamed seductively from the opposite side of the street. He crossed the street and approached it tentatively, afraid it would turn out to be some kind of optical illusion. It was not. It was an empty store. The walls were freshly painted in a soothing, non-descript color. He let his eyes wander freely from one end of the store to the other, up and down the walls. Nothing obstructed his view. Nothing held his attention.

His phone buzzed: a new message from *her*. The movers were coming tomorrow afternoon to pick up her furniture and all her boxes. There was no need for him to be there: she still had her apartment key. If he couldn't help being there, however, she would appreciate it if he told her in advance so that she didn't bother coming. It was better this way. Bruno supposed she was right. He had spent seven, no, eight years supposing that.

He wondered if her decision to leave him had something to do with a play he had written for an experimental theatre group during one of the numerous breaks he took from the drudgery of academic writing, breaks that were becoming harder and harder to justify with his tenure review coming up. He had changed the names, of course. He should have known this would make her even more suspicious.

He called the play *The Poetics of Conflict*.

Francois and Sarah are in the living room of their beautiful Paris apartment. Francois is surfing the net. Sarah is staring out the window.
Sarah: I love living in Paris.
Francois: I do too.
Sarah: I love this flat.
Francois: Yes, isn't it great?
Sarah: I love being here with you.
Francois: And I love being here with you.
Beat.
Sarah: This can't go on any more.
Francois: I agree.
Beat.

Sarah: Something's missing.

Francois: I feel it too.

Sarah: We don't fit in. If this goes on we'll lose all credibility as a couple.

Francois: An intercultural couple living in a global city: you'd think there would be multiple opportunities for misunderstanding, intercultural conflict, and just good old relationship woes. Instead, it's been smooth sailing all along.

Sarah: How do others do it? What do they have that we don't?

Francois: I wish I could say I can't bear it any longer. I mean—that would be something.

Sarah: Yes, especially if I disagreed with you and insisted that I could, and would, bear it.

Francois: Then we would have something to build on!

Sarah: Yes: a bit of resentment and restlessness, with a healthy dose of irritation on the side. We could work with that! We could blow it out of proportion! Work it up into a real conflict!

Francois: But I can't say that I can't bear it any longer. I couldn't care less if I could or could not bear it.

Sarah: Same here.

Francois: So we agree, once again.

Sarah: It's a lost cause.

Beat.

Francois starts typing.

Sarah: What are you doing?

Francois: Googling "conflict."

Sarah leans over and reads the dictionary definition out loud: "Conflict is an inherent incompatibility between the objectives of two or more forces."

Francois: Let's break it down before we try it out. I can already identify one problem that might preclude us from entering into a proper conflict.

Sarah: What's that?

Francois: You don't have any objectives of your own.

Sarah: What's that supposed to mean?

Francois: You get distracted easily. Finding an objective is an objective in itself. If you are already distracted when you already have an objective, can you imagine how much worse you would be when your objective is to find an objective?

Sarah: Fine. I have a short attention span. On the bright side, we've just identified at least one of our conflicting objectives: my objective is to find an objective. What would be yours then?

Francois: Mine should be opposed to yours. I suppose then my objective should be to prevent you from finding an objective.

Sarah: Now we're getting somewhere!

Francois (continues reading the Wikipedia definition out loud): "Conflict creates tension and interest by adding doubt as to the outcome." In other words, it shouldn't be obvious that you *will* find an objective or that I *will* prevent you from finding one.

Sarah: No worries! Given your utter lack of trust in me I'm already pretty skeptical that I *will* find an objective.

Francois: No, no, we can't afford any doubts: you should firmly believe in your objective to find an objective. You should really *want* to find an objective, because wanting to find an objective *is* your objective.

Sarah: So what you are saying is that I should really want to want something.

Francois: Correct. Now you only need to define what it is that you want to want so badly.

Sarah: How about: 'I really want to want to continue this conversation.'

Francois (taken aback): Why *wouldn't* you want to continue it?

Sarah: Perhaps because I know that, as always, you have your own narrowminded idea of what conflict is and you'll do anything to impose your idea of conflict on me. I want to want to continue talking about conflict but

I am conflicted about discussing conflict exclusively on your terms.

Francois: That's wonderful!

Sarah: What is?

Francois: You just discovered, without even meaning to, your own internal conflict: you are internally conflicted about discussing conflict exclusively on my terms.

Sarah: What's *your* internal conflict then?

Francois: How about this: I am internally conflicted because I am aware of my tendency to be tyrannical when it comes to establishing the terms of a conversation and I would like to be less so, but at the same time I know that if I relinquish even a tiny bit of my tyrannical power I risk losing all my power over you.

Sarah: Is this because you think that if I hold the erotic power in our relationship you must at least keep the linguistic power?

Francois: No, look here, it's a lot simpler. I am afraid to relinquish my linguistic power for the simple reason that in order to exercise it I need an interlocutor: you. I need you to resent me for always setting the terms of our conversations in the safety of meta-discourse, where I have full executive authority simply by virtue of the fact that I am a native French speaker and, as such, I am better at playing games of distraction. I can distract you from whatever real conflicts we might have by moving the whole conversation to a higher, philosophical ground, whose rarified air I am accustomed to breathing as an academic. Instead of working through a specific conflict I can seduce you into an exhausting academic discussion of the *nature* of conflict, the etymology of the word, its application in various media, et cetera, until you've spent all of your energy and have none left for a real conflict.

Sarah: You've always considered me intellectually inferior, as you do all non-academics, so I am not surprised that you simply assume I am unaware of your strategies of distraction. What you've failed to take into consideration, however, is that a philosophical conversation about the *nature* of conflict is a valid, *real* conflict in its own right. I might very well disagree with you on any point you make about the *nature* of conflict and my disagreement will inevitably be indicative of the other, personal—not purely philosophical or linguistic—disagreements underlying our relationship. I might even disagree on what *type* of conflict we should use to spice up our relationship. Knowing what a snob you can be, you'll probably suggest an internal conflict because you consider external conflicts too 'literal' or 'obvious' and, therefore, inferior to internal ones.

Francois: This is all very promising! The more you talk, the more internal conflicts you reveal. It seems our cultural, linguistic and educational differences have taken a deep root in your subconscious, producing a rich, promising harvest of mini-internal conflicts, and making your otherwise flat, one-dimensional character multi-dimensional. No worries, though. Not all of your internal conflicts need to be resolved. In fact, I would suggest that we don't resolve any of them: I've always been a fan of ambiguous endings. Frankly, obvious conflict resolution is vulgar. Yes, I am not ashamed to admit that I am a snob when it comes to narrative structure.

Sarah: I was hoping you would resist my attempts to pin you down as an arrogant son of a bitch, but you seem to take pride in it. This, however, is consistent with your character so I cannot really object to it.

Francois: Fine. I'll compromise. Let's briefly consider other options before choosing *internal* conflict—man against himself—as the most interesting one. Let's see. We've got man against man, man against nature, man against society, man against machine, man against fate, man against the supernatural, and man against god.

Sarah: Man against man—or, should I say, man against woman—sounds promising.

Francois: Mind you, this type of external conflict can be developed either as a direct opposition or as a more subtle conflict between our desires. Do you have a preference?

Sarah: If we are trying to spice up our relationship I think the quickest and most reliable way to do it is through a direct opposition. It's like make up sex: I am told (though I've never experienced it myself) people often use it with the same goal in mind. In fact, direct opposition almost inevitably leads to make up sex, so if we choose this option we would be doubling our points in terms of the audience's affective response. Conflict is sexier when you can see some skin.

She begins unbuttoning her shirt.

Francois: Been a while?

She stares at him coldly and buttons up her shirt.

Francois: If you ask me, "man against society" is a much more interesting type of conflict.

Sarah: What does society got to do with it? This is about me and you, not about some man-made institution we are supposedly in conflict with.

Francois: You are wrong, my dear. What we are really trying to do here is challenge two implicit social assumptions: 1) that a relationship without conflict is necessarily a bad relationship, and 2) that an intercultural relationship is inevitably predicated on conflict—i.e. 'cultural differences'—whereas a culturally homogenous one is somehow free of conflict.

Sarah: I have to give it to you: only you can make a relationship drama sound so un-dramatic. However, I must still insist that we need something more exciting. How about "man against nature"?

Francois: And what force of nature could we possibly face here, in this city of brick and grey skies?

Sarah: Fine. Let's do the one you like, "man against self." (She reads from the Wikipedia page.) "An internal conflict is one in which the titular character deals with his own neuroses and self-doubts."

Francois: Are you ok with being the antagonist? You seem to fit the role perfectly seeing as how antagonists are incapable of doubting themselves and equally incapable of suffering any neuroses because they lack the full psychological complexity of neurotic types like me.

Sarah: That's fine by me. I am worried about this requirement though: "the hero's struggle must be ennobling."

Francois: I see: you cannot imagine me being ennobled.

Sarah: No, because that would presuppose that you had some integrity or nobility in the first place.

Francois puts away his laptop and picks up a book lying on the couch next to him.

Sarah: What's this?

Francois: Aristotle's *Poetics*.

Beat.

Francois: You know, the basic principles of creating conflict are all borrowed from the *Poetics*.

Sarah: Is that so?

Beat.

Francois: What if we tried to apply Aristotle's principles to our situation?

Sarah: Use Aristotle to spice up our relationship with conflict? I suppose we could try.

Francois: How about I read out loud some of the basic principles and we try to structure our conversation around them?

Sarah: Let's put theory into practice!

Francois: Exactly. (He leafs through the book.) Let's see. Oh, keep in mind that even though he is talking about 'Tragedy,' what he says applies to drama. (He chooses an excerpt and reads it out loud.) "Character determines men's qualities, but it is by their actions that they are happy or the reverse. Dramatic action, therefore, is not with a view to the representation of character: character comes in as subsidiary to the actions."

Sarah: This should be easy to apply.

Francois: How so?

Sarah: Well, you've always lacked character so there is no need to worry about making your character subservient to the action. It already is.

Francois: I want to disagree with you but that would be completely out of character, seeing as my character is not to have one. I can't afford to veer off from my usual spinelessness: Aristotle demands that characters stay consistent.

Sarah: If it's any consolation, he says that characters don't have any essential qualities: it is only by virtue of their actions that they reveal their character. In other words, you are not spineless by nature. It is only by virtue of your spineless actions that your spinelessness is revealed. If you act in a non-spineless way—

Francois slaps Sarah on the face.

Francois: Like this?

Sarah is too surprised to react. She just sits there, holding her hand up to her cheek.

Francois (rubs his hands in satisfaction): I think I just complicated my character.

Sarah: How does it feel?

Francois stands up, walks back and forth, stretches his arms and jumps up and down a few times.

Francois: Feels great. Like something I've wanted to do for a long time.

Sarah: I want to try it too.

She motions to slap him but he steps back.

Francois: You can't copy my actions. Your actions should reveal a different character than mine.

Sarah picks up a pillow, plays with it for a while, not sure what to do, then throws it across the room. Unsatisfied, she picks up another object and throws it across the room. Another one. And another one. She is trying to work herself up into a proper fit of anger but cannot. Francois stands aside, observing her performance calmly, as though he were a judge at an audition.

Sarah: How does it look?

Francois: Your heart is not in it.

He walks up to her and turns one of his cheeks towards her.

Francois: Try this.

Sarah slaps him.

Francois: Feel better?

Sarah: Not sure.

She slaps him again.

Sarah: Almost there.

She motions to slap him again. He stops her.

Francois: Are you sure this next one is not going to be superfluous?

Sarah: I won't know until I actually do it.

She slaps him. Then she slaps him again.

Francois: What was the last one for?

Sarah: Sorry. I was trying to buy time to seriously consider the necessity of the third slap but I thought it would be awkward just to stand here, not doing anything, so I slapped you. It's an in-between slap. It doesn't count.

Francois: Of course it counts! Technically that was four slaps, not three. But, more importantly, your 'in-between slap' was not motivated. It did not reveal (he reads from the *Poetics*) "a moral purpose" and it was too much of an "irrational action," which goes against Aristotelian principles.

Sarah snatches the book from his hands and reads out loud:

Sarah: "Character is that which reveals moral purpose, showing what kinds of things a man chooses or avoids. Speeches which do not make this manifest, or in which the speaker does not choose or avoid anything whatever, are not expressive of character." And what, I wonder, was the moral purpose behind your criticism? Wait! Let me guess! Your 'criticism' merely showed that you are a stickler for the rules. You refuse to leave any room for improvisation.

Francois: Improvise as much as you want, my dear, but please make sure your actions have a purpose.

Sarah: Fine. Can you guess the purpose of this one?

She gives him the finger.

Francois: I think you are on to something here. I sense some animosity and sarcasm. A promising mix!

Sarah: I can't say the same about you. Your speeches have been falling flat from the beginning. I certainly wouldn't say they've been "expressive of character."

Francois: Perhaps my reluctance to slap you around is indicative of my mellow character, which occupies a higher moral ground.

Sarah considers this briefly.

Sarah: I can't recall a single instance of you occupying a higher moral ground.

Francois: It's been difficult to occupy a higher moral ground seeing as you have a tendency to pre-occupy even the tiniest moral hills in view. Anyhow, this is irrelevant because (he reads out loud from the *Poetics*) "it is not the function of the poet to relate what *has* happened, but what *may* happen—what is possible according to the law of probability or necessity."

Sarah: Let me get this straight. You think that even though you've never occupied a higher moral ground, it is probable—even necessary—that you will in the future?

Francois: Didn't we agree to do everything possible to introduce conflict in our relationship? If I have to occupy a higher moral ground to fulfill Aristotle's probability and necessity requirement I'm willing to do it.

The phone rings. Sarah motions to answer it.

Francois: Don't answer it.

Sarah: Why not?

Francois: Because we don't yet know how a phone call would fit into the story, plus it will definitely make this scene episodic and you know what Aristotle says about episodic narratives (he reads out loud): "Of all plots and actions the episodic are the worst. I call a plot 'episodic' in which the episodes succeed one another without probable or necessary sequence."

Sarah: We are sitting in our living room. The phone ringing is a probable event in this context. In fact, it's one of the most probable events in *any* context.

Francois: But how can we be sure that the phone ringing would logically succeed the previous episode—our discussion of a higher moral ground—thereby creating a sense of necessity?

Sarah: If you had let me answer it we would have found out how necessary it was.

The phone rings again. Sarah answers it right away.

Sarah: The Hilton? Room 219. Got it.

Sarah hangs up. She looks relieved.

Sarah: No need to worry. I can assure you the phone ringing and the preceding discussion about which one of us occupies a higher moral ground are two events linked by a strong sense of necessity or causality.

Francois: Who was it?

Sarah: Chloe. She's been waiting for you since 4PM at the Hilton. You are two hours late. You should have finished having sex with her an hour ago.

Francois: Brilliant! We couldn't have hoped for a more logical sequence of events. We just have to make sure that whatever happens next is also causally linked to the phone conversation.

Sarah: Perhaps I can go to the other room, you know, give you a chance to call her back to reschedule the sexual intercourse?

Francois checks the *Poetics*.

Francois: That's a grand idea! We can kill two birds with one stone: not only would this be causally linked to what just happened, but it would fulfill another requirement (he reads out loud): "Events should inspire fear or pity. Such an effect is best produced when the events come on us by surprise; and the effect is heightened when, at the same time, they follow as cause and effect. The tragic wonder will then be greater than if they happened of themselves or by accident; for even coincidences are most striking when they have an air of design." Calling Chloe back would prompt anyone to feel pity for you and resentment towards me for betraying you.

Sarah: Too bad the phone rang by accident. The effect would have been heightened if it hadn't been just a coincidence.

Beat.

Sarah: Was it just a coincidence? Or did you arrange for her to call?

Francois: Don't be absurd. Why would I ask my mistress to call you?

Francois goes back to reading the *Poetics*.

Francois: Unless . . .

He reads a passage to himself and appears satisfied.

Francois: Unless I wanted to turn a Simple plot into a Complex one (he reads out loud): "A Complex plot is one in which the change is accompanied by a Reversal of the Situation, or by Recognition, or by both."

Sarah: I'm not following.

Francois: What if Chloe was not my mistress but yours? What if I had found out about you and her and I knew that you were supposed to meet her at the Hilton today but I deliberately kept you here to make you late for your tryst with her? What if I was waiting for her to call you? What if I wanted to test you and see how you would deal with the situation? Would you feel trapped and confess to your indiscretion or would you keep your cool and try to deflect any doubts I might have about you by blaming *me* for cheating on you?

Sarah: Read me the definition again.

Francois: "Reversal of the Situation is a change by which the action veers round to its opposite, subject always to our rule of probability or necessity."

Sarah takes the book from him.

Sarah: Not bad. Not bad at all. It's a shame the Reversal of the Situation is not combined with Recognition (she reads out loud): "a change from ignorance to knowledge, producing love or hate between the persons." This combination is unbeatable. Unfortunately, in your version of the story your movement from ignorance to knowledge—the knowledge that Chloe and I are lovers—does not coincide with the Reversal of the Situation, because you already knew about us *before* the phone call.

Francois: Can't win them all, can you?

Sarah: No need to give up just yet. Even though Recognition does not coincide with Reversal of the Situation, we can still count on the effects produced by it, especially fear, since there is no way of knowing what you are capable of once you realize I've been cheating on you. There is fear for what you might do to me.

Francois: What about pity? Is there absolutely no pity for me?

Sarah: Can't win them all, can you?

Francois takes the book from her.

Francois: Anyway, I think we're safe as long as we have ourselves a Scene of Suffering (reads out loud): "a destructive or painful action, such as death on the stage, bodily agony, wounds, and the like." Do we still have that power drill in the basement?

Sarah: Yes.

Francois: We're good then. We could even have several Scenes of Suffering, just to be on the safe side.

Sarah takes the book from him.

Sarah: The more pressing issue now is figuring out which one of us is actually going to experience this Reversal of Fortune. "The change of fortune presented must not be the spectacle of a virtuous man brought from prosperity to adversity: for this moves neither pity nor fear; it merely shocks us. Nor, again, that of a bad man passing from adversity to prosperity: this neither satisfies the moral sense nor calls forth pity or fear.

Nor, again, should the downfall of the utter villain be exhibited. There remains, then, the character between these two extremes—that of a person who is not eminently good and just, yet whose misfortune is brought about not by vice or depravity, but by some error or frailty."

Francois: I should think your inherent vice and depravity automatically disqualifies you from consideration.

Sarah: Since you are, once again, occupying the higher moral ground, claiming to be eminently good and just, you are also disqualified.

Francois: Logically speaking, this leaves only one option: Chloe must experience the Reversal of Fortune.

Sarah: She is neither eminently good and just, nor inherently depraved. She is perfectly positioned to experience the Reversal of Fortune, with Recognition on the side, when she finds out that her husband (she looks at Francois significantly) was having an affair with her best friend.

Francois takes the book from her.

Francois: Fuck! It says here: "The law of necessity and probability demands that the unraveling of the plot, no less than the complication, must arise out of the plot itself. It must not be brought about by Deus ex Machina." Isn't making Chloe the victim an example of Deus ex Machina?

Beat.

Sarah (reluctant): I forgot about that one.

Sarah takes the book from him.

Sarah: According to this, "every tragedy falls into two parts: Complication and Unraveling. Complication includes everything that extends from the beginning of the action to the part, which marks the turning point to good or bad fortune. The Unraveling is that which extends from the beginning of the change to the end." What if Chloe's discovery of her husband's marital indiscretion is only the Complication, followed by her decision to take revenge on her husband by having an affair with his mistress? That would then be the Unraveling.

Francois: Not bad.

Sarah (blushes): Thanks!

Francois: Though we would still have to evaluate whether Chloe finding out about her husband and her best friend is a probable impossibility or an improbable possibility. "The poet should prefer probable impossibilities to improbable possibilities. Everything irrational should be left out."

Sarah: In that case, we would have to leave out Chloe completely.

Francois: She does seem to act irrationally most of the time, doesn't she?

Sarah: I suppose before we evaluate the probability of Chloe finding out about your indiscretion, we should first evaluate the probability of you having an affair with me, as well as the probability of me having an affair with you.

Francois: Would you please stand up and walk around a bit.

Sarah stands up and walks from one corner of the room to the other. She sways her hips demonstratively and in general does everything she can to appear desirable.

Francois: I'll write down your score. You do the same.

He writes it down, then stands up and walks around the room. Sarah writes down her score.

Francois: What did I get?

Sarah: Let's do it together.

They raise their scorecards at the same time. They both gave each other a 10.

Sarah: So would you say it's a probable impossibility?

Francois: No.

Sarah: No?

Francois: I would say it's both probable and possible.

Sarah: I would agree.

Francois: So we agree once again. Has everything been
in vain?

Sarah: Unless we disagree to agree.

Francois: I think we can build on that.

The phone rings. They stare at it. It keeps ringing.

THE END.

2

For some reason *she* had taken the play to be autobiographical, though she never came out and said it. Instead, she had criticized him for his "flippant" treatment of romantic relationships, a sign of his seemingly incurable skepticism about human relationships, and his stereotypical views of women, American women in particular. What she found particularly unsatisfactory, she had told him, was that the nature of Francois's relationship to Sarah was never made clear, just as Bruno had never made clear *his* relationship to *her*. What on earth did she mean? He was married to her, he reminded her. Not for that much longer, she informed him. When he tried to explain to her the roots of his skepticism, she wanted to know whether the very fact that the way things *were* differed from the way *he thought they were*, or the way *he wanted them to be*, was not sufficient evidence that the world was not just in his mind. He demanded that she define her terms, 'evidence' and 'skepticism' in particular, because, he explained, he was skeptical there was evidence that they understood the terms in the same way.

They met during his last year of graduate studies in San Diego, right around the time when he became aware of a strong correlation between the climate in a given place and the sensitivity and emotional maturity of those inhabiting it. He was convinced that if one were to conduct a comparative study of people living in parts of the world with four well defined seasons and people living in parts of the world with very slight variations in temperature, one would find the emotional experiences of the former to be more varied (covering a wider range of feelings but also the feelings themselves being more nuanced) than those of the latter. Certain feelings were literally missing from the So Cal emotional continuum: for example, while he was living in San

Diego he found it almost impossible to experience melancholy, anger, or despair (not counting his despair over his inability to experience despair). The pleasant California weather dulled the senses, submerging everything into a kind of perceptual fogginess. Nothing stood out. Precisely because everything was so bright and colorful it remained abstract: all he saw were silhouettes, outlines, and surfaces. Everything—himself included—was part of a fat, anonymous, perennially sunny BLAH, a pretty accurate description of their romantic relationship as well, at least before she began to catch up to his "Continental cynical ways" during their long weekend walks in San Diego, her hometown, a place to which he was developing a growing aversion. On Friday and Saturday night downtown San Diego was lit up like a menagerie. Upper middle-class citizens circulated between quasi-Irish pubs, quasi-French bistros and quasi-Spanish taverns, all with valet parking. Middle-class couples of a lesser extraction crowded the ice-cream parlors decked out like movie theatres, dragging behind them unbearably cute children, faces smeared with quadruple-chocolate ice cream, little hands sticky from their fifth large milkshake, bright eyes staring with insupportable enthusiasm into the near future where another cookie-&-cream-strawberry-angel-hash ice cream or banana split loomed big over the fattened horizon. There was a general sense of well-being that made the streets bend outward, as though unable to contain so much happiness. The balmy evening air was suffused with the stench of expensive ultra-sweet perfumes and the promise of a hearty yet sophisticated meal at the quasi-Persian restaurant, where one could stare, without feeling uncomfortable, at the belly buttons of Middle Eastern dancers. On weekdays, however, the downtown area belonged to the homeless and the ugly, pushing their carts around Horton Plaza, smoking cheap cigarettes and scratching their bare toes in front of the Kodak Moment Horton Plaza fountain, hanging out at the bus stop; the devoted clientele of the Payless Shoe store; the city freaks; the groups of unattractive but eager tourists of a recognizably Midwestern circumference.

Bruno recalled a line by Stendhal: "In love, unlike most other passions, the recollection of what you have had and lost is always better than what you can hope for in the future." At least he could console himself with the thought that even if that future didn't seem so bright from his present vantage point, once he had 'reached' that future moment it would inevitably be tainted by the seductive glow of remembrance. And if now it seemed that he had nothing to look forward to, there was still the promise of imagining retrospectively that he had lost something and that, therefore, he must have had it in the first place.

The movers arrived at the appointed time and methodically checked every item off the list *she* had given them. The landlord, Girard, an old man who should have been dead a long time ago, climbed the stairs all the way up to the fifth floor to inquire if Bruno was moving. A few of the neighbors, who had mustered enough courage to drop the pretense that this was none of their business, gathered behind the landlord, forming a small army of concerned citizens. Girard was blabbering about something or other while the rest of them nodded their heads in automatic approval of every meaningless word that dropped, infused with bad breath, from his meaty lips. Bruno took a step back, glancing wistfully at the half open door of his nearly empty apartment, in which nothing obstructed his view and nothing held his attention. Girard demanded that Bruno elaborate on his decision to free himself of his material possessions. What drove him to make that decision? Was he seeking a simpler life? Or was he just tired of his old furniture? Had he finally surrendered to Ikea? Bruno mumbled a few incoherent 'yes's and 'no's, which proved inefficient against the slurred barrage of words coming his way (the landlord had been drinking again, something he did with the exact same regularity with which he denied it).

Over the next few weeks the newly found serenity of his ultra-minimalistic abode sent Bruno through several stages of increasing numbness as he circulated through his apartment like an unjustified, weightless mass floating above the hardwood floor, instinctively adapting its irregular shape to the dull angles of the remaining few pieces of furniture. It was fairly easy to avoid any undesirable contact with the outside world: the little food he consumed he ordered over the phone and had delivered straight to his apartment. In the afternoon he would take long, unnecessary naps or read random books.

The first weekend after *she* left he read a little book about Colin, Chick, Alice, Chloe, Nicolas and Isis. Jean-Sol Partre was also there. Colin's friend Chick is dating Alice. Alice is pretty in her green skirt and white blouse. Colin wishes he were dating Alice, not because he is in love with her but because he wants to fall in love. He decides to fall in love so he goes skating with Chick and Alice. At the skating rink he meets Chloe and falls in love with her. Chloe is pretty in her green skirt and white blouse. Colin and Chloe get married. They go on a honeymoon. Chloe begins to feel ill. She coughs a lot. They return to Paris. Colin despises work but now he has to start working because he needs money to buy flowers. Chloe has a water lily in her left lung. It's making her cough. To prevent the water lily in her lung from growing she must not drink any fluids. Also, she has to be constantly surrounded by other flowers, which are supposed to suffocate the water lily in her lung. As the days go by Colin and Chloe's apartment begins to change. There used to be a lot of light in the apartment. Now the rooms are dark. The room where Chloe lies in bed all day is getting smaller and smaller: the walls are pushing in, the ceiling is sinking, and the floor is rising. One day Chloe asks Colin to put on a record. He puts on a song by Duke Ellington. The song is called *In the Mood to Be Wooed*. They used to listen to that song when they first met. Colin and Chloe embrace. The room continues to shrink. It is no longer square. Now it is round. How will the doctor enter the room now that it's round? Time passes. Colin changes several jobs. His last one pays well. He is able to buy a lot of flowers. His job is to break bad news to people. He keeps a list of his clients. One day he sees his own name on the list. He knows Chloe is dead. By that time, the room where Colin and Chloe used to live has shrunk completely. The little mouse that used to live with them barely manages to escape before the ceiling hits the floor. The mouse finds a cat and asks the cat to eat her. The cat has just eaten and is not really hungry. The mouse puts her head in the cat's mouth, the cat unrolls her tail on the street, and they wait for someone to step on the cat's tail, causing the cat to close its mouth instinctively and thus killing the mouse. As the cat and the mouse wait, the mouse's head buried deep in the cat's mouth, eleven blind girls from the nearby orphanage approach them, singing.

In the evening he would lie down on the sofa—the last piece of evidence of his conjugal life—while a little word hung like a small but efficient guillotine over his head: despair (*despeiren,* from Middle French *desperer,* from Latin *desperare,* from *de-* + *sperare* to hope; akin to Latin *spes* hope). 'Despair' was the kind of word that made for an excellent title of a treatise. There was something 'treatisely' or 'discoursely' about 'despair,' indeed something monumental and magnificent. It was a word that did not need any qualifications or explanations. It stood on its own. It weighed in its place. It was self-sufficient and final. It evoked noble sentiments and extreme measures. In fact, it demanded a different font altogether: DESPAIR.

In *Sickness unto Death* Kierkegaard points to the ambivalent nature of despair. On one hand, despair distinguishes men from animals, testifying to the spiritual destiny of men, their relation to God, their own infinity, but on the other hand despair is the most miserable state to be in: "To despair is a qualification of spirit and relates to the eternal in man. But he cannot rid himself of the eternal: no, never in eternity. The eternal in man can be demonstrated by the fact that despair cannot consume his self [and] . . . precisely this is the torment of contradiction in despair."[11] For philosopher Pierre Michel, despair is the opposite of naivety: he calls it 'lucidity,' and thinks of it as an act of 'demystification of the world,' 'an act of revolt.'

To Bruno, however, this notion of lucidity reduced despair to nothing more than a defense mechanism: to be in despair was simply to guard oneself against deception or self-deception, to stay lucid about one's options. He appreciated much better the connection Michel drew between despair and writing: lucidity, Michel argued, is a rhetorical choice, and not one that necessarily makes for the best writing. To despair over one's failure to attain absolute lucidity is the sign of a great writer rather than proof of literary incompetence. As Flaubert puts it, "Pour être vrai, il faudrait être obscur, parler charabia."[III] Whenever he shared samples of his academic work with his colleagues Bruno would advise them that if they ever felt frustrated by the obscurity of his analysis they would do well to remember Flaubert's words and find satisfaction in the knowledge that obscurity is necessary to excellence.

Another philosopher, André Comte-Sponville, believes despair to offer deliverance from what he considers, under the influence of Buddhism, an ever greater misery, hope. The enlightened man (the one who has attained the state of nirvana) is one who has freed himself of all hope, embracing despair as the greatest happiness there is: 'Que ce désespoir puisse être lumineux, oui paisable et lumineux, comme un ciel de printemps, c'est ce que j'ai essayé de montrer. [...] Seul est heureux celui qui a perdu tout espoir; l'espoir est la plus grande torture qui soit, et le désespoir le plus grand bonheur.'[IV] As he no longer expected or hoped to be happy, he found himself, paradoxically, already happy: 'Telle est la bonne nouvelle du désespoir ... précisément parce qu'elle n'annonce rien'.[V] To live in despair is to live life *as it simply is*: 'La béatitude n'est pas autre chose que le désespoir, et je l'avais dit en commençant; ni pourtant, avouons-nous, tout à fait la même chose: elle est le désespoir *sub specie aeternitatis*, si l'on veut, c'est-à-dire la vie elle-même, cette vie, la vraie vie, la seule vie, avec ses tristesses et sa finitude, mais délivrée enfin de l'attente, du manque et du sens: la vraie vie, donc, mais vécue enfin en vérité. [...] Il n'y a que le réel, et c'est la seule doctrine en vérité. Accepter. Aller au fond de la souffrance: là où plus personne ne souffre. Au fond du désespoir: là où plus personne ne désespère. Au fond de la vérité: là où plus personne ne connaît.'[VI] Despair then became beatitude: the greatest happiness, the absence of all hope. In his later book titled, appropriately enough, *Le bonheur, désespérément*, Comte-Sponville went beyond the comparison between despair and certain states of Eastern religious enlightenment to consider despair on analogy with Nietzsche's 'gay science', calling it instead 'gay despair'. Bruno did not subscribe to this kind of therapeutic, recuperative view of despair, which trivialized it into a placid contemplation of ultimate reality, one eternally smug "Ommm."

Time passed. How much time? Bruno couldn't tell. A familiar feeling started creeping up on him.

He was bored.

His usual way of dealing with the eventual onslaught of ennui was to perform every minor daily routine, every trivial gesture, with the utmost concentration, as though it required unprecedented mental effort. When this time-honored strategy proved insufficient he began recording, by hand, every individual thought that sluggishly crossed his mind, from the first flicker of meaning to its ultimate extinguishment, but since he found it impossible to disentangle one thought from the one preceding or following it he was soon forced to declare defeat.

At some point it occurred to him that he had not checked his mailbox for a while. One stormy night he sneaked downstairs undramatically. The mailbox was empty except for a simple white envelope. Bruno tore it open with the lack of enthusiasm he usually reserved for opening his bills. It was a 'friendly reminder' that his identity card was about to expire and that he needed to apply for a new one 'at his earliest convenience.' The application for a new card required two recent photographs. Under normal circumstances Bruno would have responded to this type of request at his latest convenience. However, the idea of leaving his empty apartment to run an errand no longer struck him as repugnant. On the contrary, after a long, self-imposed exile a visit to the photo studio suddenly assumed the aura of an exotic adventure.

One shockingly sunny December afternoon he found himself sitting in a chair far too big for his delicate frame, moving his head "slightly to the right, now slightly to the left, chin up, now hold still." He had had a lot of experience holding still in the last several weeks, which is why when he noticed the frustrated expression on the photographer's face he was certain it could not be attributed to his poor performance as a model. The photographer fiddled with the camera and kept changing the settings, seemingly to no effect.

"Could you please move a bit closer to the camera?"

Lifting up the chair and moving it a step forward turned out to be not as easy as Bruno had imagined it would be. His bony fingers, long and limp, hung from his hands like unlikely appendages. Had he lost weight?

"A little closer please," the photographer said as he waltzed over to the window and pulled the curtains apart to let in more light.

. Still out of breath Bruno managed to move his chair another inch forward. When the photographer looked through the viewfinder his face morphed through an informative—and impressively nuanced—display of the different stages of bewilderment. He shook his head and looked gravely at Bruno as though he had just been informed of the untimely demise of someone or other.

"Problem with the camera?" Bruno asked.

"There is nothing wrong with the camera. Do you mind standing up and walking slowly towards me? I want to do a little test."

"I thought you said there is nothing wrong with the camera."

"I am not testing the camera."

Bruno stepped forward. The photographer motioned to him to continue moving. Bruno walked forward until he stood very close to the camera lens.

"No," the photographer said and switched off the camera.

"How complicated can it be to take a picture?" Bruno exclaimed.

"It gets complicated when the subject doesn't register."

"What do you mean 'doesn't register'?"

"The camera is not registering your presence. I tried to *boost* your presence digitally but unfortunately . . ."

He turned the camera screen toward Bruno.

"Take a look for yourself. There are some slight, almost imperceptible, variations in the amount of light that gets reflected off of you. When I asked you to move closer the camera did record something like a dark stain right in the place where you should have been. Unfortunately, when I asked you to move even closer, the stain vanished. It's as if you are not present, except for a few fractions of a second perhaps."

Outside in the street Bruno stopped in front of a shop window to examine the reflection of his rain-coated silhouette: it did look a bit vague and rough around the edges. He pondered what options were available to a man in his predicament. Nothing came to mind, perhaps because there was no mind it could come to, he reasoned. But then who, or what, was reasoning this way? Who, or what, was entertaining the possibility that his mind had suddenly vanished? Should he feel reassured by the infinite regress his mind had run up against—thereby demonstrating that there was, indeed, still something there, something that was doing all this rambling-thinking—or should he assume that the inexplicable case of 'physical absence' he had contracted would be eventually accompanied by its mental equivalent? The question of his—and others'—presence/absence, had always occupied his mind of course, but always in the form of a pleasant diversion, something to ponder distractedly as he waited for the bus or listened to a student's oral presentation. The existence of other minds—and of his mind—had never, until now, demanded his attention with such urgency.

Skepticism's fundamental error, some of his colleagues from the Philosophy Department would have him believe, was to assume that the subject's relationship to the world, to itself, and to other subjects, was purely cognitive when, in fact, it was *ethical*: a matter of reciprocity and acknowledgment rather than of knowledge. The real question was not whether I—or others—exist, but what claim I make upon them and what claim they make upon me, and how we respond to these claims (by acknowledging them or by refusing to). Supposedly, even others' refusal to respond to the claim Bruno made upon them was also a kind of response simply because it was impossible for them to assume a neutral (i.e. cognitive) attitude to him: *he made a claim upon them simply by virtue of existing*. Skepticism was thus a phantom philosophical problem. For Bruno, however, this alleged 'victory' over skepticism depended on cheating one's way out of the real issue by bringing the concept of skepticism from the realm of metaphysics (proving one's existence, the existence of the world, and of other minds) down to the human/ethical realm (psychological responses such as shame, guilt, or embarrassment).

The ultimate guarantee of one's existence, the cogito's *condition of possibility*, was, supposedly, the body with its everyday, automatic, unconscious movements and gestures. The body, Bruno was supposed to believe, could never be completely fictionalized: its inherent lucidity guaranteed that it would always exceed the meaning others ascribed to it on the basis of established conventions of communication. The mind *automatically* expressed itself through the body: if it wished *not* to express itself, the mind would be forced to suppress its behavior or pervert it. The falsification of one's behavior was thus incontrovertible evidence of the cogito's *automatism* (self-evidence) or *transparency:* one falsified one's behavior precisely because one assumed that if one didn't, his body would betray him. Shame, exposure, betrayal and embarrassment were ontological facts rather than feelings associated with particular uncomfortable or traumatic experiences. If there was a danger to speak of here, it was not the danger of skepticism but that of the cogito *overexposing* itself through its automatic gestures and movements, which could never be concealed. At this point his philosopher friends would throw in some Stanley Cavell: "If the price of Descartes' proof of his existence was a perpetual recession of the body, the price of an Emersonian proof of my existence is a perpetual visibility of the self, a theatricality in my presence to others, hence to myself. The camera is an emblem of perpetual visibility. Descartes' self-consciousness thus takes the form of *embarrassment.*" [VII]

As he turned away from his ghost-like reflection in the shop window Bruno felt robbed of the "perpetual visibility" to which the camera was supposed to condemn him, a sentence he would have gladly accepted right now. Walking down the street he closed his eyes occasionally and walked straight into people, hoping to crash into another body—*any* body—and feel the warmth and resistance of his own. Back home he locked himself in the bathroom where he spent a considerable amount of time taking care of the self-inflicted bruises he had suffered in his desperate attempt to measure and regulate the unexpected 'fluctuations' in his existential being following (or perhaps brought about by) his post-conjugal existential fast. He had somehow managed to cut his left cheek, probably brushing against a woman's brooch or a man's cufflinks. He patched himself up rather sloppily but not before he took a photograph of his bruised face with the instant print camera *she* had given him for his last birthday. He then took a photograph of his bandaged face, Band Aids crisscrossing his concave cheeks, and another one of the reflection of his face in the bathroom mirror.

He arranged the vacant photographs on the edge of the bathtub and sat on the toilet, studying his multiple states of invisibility. Think like a historian, he told himself. Imagine this is a 19TH century case you are reading about in a scholarly article. Situate the case historically. Are there any precedents? Yes, of course: the famous 'ghosting' of photographs, latent images, overexposure, et cetera. But his case did not belong in this category, because there were no technical problems with the camera. There had been considerably more precedents in the opposite category: photographic records of super-abundance—the presence of too many selves rather than the absence of a single one. In 1885, ten years before the first film screening of the Lumière brothers, the first clinical case of a multiple, Louis Vivet, was photographed in his ten personality states. Two years later Albert Dad, the first person whose dissociative fugues were studied in detail, was photographed in his three states (normal, hypnotized and during a fugue). One hundred and twenty five years later Bruno Leblon, a history lecturer at a prestigious university, produced photographic records of an ocular-metaphysical condition for which there was (as yet) no explanation.

Situating his condition in a historical context did not have the salutary effect Bruno had hoped for. Perhaps not all was lost, however. Perhaps this super-abundance—the self's ready visibility, its constant state of exposure to the camera's omniscient eye—was not all it was cracked up to be. With the introduction of the camera in fin-de-siècle, 'thinking' and 'subject' could no longer be defined in terms of the Cartesian privileging of pure thought. By registering automatically both our conscious and unconscious movements/gestures, the camera would condemn us to a perennially exposed mode of existence, of which it would provide an inevitable surplus of proof. The entire burden of proof of our existence, and of our sanity would, from now on, rest with the camera, which would render the notion of the cogito as 'hidden' or 'invisible' obsolete. If Cavell was right that photography had provoked a shift in our understanding of rational thought, a shift away from the Cartesian notion of the cogito as a perpetual recession of the body toward a photographic notion of the cogito as the perpetual visibility of the self, a *theatricality* in my presence to others and hence to myself,[VIII] then perhaps perpetual *invisibility* held the promise for regaining some modicum of the authenticity that was lost with the camera's theatricalization of the cogito. Perhaps the fact that Bruno was not constantly present to himself and to others, except in the form of a shapeless smudge easily confused with a smudge on the camera lens, was a sign that he was evolving toward a different form of selfhood, one that would escape the specular process that was the construction of a Self. The Self, as is well known, is constructed by adopting the gestures and behaviors of those around it in a process similar to taking photographs. Selfhood originates in imitation, a process sociologist Gabriel Tarde compared to 'inter-psychical photography'—"a quasi-photographic reproduction of a cerebral image upon the sensitive plane of another brain."[IX] Perhaps Bruno's failure to 'register' photographically was the first step toward achieving the absolute autonomy of his Self.

Before considering this exciting possibility, however, Bruno was determined to exhaust all other options for boosting up his presence.

The windows of his apartment, like those of everyone else living on this side of the building, overlooked a little courtyard in the middle of which stood a single bench that was supposed to offer the building's residents the rare opportunity to spend some quality alone time while being observed by everyone else. Bruno had not yet taken advantage of this little perk since he (and *she*) moved into the building eight years ago. Mrs. Damier, a sheepish little woman living in the apartment opposite his, had left her window open. The sounds of her favorite detective TV series reverberated in the empty courtyard. Bruno tried to make out the TV screen through the cigarette smoke: all he could see was the dark silhouette of a small man in a trench coat and a fedora hat hanging low over his eyes. He closed the window and picked up the phone. No dial tone. He pulled on the phone cord: it broke off like an unnecessary umbilical cord.

Minutes later he pressed Mrs. Damier's buzzer. Her round face, lit up auratically by the intense light coming from the TV screen behind her, appeared in the half-opened door.

"Good evening," he said politely.

She didn't seem impressed by his manners and glanced back at the TV.

"Bruno Leblon. I am in the apartment right across from you."

"New tenants should speak with Monsieur Girard, third floor, apartment seven," she said curtly and motioned to close the door.

"I am not a new tenant," he pleaded with her.

Mrs. Damier searched the pockets of her misshapen woolen cardigan and produced an old pair of glasses, whose frames had been broken and glued back together more than once. She put them on and looked him up and down.

"I've been living here for the past eight years with my wife, I mean my ex-wife . . ."

His voice trailed off. Mrs. Damier furrowed her eyebrows as if she was trying to solve an incredibly difficult math problem. Finally she took off her glasses, folded them carefully and put them back in her pocket. She seemed to have found a satisfactory solution to the problem. Bruno waited for her verdict.

"I don't think so," she said simply.

Franz Joseph Gall, the 'father' of phrenology, maintained that personality could be assessed from the shape of a person's skull and that the brain is a system of connected but individual organs, each corresponding to a specific faculty (hope, language, self-esteem etc.) One look at Mrs. Damier was enough to discredit Gall's theory: her soft baby skull, free of any bumps or unidentifiable growths, did not prepare one for her willful refusal to even conceive the possibility of ever being wrong about something. Bruno sensed that any attempt to extend the argument further and deprive her of another second of her viewing pleasure would be detrimental to his plans.

"May I please use your phone? I urgently need to speak to Monsieur Girard."

Mrs. Damier hesitated but then pointed to a room on the left. She walked back to her room and he heard her turn up the volume on the TV. He leafed through the phone book looking for the "private investigators" section. There were twenty-six listed. He picked one at random: "Jacques Fontaine, private detective. Reasonable rates." The phone rang only once before a deep male voice said:

"Fontaine."

"I am looking for a private detective. I must insist on absolute discretion."

"I respect the privacy of all my clients, Monsieur . . . ?"

"Louis Villiers," Bruno said after a short pause.

"Monsieur Villiers, please stay on the line while I get a pen and a piece of paper."

"My request is very simple," Bruno said quickly.

"Even if that is the case, and in my experience it never is, I do need to jot down a few things if you don't mind."

Bruno heard Fontaine rummage through some papers. Finally, he came back to the phone.

"Go ahead."

"I need you to follow someone."

"A man or a woman?"

"A man."

"Do you know this person?"

"I do."

"Is he a family member, a distant relative, a colleague, or an acquaintance?"

"A family member."

"A close family member?"

"A very close family member." Bruno paused, not sure how to explain his predicament. "Over the last several days it's been increasingly difficult to get a hold of this man."

"You mean he's been hiding?"

"Not exactly."

Bruno waited as Fontaine paused.

"Monsieur Villiers, you are not being forthright with me. If you want me to find this person, you need to tell me as much about him as you can."

"It's not a question of finding him but simply confirming that he is present."

"Present where?"

Bruno put down the receiver and wiped his sweaty hands on his pants. He picked it up again and held it at a distance from his ear, afraid that Fontaine might hear his nervous breathing.

"I can assure you that you will find your honorarium more than generous."

"You have a way with words, Monsieur Villiers," Fontaine said. "A beautiful way with words if you don't mind me saying so. Please go on."

"The man lives at thirty-seven Bosquet Avenue, fifth floor, apartment twelve. Single, white, thirty-seven years old."

"Any birth scars?"

Bruno reattached the Band Aid that had come unglued from his cheek.

"No," he said.

"Where does he work?"

"He is not working at the moment."

"How would I recognize him? Do you have any photographs?"

"I am afraid not. You will have to rely on my description. Tall, thin, short dark hair, grey eyes, thick eyebrows, high cheekbones." Bruno looked away from the mirror.

"How exactly would you like me to report back to you?"

"I'll rent a mailbox at the Central Post Office where you will leave your written reports every evening."

"How detailed do you expect them to be?"

"Monsieur Fontaine, I expect you to be a man on whom nothing is lost."

As soon as he put down the receiver Bruno felt slightly embarrassed about ending the conversation with a pretentious literary reference. At the opposite end of the hallway Mrs. Damiers opened the door. Something dramatic was happening with the little man in the fedora hat. The suspense music escalated to a predictable crescendo.

3

Early morning. Grey calm. His neck felt stiff. After a quick survey of his closet Bruno opted for a grey suit and a grey raincoat. It occurred to him that wearing all grey might make following him difficult for Fontaine, especially on an overcast day like this. He took off the raincoat and put on a green jacket. No, he should first test Fontaine's detective skills. He took off the green jacket and put on the grey raincoat again. It was ten minutes to nine. He walked over to the window and pulled the curtains aside. Down below, identical looking grey silhouettes holding up oversized black umbrellas moved in numbing synchronicity, sloshing and splashing from puddle to puddle before disappearing down the stairs leading to the subway. A single figure detached itself from the others and stood under the street lamp right across from Bruno's apartment. The man was dressed immaculately, down to the white handkerchief in his front pocket. Bruno stepped away from the window, counted to ten and looked out again. Fontaine was pacing back and forth, occasionally checking his watch. Bruno put his hand on the doorknob. He would come out of the building, turn right immediately and walk toward the subway station without a hint of hesitation. His body movements had to appear habitual. Fontaine should not suspect Bruno was aware of being followed.

Out in the street, instead of 'instinctively' turning right as he had planned, Bruno closed the door behind him and stopped in front of the building, facing Fontaine. He told himself not to look at Fontaine. Of course, this is exactly what he did. Out of the corner of his eye he saw Fontaine step back and hide behind a tree. To guard himself against any further self-sabotage Bruno turned around abruptly. Now he was facing the wall. When he was finally able to collect himself he turned left and walked toward the bakery, where he waited for Fontaine to catch up with him.

He had absolutely nowhere to go, nothing to do, no one to see. The Fall term had just ended and the Winter term did not start for another month and a half. No one expected anything from him. No one, that is, except Fontaine, who was expecting to witness a typical day in the life of Bruno Leblon. As he watched Fontaine swim across the morning waves of sleepy commuters Bruno searched his memory for 'typical day' scenarios. Fontaine was getting closer and closer. Running out of options Bruno walked into the bakery. The familiar smell of cinnamon, roasted almonds and freshly baked dough enveloped him like a warm blanket, bringing back random images of winter holidays spent at his grandparents' house in the countryside. In the corner a sullen-looking boy was drinking milk from a glass and then spitting it back inside. His mother was putting on lipstick using her empty coke bottle as a mirror. The third seat at their table was empty. Bruno imagined himself sitting there, sipping his coffee and giving stern yet gentle fatherly advice to his son about the proper way of consuming milk in a public place. He would then lean over and kiss his attractive wife on the cheek before standing up with an air of gravity, checking his pocket watch, a gift from his dead father of course, and walking to his company's office where, sleeves rolled up to the elbows, cigarette, no, cigar, hanging from his lips, he would begin his working day. . . . His family reverie was cut short by a strong whiff of body odor as his hypothetical wife waltzed past him followed by her son, whose face, post-milk, looked even surlier.

Fontaine stood outside the bakery, smoking a cigarette in an ostentatiously unself-conscious way, like a bad actor. It started raining. Fontaine raised his collar and moved under the awning. Bruno ordered another coffee and began drawing up a list of errands. Never underestimate the importance of the Errands List, one of the founding documents of sanity. First he would go to the bank. Yes, the bank seemed like the most logical place to start: all subsequent errands were bound to involve some kind of monetary transaction. But if the majority of his errands depended on the exchange of money, Bruno reasoned, the order in which he completed the errands was irrelevant: it didn't matter if he first went to the grocery store and *then* to the library, or he first read a few books on fin de siècle Paris and *then* bought some pork for dinner. No, what he had to focus on was the *execution* of these errands, in whatever order, with *the greatest possible dedication*, as if he *believed* in them or, better yet, as if the question of belief had never even presented itself to him.

By the time Bruno came out of the bank the sun had pierced the clouds, drawing out of their hiding places a dozen homeless men and women and their extended families, who were now busy setting up their 'work stations' along the sidewalk and rolling up their sleeves to make it easier for begging arms to extend and move in a wide variety of supplicatory gestures. The younger ones rehearsed their plaintive songs and wails while inspecting the garbage cans for any recent breakfast additions. Bruno stopped in front of a group of street kids playing house with discarded, imaginatively mangled Barbie dolls. He observed them for a while, admiring and envying the seriousness with which they invested their meaningless game. He stepped forward and squatted in the middle of their group, feeling the pressure of their earnest looks as they turned their dirty little faces toward him. He picked up one of the dolls and held it up in the air, its long blonde hair hanging upside down. He had no idea what he was going to do next—he only sensed a light, nervous energy coursing through him, infusing this random moment with an almost unbearable portent. Holding the doll with one hand he used his other hand to tear its head off. It rolled down the slanted sidewalk and landed at the feet of a little girl with greasy hair. She licked her lips where the snot drizzling from her nose had collected in tiny pools. Bruno put his finger inside the decapitated plastic body and waved it demonstratively in front of the kids' stunned faces. He then freed his finger from the decapitated plastic corpse, adjusted the creases of his pants, and walked away. He looked back: one of the kids was jumping up and down on Barbie's severed head.

The imposingly kitschy building of the Public Library dominated Avenue de Verzy. Through the half-opened shutters Bruno could see several heads, propped up by one or two hands, bent over books and newspapers. Although it was a sunny day all reading lamps were on, creating a cozy, scholarly atmosphere. Libraries are designed for rainy days, Bruno thought. More specifically, they are designed for lonely people for whom the idea of snuggling up with a good book at home, an idea most people find appealing, is so depressing that they must gather together and snuggle collectively, each in their own solitary pool of *Geselligkeit* provided by quasi-antique reading lamps, under a high dome painted to resemble a blue sky whose sun never shines (except every two years when the library brings in specialists to restore the darkening golden patina) and whose stars never twinkle. In the course of his academic studies Bruno had spent endless hours in this artificial heaven, breathing in the musky smell of forgotten books, looking up from under his pool of light at the other miniature planet systems hovering at the edge of his solipsistic system.

He approached the front desk. The librarian looked up from the book she was reading.

"Can I help you?"

Bruno noted the dissonance between her unexpectedly sexy voice and her wrinkled face, which placed her in two cognitively dissonant mental categories, that of voice-over actresses for public service announcements and that of long extinct prehistoric beasts. He handed her a copy of the bibliography he had compiled last Spring when he first began doing research. She slowly unfolded her arms and lifted up her chin like a marionette that had been long out of use and was suddenly coming alive again, ready to perform whatever feats of public duty the state had entrusted her with, allowing her, an old spinster, to continue to occupy a small niche in the social fabric and feel like a useful member of the community for a little while longer. While she studied his bibliography she made strange noises, mostly nasal, which Bruno interpreted as possibly signifying reluctant approval. Apparently he had excellent taste when it came to books. Finally, she descended from her throne, revealing a miniature height or, rather, not really revealing anything since she was so short that she immediately disappeared behind the counter, leaving Bruno to deduce what her height might be. Having spent the last several days in self-imposed exile Bruno had become a master at deducing things based on even less evidence than that he was presented with at the moment.

A few minutes later she re-emerged from behind the counter and put down a pile of books on one of the tables-on-wheels parked by the check out desk. Bruno rolled the books over to a table at the other end of the Reading Room. He made sure the neighboring tables were empty so Fontaine would have a good vantage point for observing Bruno. The other academic planetary systems, each ruled by the solitary sun of a reading lamp, revolved at a steady rate around his to the accompaniment of scribbling pens and laptop typing muzak. Bruno felt warm and relaxed, as if he had just drunk a glass of warm milk. He closed his eyes and allowed himself to be lulled to sleep by the pleasant sound of whispering library voices spouting out unpronounceable academic jargon that sounded as beautiful as nonsense always did.

He woke up abruptly and looked around, randomly locking eyes with a man sitting at the table across from him. The man looked away. Bruno reached toward the pile of academic books in front of him but at the last moment his arm changed direction and moved to the fiction pile instead. He opened one of them to a random page and began copying down the first sentence he happened to read: "He spent the afternoon in a mood of anguish and anger" (*The Pigeon* 85). He could have chosen a much longer sentence—thereby delaying the guilt trip he was inevitably going to embark on as soon as he ran out of words to copy and had to actually work on chapter one of his own book—but a dogmatic sense of loyalty to the randomness and meaninglessness of what he was doing forced him to keep the sentence. He opened another book at random: "Laughing aristocrats moved up and down the corridors of the city" (Barthelme, *Sixty Stories* 151). And another one: "Seeing a past action as meaningful meant attributing reasons for it to one's past self" (*Perlman's Silence* 148).

He looked up. The man sitting opposite him was inspecting an old photograph under a magnifying glass. Bruno studied his balding head, his long thin arms, his retro—yet surprisingly unfashionable—brown jacket and the checkered beige shirt he was wearing under it. The next sentence was longer: "In all the

reconstructive or restorative arts—forensics, forensic anthropology, paleontology, archaeology, art restoration, fields into which
scholars have put enormous work, defining methods, freedoms,
and boundaries as they strive to fill in the blanks of history—people make the best educated guess as to what 'really' happened"
(*Reality Hunger* 71). And finally: "Isn't it strange to see an event
happening precisely because it was not supposed to happen? What
kind of defense do we have against that?" (*The Black Swan* xix).

He spent the rest of the afternoon copying random sentences
from random books. In the evening one of the expectedly
bespectacled library assistants walked down the isle switching off
all reading lamps. A dozen of somber library patrons descended
reluctantly from their cozy orbits, fiddling with pens and coats,
trying to delay the moment when they would have to leave the
library and be left to their own resources. Before exiting the lobby
they exchanged awkward glances mutually reassuring one another that they would reconvene again the following morning at 9AM
sharp.

As Bruno walked out into the depressing evening-commute
night the lights inside the library behind him died one after the
other and multiple temporary galaxies of imaginary worlds heav-
ing within the pages of dusty old tomes slowed their steady rev-
olutions, eventually grinding down to a halt. He had spent the
afternoon in a mood of anguish and anger. Laughing library
patrons had moved up and down the corridors of the public
library. Seeing Bruno's past actions as meaningful meant attributing reasons for them to Bruno's past self. In all the reconstructive
or restorative arts—forensics, forensic anthropology, paleontology,
archaeology, art restoration, fields into which scholars have put
enormous work, defining methods, freedoms, and boundaries as
they strive to fill in the blanks of history—people made the best
educated guess as to what 'really' happened with Bruno. Wasn't it
strange to see an event happening precisely because it was not
supposed to happen to Bruno? What kind of defense did Bruno
have against that?

There was an Italian cinema retrospective at Cinema
Paradiso. Perhaps he could see a Visconti flick. He had a soft spot

for laughing aristocrats drinking themselves to sexual and moral abandon. The Visconti film was sold out. Without looking at the program he bought a ticket for the only other film playing—*The Naturals*, screened as part of the 2012 *Experimental Film Festival*— and sat in the last row without bothering to brush the stale popcorn from his seat. The film had already started. Up on the screen two men sat in a prototypical diner somewhere in cornfield America.

"Let's try to have a conversation naturally, without putting any effort into it, just letting the words roll off our tongues," one of them said.

"But words don't come naturally to me. I have to make an effort," the other one explained.

"Fine, but try to be discreet about it, will you?" the first one said.

There was a long pause, during which the two men were preparing to be 'natural'. Fontaine, sitting three seats over from Bruno, was snoring discreetly.

"The MOMA collection *Home Accessories through the Ages* is currently on tour," the first man finally said.

"Really?"

"Yes."

There was another long pause.

"If we exhaust our topic do we just move on to the next one?" the second man asked.

"Are we sure we have exhausted our topic? Isn't there anything else we can say about the MOMA collection?"

"Does it have to be about MOMA or can we talk about museums in general?"

"You want to talk about the *nature* of museums?"

"It's not that I want to talk. I just want to be clear about the rules."

The first man held his head between his hands.

"There're no rules. The whole point is to try to have a spontaneous, natural conversation. How many times do we have to go over this?"

"I'm sorry. It's just that I don't know much about museums."

"There are dozens of common sense things everyone—even you—knows about museums. I am pretty sure we can have an informative, even meaningful conversation about it. At least two hours long!"

"Why don't we actually go to MOMA? If we are at the scene of the crime, so to speak, it will be easier to talk about it, right?"

"Wrong! We should be able to talk about anything, regardless of whether it exists or not. From what I've read most natural conversations are about hypothetical things."

"So it doesn't matter if what I say is verifiable or not? I can say absolutely anything about museums?"

"Yes, as long as it keeps the conversation going."

Bruno did not stick around to see whether the two men managed to keep the conversation going or whether it got more 'natural'. He had to wait ten minutes before Fontaine stumbled out in the street. The street was deserted except for one man walking a few hundred meters ahead of Bruno. His slouched shoulders and lanky frame looked familiar. The bright streetlights divided his balding head into irregular shapes, transforming it into an impressionistic phrenological map. Bruno recognized the man from the library. The man quickened his pace. Bruno instinctively did the same. He heard Fontaine do the same behind him. The three of them dived into the labyrinth of narrow streets on the other side of the river. After several blind turns the man walked into Hôtel Dauphine. The receptionist, a middle-aged woman with excessive amounts of lipstick splattered over her otherwise inconspicuous lips, handed him a room key and he walked up the stairs. Disappointed that his quasi-detective adventure had ended prematurely Bruno walked into the nearest bar. Fontaine had disappeared: he was probably writing his report. Around 11PM Bruno settled his tab at the bar and headed over to the Post Office.

In the mailbox he had rented there was a slim white envelope with his name on it. Back in his apartment Bruno lay down on the sofa and opened the envelope containing Fontaine's report:

> At 9AM in the morning of December 10 the subject emerged from his apartment building at 37 Bosquet

Avenue. His physical appearance conformed to the description I was given. He was dressed entirely in grey, which a lesser detective might have interpreted as an attempt to maintain anonymity, but which, upon further reflection, revealed X's intimate familiarity with current fashion trends (cf. the Spring 2012 and Autumn 2012 issues of *CQ*) and, by virtue of that fact, a vain and narcissistic personality. The scant preliminary evidence I was provided with did not specify the subject's occupation. I was told he is currently unemployed but not what his previous occupation might have been. I would wager, on the basis of my observations of his general demeanor, which consistently betrayed a deliberate desire to maintain a distance between him and the rest of the world, that he has never been employed in the service industries.

The subject first stopped at a bakery where he purchased a cinnamon roll and two cups of coffee. Judging from the quick exchange between him and the cashier—he didn't even have to point to what he wanted—I would venture that he is a regular there. In short, he is a man of habit and, from the looks of it, not that concerned about his diet. While he drank his coffee he pretended to write something on a piece of paper but, in fact, he was watching a beautiful young woman and what seemed to be her son sitting at the next table. The woman pretended to be busy putting on make up but the cursory glances she exchanged with the subject while she was thus occupied made it clear that they only appear to be strangers. In the absence of further evidence, and taking into account the young woman's provocative and tasteless attire, I can surmise that her relationship with the subject is of a sexual nature, that is, he occasionally takes advantage of her services in exchange for money. I would also venture that, despite the financial power he wields over her, in all likelihood she holds the erotic power in the relationship as evidenced by his reaction when she stood up and left. She walked past him slowly, swaying her hips (as skillfully as any other woman of her trade) while he, obviously enthralled by her sexual charisma, stepped back and deliberately looked away, as though he wanted to show everyone how little he thought of women like her, but his act was so exaggerated that it exposed, instead of concealing, the real depth of his animal attraction to women precisely of her type.

The subject then went to the bank across the street. When the bank-teller handed him the cash he did not count it, which suggests he is a regular there as well. He did not look at the receipt either: financial security is not something he concerns himself with. The bank-teller's attempt to engage the subject in small talk—the usual, nothing fancy—was met with undisguised hostility on his part. She was wise enough not to insist. Upon leaving the bank the subject walked directly to the little street, off of the square, where many of the city's homeless citizens gather. It was immediately obvious that this was not the subject's first encounter with them. His interaction with a group of street children demonstrated the great deal of respect and trust he enjoys among them. I would not be surprised to find out that he regularly volunteers at one of the homeless shelters in town as a way of dealing with the guilt and regret he feels for not having yet adopted one of these street kids.

The subject spent the rest of the day at the Public Library. He was so focused on his research that he made no notice of a bald man sitting across from him, who kept glancing up at the subject. The subject left the library just before it was about to close. He walked fast, like someone who knows exactly where they are going. It didn't take me long to realize that he was following the man walking ahead of him, the same bald man to whose presence in the library the subject had previously seemed oblivious. This confirmed what I already half-suspected, namely, that the subject excels at feigning obliviousness.

Although I am fairly certain he is not aware of the fact that I am following him I must take all necessary precautions not to arouse his suspicion. There is always the possibility that he may find out I am following him but feign obliviousness, letting me go on with the investigation, which will be then irreversibly compromised. Some form of minimal disguise might help me maintain the anonymity on which my work depends. Needless to say, I expect to be fully reimbursed for any extra charges incurred to secure such a disguise. The present report is a true record of the events of December 10. Please forward the first check in my name to the following address: Jacques Fontaine, Mailbox 23, Central Post Office.

Had Fontaine been a writer, rather than a private investigator, Bruno would have commended him for his straightforward style and his firm grasp of the mechanics of creating psychologically believable characters. Bruno folded the letter and put it back in the envelope. Only this morning his existence had seemed blank, his actions unmotivated and meaningless. Not any more! Fontaine's report had infused Bruno's random actions and gestures with numerous meanings, conflicting motivations, and a potentially infinite number of possible outcomes. And at the center of it all was he, Bruno. He was gradually beginning *to appear*, to come into focus. This whole day *he had been—beyond any doubt—present*. He had been present as a man with particular beliefs on prostitution, a regular bank customer, a man of habit with a favorite breakfast spot—and with a soft spot for the homeless—a man with plans, intentions, reasons, motivations, hopes and regrets, finally, a man with an *objective*: to find out the identity of the bald man from the Public Library.

What about tomorrow? And the day after tomorrow? Would Bruno still be able to insert himself effortlessly into the rich world the report had unveiled before him as his own? Or would he start disappearing again?

4

Bruno gulped down yesterday's coffee and glanced at his reflection in the mirror: his face was unshaven, his clothes wrinkled (he had slept in them), and the hair on one side of his head was sticking out. He turned on the hot water in the bathroom and shoved his head under it. The clock struck nine. He rubbed his head energetically with a towel and ran down the stairs.

The Public Library welcomed him with its leather armchairs, the warm glow of reading lamps, and the musty smell of old books that hadn't been opened for years. He sat at one of the tables, plugged in his laptop, pulled out a random book from the pile in front of him and pretended to read. The book was called *The Black Swan*. Apparently it had been a bestseller when it was first published. The black swan theory, he read, was an attempt to account for the human tendency to explain retrospectively random, unexpected, unpredictable phenomena—such as the existence of a black swan—by inscribing them into some kind of logical scheme thereby denying their randomness.

Fontaine sat by the window, busy writing a rough draft of Bruno's future past, which Bruno would read later that evening. How did he know where to look, which details were important and which ones were not, how to get the overall feeling of *this* place, *this* moment? Bruno surveyed the room discreetly: typing with one finger the librarian was entering data in the computer, two young library assistants were reordering a stack of index cards, and numerous pairs of myopic scholarly eyes moved across the brittle pages of rare books and manuscripts propped up on special stands in front of them. He imagined the scene as a photograph with a blurry background, his own figure standing out in embarrassingly sharp focus. The image gradually acquired the familiar sepia tone of old photographs. It was now glued to a page of a forgotten library album telling the history of the Public Library, locked up in an elegant glass case in the library's Rare Books collection. Library patrons passed by, bent over the glass case, and pointed to the photograph. A bald man wearing a retro brown jacket and a checkered beige shirt studied the photograph under a magnifying glass and diligently recorded his interpretation of the lives of the people in the photograph, including one Bruno Leblon.

Fontaine put down his pen and stretched back in his chair. Only now Bruno noticed the bald man from the day before. He was sitting behind Fontaine, studying a photograph under a magnifying glass, exactly like the day before.

Bruno opened his laptop and clicked on the file containing the rough draft of chapter one of his book. He had begun doing research for the book last April. It was supposed to be a cultural history of fin de siècle Paris told through the story of Bruno's own family, Leblon, one of the oldest aristocratic families in Paris.

Early photography was more often than not discussed as a 'discovery'—"a discovery of nature's capacity to register its own image"—rather than as an 'invention'. Photographs were said to be "'obtained' or 'taken', like natural specimens found in the wild." [X] *However, the discourse of scientific objectivity to which the new medium seemed to belong was from the very beginning enmeshed with another, contradictory discourse of the uncanny and the magical, as evidenced by the 'ghosting' of nineteenth century photographs—the appearance of incomplete, blurred images—and by photography's basic technical property, the latent image. Thus, the notion of photography as nature's "spontaneous reproduction," which took the medium's inherent <u>automatism</u> as proof of its <u>objectivity</u>, was from the start undermined by the opposite reading of the very same characteristic of the medium—its <u>automatism</u>—as an instance of <u>natural magic</u>. Not surprisingly, in slightly more than a decade after its invention photography became associated with the idea of the double and the uncanny.*

This was followed by a note-to-self: *Find a transition to the Leblons' family history!*

The transition from a general analysis of fin de siècle visual culture to Bruno's own family history had proven the main obstacle in his research from the very beginning. He scrolled up to the top of the paragraph and italicized a few key words, then un-did the italics and italicized several other words, before finally going back and re-italicizing the original words. Was this really all he could hope to achieve this afternoon? He picked up his bibliography and walked over to the librarian's desk. She glanced at the titles on his list.

"I am sorry but none of these are currently available," she said and went back to the unrewarding task of re-filing old paper index cards.

"Have they been moved somewhere else?"

"Someone else is using them at the moment," she said without looking up.

"Someone else is doing research on my family history?"

She looked up. Her customary curtness was now tinged with unmistakable irritation.

"Do you really find it strange that another scholar is using the same library resources?"

"Do you mind telling me who is using them?"

She searched the room and pointed to the bald man.

"Monsieur Leblon. He is sitting over there."

Bruno stared at her.

"Leblon? Is this a joke? I am Monsieur . . ."

He took a deep breath.

"I'll wait till he is finished," he said.

The librarian resumed her pointless task and Bruno returned to his seat. 3:45PM. Better do some more work.

Dr. Hugh W. Diamond pioneered the use of photographic portraits in the study and treatment of the insane. His patients had to pose for their photographs because the available technology depended on long exposure times. However, Diamond believed that even the use of professional models did not undermine the evidential value of photography. In La Photographie Moderne Albert Londe argued that photography was particularly well suited for the study of a range of psycho-somatic disturbances on account of a certain correspondence between the object of study (the illness, which proceeds through different stages) and the very mechanism of photography (its capacity to divide and analyze movement into

its constituent parts/instants).[XI] On one hand, then what made photog-
raphy such an invaluable scientific instrument was the photographer's
control over his instrument. On the other hand, however, controlling the
recording apparatus did not guarantee an objective record of the illness:
since the photographer had the power to choose when to turn on the cam-
era, he would end up with a selective record of the progression of the
hysterical or epileptic attack he was recording. By dividing the attack into
concrete stages otherwise imperceptible to the human eye, in order to ana-
lyze it better, he was 'narrativizing' or 'fictionalizing' it, rather than sim-
ply 'recording' it.[XII]

His backside was getting warm. He didn't realize he was sitting in front of the fireplace. His heartbeat slowed down. The only
sounds that reached him now were the crackling of the fire and
the half-whispered words the library assistants exchanged with
patrons. Someone tapped him on the shoulder.

"The materials you requested are available now."

The librarian placed a box of 19TH century family albums on
his table. The photographs he remembered most vividly, since his
last research trip to the library back in April, were several portraits
of dead babies—to whom he was apparently related by blood—
propped up against a bed frame or a wall, their faces turned artistically towards the camera. Although he had not yet identified all
the people in the photographs by name, back in April he had
drawn up a preliminary genealogical tree—based on what he had
read in secondary accounts—which showed the marriages, births
and deaths in the Leblon family over several generations. The
genealogical tree was now missing from the box. But this was not
all. The last time he had seen the photographs they were lying in
a loose pile at the bottom of the box. Now, about a third of them
were attached with paperclips to the pages of a family album in
what looked like a chronological order judging by the date written at the bottom of each photograph. Sheets of paper filled with
handwritten notes were folded neatly and attached to each photograph. None of these notes had been there last April. Bruno
selected several photographs at random and placed them next to
each other, hoping to rediscover the family resemblance he had
once discerned, something in the structure of the faces or in the

dignified postures, perhaps a certain look in the eyes that survived across generations, but the longer he stared at the faces the more unfamiliar they seemed to him.

He looked more closely at the first photograph in the chronological order the bald man calling himself 'Leblon' had established. It was a photograph of a young woman. On the back someone had written a name—*Gaspard Leblon*—followed by a date, *1876*. The name was unfamiliar to Bruno. Underneath, in a smaller font, was the word "melancholy." Bruno had read somewhere that Diamond's photographs had inspired a series of essays by John Conolly, *The Physiognomy of Insanity*, published in 1858 in the *Medical Times and Gazette*. Conolly's essays were illustrated with lithographs based on Diamond's photographs, but there were some significant differences between the two. One of Diamond's most famous photographs, which Bruno remembered well, was that of a woman suffering from melancholy. In the photograph the woman gazed directly into the camera; however, in Conolly's lithograph she looked down, presumably because her downward gaze fit better the classical image of the passive and withdrawn melancholic. In this case, as in most of the cases from that period, the medical diagnosis was deduced from the woman's pose rather than from the camera's supposedly inherent objectivity.

The (melancholy?) woman in the photograph was sitting at one end of a settee with exquisite curved legs. With one hand she was propping up her head, while in the other one, lying in her lap, she was holding a hairbrush encrusted with precious stones. Her hair, arranged in an elaborate bun on top of her head, seemed like it was going to come undone any moment. She was looking down. Her blue evening gown, sleeveless and low-necked, was perfectly matched with white, long suede gloves that reached well over the elbow. Behind the settee the room extended further back, filled with numerous elegant pieces of furniture typical of the period: a writing desk, a grand mirror with a golden frame, several smaller sofas and tables, a miniature dollhouse. A sheet of paper with handwritten notes was attached to the back of the photograph with a paperclip. Bruno removed the paperclip and

began reading the text, which, he soon realized, was—or purport-
ed to be—a description of the photograph.

*Mrs. Leblon sits on an elegant settee in the middle of a large room,
most likely the sitting room in the Chateau. On the wall behind her we
can see a beautiful clock dating back to the middle of the 19TH century.
The heavy pendulum remains frozen in the upper right corner of its trajectory. An unfinished letter lies on top of the writing desk visible just to
the side of the clock. The ink pen is propped up against the edge of the
inkwell, as if the writer—Mrs. Leblon herself?—was interrupted in the
middle of writing and forgot to return to the desk. The curtains are drawn,
allowing only a tiny ray of light to reach the center of the room, just
behind the settee, where a tray with exquisitely drawn teacups and tea
plates sits on top of a mahogany table. Tea has been served and abandoned. The dignified faces of men and women of the family look down
from the portraits on the walls, their looks intersecting somewhere in the
center of the room, where Mrs. Leblon is sitting with her back towards
them. If we look closely we can see several of her hairs stuck in the hairbrush in her hand. With her other hand Mrs. Leblon is supporting her
lovely head, as if afraid that her whole body might fall apart if she accidentally forgets to prop it up. She is alone.*

*Or is she? In front of the right leg of the settee a ray of light is reflect-
ed off of something small and round. A marble ball. A bit further to the
right there is another one. And another one. Our eyes move instinctively
to the right where the heavy draped curtains hang oppressively over the
edge of the frame. There is something there. We can only see the contours
of a small human figure receding in the deep shadows. One look through
the magnifying glass confirms our suspicions. Someone is sitting there. A
child. Knee-length breeches. A jacket with a round-collar shirt. He looks
to be about nine. He is sitting on the floor, both legs tucked under his
body. His light brown hair is combed to one side, sticking ruefully to his
pale forehead. He is playing distractedly with marble balls but his head is
turned to the right. He is looking in the direction of the settee. Mrs. Leblon
remains oblivious to his presence.*

The text ended here. Bruno examined the photograph
through his magnifying glass. If there was a child in the corner his
face and the upper part of his torso receded in the irreversible
darkness of fickle early film exposure. He flipped the photograph:

now he noticed there was something else scribbled in the lower left corner. With a little bit of effort he was able to decipher the following sentence: *The scene depicted in the photograph might be helpful in establishing an early symptomatology of the psychopathology under investigation.*

Bruno moved on to the next photograph—a long dining table over which hung a heavy chandelier. He unfolded the sheet of paper attached to the photograph and began reading.

The dining room in Chateau de Lourps, lit by a grand chandelier hanging ominously over the dining table, was exactly fourteen meters long. Gaspard had measured it several times over the years. His father, Duke Philippe Leblon, was busy inspecting the chicken carcass before him. His mother, hands crossed peacefully in her lap, stared at the drawn burgundy curtains. The Duke put down his fork and announced without a hint of disappointment that he had to go to Paris tonight. He walked over to his wife and awkwardly kissed her on the cheek. On the way out he distractedly patted his son on the head. Gaspard dragged his fork across the empty plate. His mother held her head between her hands and closed her eyes.

The next photograph in the sequence featured several inconspicuous buildings huddled together at the bottom of a valley. It was taken from a distance, making it impossible to identify the people walking through the courtyard. The text accompanying the photograph read:

The Jesuit seminary crowded itself into the nooks and crannies of an ancient abbey, a three-storey structure that served as a study hall and dormitory, and two houses near the main property. The Duke walked side by side with the Father Rector, a portly man in his sixties.

"You've made the right decision in bringing your son to us," the Father Rector said. "A royal college is no place to be for a young Christian. You can never be too careful with these Voltairian skeptics, with their vicious habits and loathsome morals. Students come out of their college spiritually and intellectually malnourished, glorifying incest, adultery, and revolt. Rhetoric is the core of our curriculum," he raised his hand. "Ad perfectam enim eloquentiam informat."

It occurred to the Duke that he was expected to show some interest in his son's future education.

"What about the gentlemanly accomplishments: music, drawing, fencing?" he asked unenthusiastically.

The Father Rector rewarded him with a faint smile.

"Those are taught only during times of recreation. And now let me show you some of the classrooms."

The Duke checked his watch. He had to be in Paris in less than an hour.

At the opposite end of the Seminary Gaspard was dragging his feet behind a young seminarian in a black frock coat. He had the unenviable task of showing the boy around and introducing him to the basic rules of seminary life.

"You get up at 5AM. You have an hour and a half of study before attending Mass, followed by breakfast at 7:30 and recreation until 8. The rest of the morning is taken up with study until lunch at noon, followed by recreation, then the rosary and study at 1:30. In the afternoon there is another class, a half hour of recreation, ten minute reading of a religious book, study until 7:20, supper at 7:30, and at 8:15 night prayers and bed. Any questions?"

Later in the afternoon Gaspard stood in the middle of the empty courtyard and watched his father's carriage disappear in the distance raising a lot of dust in its wake.

Bruno picked out two random photographs that had not yet been included in the chronology. The first one featured a young man in a fancy waistcoat walking down a street with another, considerably older man, who sported a beard and a pair of glasses. The men were walking away from the camera: their faces were not visible. Bruno flipped the photograph: "Gaspard Leblon and Doctor Gautier." The second photograph was of a group of young men listening to a lecture. A tiny black circle was drawn around one of the faces in the back, right where the image began to get out of focus. Bruno checked the back of the photograph: "Gaspard Leblon, university years." The same handwriting. He placed the two photographs side by side and tried to compare the blurry face at the back of the classroom with the back of the young man's head in the first photograph. It was impossible to tell if this was one and the same person. He rubbed his thumb over the name 'Gaspard Leblon'. When he removed his hand the words were slightly smudged. They had certainly not been written over a hundred years ago. Several days ago seemed like a better estimate.

Bruno went through all photographs in the box, selecting only those featuring men: a group of men hunting; two men sitting in a café; dozens of men getting on a train; a man in a shaving salon; a young boy dressed in a seminary uniform standing alone in the middle of a courtyard; dozens of young boys in seminary uniforms posing for a group photograph; patients in white robes lying in hospital beds; an old man giving a lecture in a crowded auditorium; men standing around a freshly dug out grave in the back of an old chateau; a child sitting, forlorn, at the dinner table. On the back of all photographs the same hand had written the name "Gaspard Leblon" followed by different dates and brief explanatory notes: "Gaspard Leblon hunting," "Gaspard Leblon, Café des Flores," "Gaspard Leblon, trip to London," "Gaspard Leblon, Opera House," "Gaspard Leblon, the Jesuit Seminary." The name was written even on the back of photographs featuring only women, as if Gaspard Leblon existed as an afterthought in the mind of everyone photographed.

In all the manuscripts and letters he had read there hadn't been a single mention of a Gaspard Leblon. Perhaps Gaspard Leblon was known under a pseudonym? Or perhaps the man's real name was something else and 'Gaspard' *was* his pseudonym? Even if Laetitia and Philippe Leblon did have a son, and the baby happened to die very young, as was often the case at that time, surely there would have been a record of that in the annals of family history. There was no evidence that a child by that name had been born. And yet, spread out before Bruno was Gaspard Leblon's entire life, from his earliest days (evidenced by a baby photograph, which had somehow gotten misplaced among the numerous dead baby photographs in the box, although the conventions peculiar to that genre of photography made it difficult to tell the living baby from the dead ones) to his last day (a photograph of an open grave). But which one of these men, now long dead, was Gaspard Leblon? Bruno slowly moved the magnifying glass over the images, looking for a pattern, something that the man circled in every photograph had in common with the men circled in the other photographs, something in the posture, height, haircut, the shape of the head, or the style of clothing. Then he tried the opposite: looking for obvious differences between the men, for any kind of inconsistency that would establish beyond reasonable doubt that these were *not* all one and the same man. It was useless. He could not prove conclusively either that it *was* the same man or that it *was not* the same man.

Last Spring Gaspard Leblon had been no more than a speck of film grain, the result of underexposure or overexposure, part of the background against which the more important and well-known stories of the Leblon family unfolded. Now he had suddenly come into focus, and into existence, linking all photographs in a loose narrative whose beginning, middle and end were still unknown.

The next photograph in the sequence was that of a classroom filled with young seminarians.

The Rector and the Prefect walked to the front of the classroom and surveyed the students' apathetic faces. The Rector cleared his throat.

"Mundus transit et concupiscentia ejus: qui autem facit voluntatem Deiy manet in ceternum. *Mes enfants, the college must seem to you like a sad prison. But we are not jailers. Although we are charged with teaching you, the name we seek above all is the name of Fathers. Obey us, respect us, but do so as children. Despite all the care with which your previous upbringing was surrounded, the very air breathed in this century, so charged with insubordination and pride, has perhaps touched even you. You have to obey. It is the very law of your age, of your weakness, of your inexperience.*"

Later that evening the seminarians were praying the rosary. They began by making the cross and saying the Apostles' Creed. Gaspard watched their lips closely as he tried to remember the words: 'I believe in God, the Father Almighty . . . his only Son . . . conceived . . . suffered . . . crucified, died and . . . descended into hell.'

One of the senior seminarians made a last round of bed checks before turning off the lights. Lying in bed, eyes wide open, hands clasped over his chest like a dead man, Gaspard stared at the ceiling.

Bruno flipped the photograph and studied the young seminarians' faces. The name 'Gaspard Leblon' was clearly written on the back of the photograph but which of the boys did it refer to? Was it the handsome, athletic boy sitting in the first row or the plump one staring, mouth half-open, at the teacher? Or the one sitting in the last row, his face disintegrated by bad film exposure? Bruno picked up the next photograph: a row of simple wooden desks illuminated by bright morning light. A puny old man stood, arms akimbo, at the front of the room. The written account accompanying the photograph identified him as 'Father Charles'.

Gaspard closed his eyes and watched the play of shadows on the inside of his eyelids. Father Charles surveyed the rows of heads before him.

"Which one of you will tell us about the doctrine of ontologism? Gaspard Leblon?"

Father Charles walked over to Gaspard's desk and stood there, demonstratively playing with a wooden ruler.

"What was the question?" Gaspard asked.

Father Charles produced a nasal sound that was meant to express his contempt. He feigned a kind smile.

"The question was about ontologism, though I seriously doubt your current ontological state allows you to speak with any authority on the subject."

Gaspard looked at him provocatively.

"The General published a directive forbidding the basic propositions of ontologism . . ."

He enunciated every word so clearly that Father Charles could not but suspect Gaspard was mocking him. Father Charles raised his hand.

"Benoit will now read it to us."

Benoit began reading in a monotone voice.

"God, as simply being, is every existent being. Also, outside of and besides God, nothing is . . . nothing. . . . Nothing is. Being . . . when being . . . when being exists, it could never be said to be . . . or not. . . . it cannot be . . ."

Father Charles motioned to him to stop and finished reading the passage himself:

"Being, as being, exists in such a way that it could never not be."

Gaspard raised his hand. Frowning, Father Charles motioned to him to speak up.

"What does 'being could never not be' mean? Does it mean I am immortal?"

Father Charles failed to hide his irritation.

"I'm afraid there is no time to speak of immortality or to comment on the arrogance of your question. I want everyone to turn to page three of Feller's Philosophical Catechism.*"*

Ten minutes before closing time Bruno brought the box of photographs back to the check out desk. While he waited in line he saw the impostor, the bald man who claimed his name was Leblon, walk out of the restroom and head toward the main exit, carefully raising his right arm, then the left one, as though he were trying to hang on to something invisible in front of him and using his arms to pull himself forward. As he walked forward, with a somnambulistic expression on his face devoid of any vitality, mouth slightly open, his frail body failed to make any impressions on the polyester material from which his suit was made: his silhouette, made entirely of straight lines, simply transformed from one geometrical configuration into another. Although his feet and arms were moving, his torso and face appeared mummified.

Bruno asked the librarian if she was aware of the nature of Monsieur Leblon's research. Monsieur Leblon was researching his family history, she informed him.

"Yes, I am," he said impatiently. "I was asking about *his* research."

"He is writing his family history," she repeated.

"What do you mean *his* family history?"

"We are closing in ten minutes," the librarian reminded him.

Perhaps the bald man was one of those distant, unfortunately real family relatives one reads about in novels, a relative so distant that years go by with no one suspecting their existence until one day they appear, out of nowhere, claiming their share of the family's collective memory or, more often, its fortune. Or perhaps he was a con artist trying to insinuate himself in one of the oldest, most affluent aristocratic families in Paris by claiming to be a descendant of this Gaspard Leblon. In any case, if he wanted to understand the bald man's motivation for claiming to be a Leblon Bruno had first to find out who the mysterious Gaspard Leblon—he decided to call him "X"—was.

In *Physiognomy, or the Corresponding Analogy between the Conformation of the Features and the Ruling Passions of the Soul*[XIII] the Swiss pastor Johann Kaspar Lavater writes that because of nature's transitoriness, one can obtain a better scientific knowledge of man from studying representations of man rather than studying the man himself: "If we could indeed seize the fleeting transitions of nature, or had she her moments of stability, it would then be much more advantageous to contemplate nature than her likeness, but this being impossible, and since likewise few people will suffer themselves to be observed, sufficiently to deserve the name of observation, it is to me indisputable that a better knowledge of man may be obtained from portraits than from nature, she being thus uncertain, thus fugitive." Photography was thus said to be capable of distinguishing what is constant and typical in the character from what is habitual, and what is habitual from what is accidental and ephemeral. But what could anyone possibly say about the permanent, habitual and the accidental in Gaspard Leblon's character based on a series of photographs from all of which he was visually exiled? If X was writing the history of the Leblon family using the photographs in the family archive, why would he pick a member of the family who was, for all intents and purposes, absent from the family's photographic memory?

In the lobby the last few patrons waited silently for their coats. The coat check girl yawned and secretly turned up the volume on her iPod as she handed Bruno a uniform jacket with the initials *MDI*. Bruno showed her his coat number again. She apologized for her mistake half-heartedly and after some searching brought out his coat.

Across the street from the library tiny shopper silhouettes moved up and down the stairs inside a transparent mall that resembled a dollhouse filled with carefully positioned miniature humans dramatically lit by miniature chandeliers. The city was now entering the part of day Bruno dreaded the most, early evening, which reunited friends and families for shopping, dining, entertaining and other foreign (to Bruno) social activities.

The movable 'homeless city' had migrated to the other side of the street, closer to the mall. The women were putting the last touches on their sons and daughters before sending them out to assume their evening posts at the mall entrance, where they would spend the evening retelling the same orphan tale—full of pathos and celebrating the strength of the human spirit—in hopes of appealing to Christmas shoppers' guilty conscience. Two street kids were getting a special treatment by what Bruno assumed to be their father, a tall, muscular man with an incongruously small moustache. The man was completely engrossed in slapping one of the boys with the back of his hand. The boy staggered back but managed to keep his balance. The man stepped forward and gently lifted up the boy's chin, inspecting the damage he had wrought. Content with the result he pushed the boy toward the other kid. The first boy raised his arm. The man stopped him, repositioned his body, raised his arm again and repositioned it at several different angles, demonstrating the different types of blows the boy could deliver and their respective degrees of effectiveness. The boy listened carefully, his dirty face focused and serious. The man stepped back and crossed his arms in front of his chest. The boy raised his arm again, held it up there for an instant before letting it fall across the second kid's face. The second kid screamed in pain and fell down. The man pushed the first boy aside and bent over the other one to inspect the damage. He then stood up, satisfied with the result of his training, and patted both boys on the back. They were ready to play the lucrative pre-Christmas abused-and-abandoned role-play.

The older, more experienced street kids assumed their positions. The adults huddled together to watch their pride and joy. One of them waved a ten-euro bill. Bruno wondered if they were betting on whose child would bring home the juiciest bacon. Fontaine stood by the mall entrance, eating roasted chestnuts. Bruno felt a dull pain in his abdomen: he hadn't eaten all day. He sat down on a bench. He would rest there for a while and then look for a place to eat. The metal bench hurt his bony back so he leaned forward, letting his head sink between his shoulders and his arms dangle freely in front of his knees. The repetitive, maudlin melody of the merry-go-round lulled him to sleep.

He woke up abruptly and raised his hand to check the time. Something small and shiny dropped from his hand on the ground. He picked it up. Two euros. A dozen other coins were lying on the ground in front of him. Must have fallen out of someone's pocket. He was about to stand up when another coin landed in his hands. He looked up. A young woman smiled at him reassuringly and walked away. A teenage girl stopped in front of Bruno's bench and took a picture of herself.

"Has no one ever told you that if you are taking a picture in public you must ask the people who might end up in your picture for permission?"

The girl blushed.

"I'm sorry. I'll delete it."

She pushed a button.

"Oh, you are actually not in the picture!"

She showed him the picture and zoomed in several times. She was right: he was not there. An underwhelming feeling of the uselessness of it all gripped him. The night before, while reading Fontaine's report, he could have sworn he felt a slight inflation in his presence, as if someone had redrawn the contours of his silhouette with a black marker. Apparently it was an erasable one.

Tomorrow he will buy one of those cheap cell phones and call Fontaine to tell him the whole thing is off. The truth is he was finding the little detective investigation he had slipped into inadvertently at the Public Library—his investigation into the mysterious, *equally invisible* Gaspard Leblon—a welcome distraction him from his own existential crisis.

Someone grabbed his shoulder. The man with the tiny moustache loomed large over him.

"Find yourself another spot," he hissed. "I've got a family to feed."

The man picked up the money from the ground and showed it to Bruno, as if he was going to do a magic trick, before slipping it in his own pocket.

On the way home Bruno stopped at a liquor store, whose freshly painted shelves stacked up with attractive looking bottles promised escape in a wide range of spirit concentrations. He tried to pay for a bottle of whiskey with the money he had inadvertently 'earned' that night. The cashier gave him a dirty look and took her time counting the pennies and dimes. He was two dollars short.

When he finally got home, after stopping by the Post Office to pick up Fontaine's second—and last—report, it was close to midnight. He poured water in the teakettle, turned on the oven and opened the oven door: this was his alternative way of heating the apartment.

The subject spent the day at the library pretending to read a book titled *The Black Swan*. As a side note, I wish to point out that the book's argument is rather poor. The author claims that when faced with an absolutely random, unpredictable event or phenomenon the human mind has an urge to tame the randomness and explain the event retrospectively inscribing it in a series of causes and effects we can understand rationally. I find the book a poorly disguised mockery of the detective method under the pretext of being a critique of the scientific method. The subject was also actively, yet discreetly, keeping an eye on the same bald man he had followed the night before. Of course, it is perfectly possible that the subject is not yet consciously plotting anything against that man. Nevertheless, it is equally likely that he is doing just that.

Upon leaving the library the subject walked over to the 'homeless city' opposite the mall. He sat down on one of the benches near the mall entrance, bent forward and extended his hands, palms up. Many of the shoppers coming out of the mall dropped change in his hands. Some of it fell on the ground but he didn't make any effort to collect it. Too embarrassed to acknowledge what he was doing (begging) he pretended to be oblivious to the money. When he finally looked up he acted surprised to find all that money in front of him but then quickly collected it. Here we have yet another fitting motive—money!—for a potential crime, though, as I pointed out earlier, the exact nature or time of the future crime is yet to be determined. I hope once the crime has been committed the police will review my report and acknowledge that I identified two possible motives for the crime (yet to be committed) very early on.

The subject had one more encounter, this time with a teenager who tried to take a picture of herself in front of the mall. For no apparent reason the subject demanded that she include him in the picture but when she did he seemed sorely disappointed with the result. Indeed, his reaction to the photograph she took was so out of proportion with the situation that it can only be read as a sign of his latent narcissistic personality: apparently the subject needs to be constantly presented with new evidence of his existence.

5

9 AM. Fontaine was already waiting outside, indifferent to the revolting drizzle that had already set the lethargic tone for another December day. Bruno picked up the cell phone he had bought the day before and dialed Fontaine's number. He informed Fontaine that the man he had been hired to follow had finally reappeared.

"You mean his existence has been conclusively re-established?" Fontaine asked skeptically.

Bruno answered in the affirmative and then assured Fontaine he would receive the remainder of his honorarium by the end of the week. Ten minutes later, after waiting for Fontaine to call a cab, Bruno jumped into another one. The driver, an old Moroccan whose cheerfulness and gregariousness Bruno found uncalled for, tried various techniques for initiating small talk, apparently undeterred by Bruno's uncooperativeness. Bruno listened sullenly to the man's accented monologue, which included, among other things, a brief personal history of his immigration to Paris and his current, allegedly well-deserved marital bliss.

The librarian brought out the box of photographs and set it down on Bruno's reading table. He began arranging the photographs in front of him.

"I apologize for interrupting your work," the librarian whispered unapologetically, "but the other day you forgot to give me your library card. If you don't have a card yet I am going to prepare one for you but I need your name and address."

There was no time to buy time. He told her the first name that popped into his head.

"Fontaine. Jacques Fontaine."

He then gave her a fake address and phone number. She returned to her desk and began entering the information in the paper catalogue and then in the electronic database. Jacques Fontaine. Jacques Fontaine. He saw the name writing itself infinitely across his mind's screen, Caligari style. Had he just planted a clue in his own future criminal investigation? He imagined a detective, perhaps Fontaine himself, investigating Bruno's (murder? disappearance?) for years without success until one day, having searched the Public Library database numerous times, Fontaine decides to review all library records one last time and suddenly stumbles upon his own name on a yellowish library card.

Bruno sat up straight. He should worry about what to do with Fontaine when and if the time comes to eliminate any possible suspicions, which might have nothing to do with . . . what to do with Fontaine . . . how to eliminate any possible suspicions . . . what to do about any possible suspicions . . . how to eliminate Fontaine? Bruno stopped his ears. Why? Did he think he was hearing voices?

He opened the box. The description of the photograph of the young woman and the apparently invisible little boy was on top of the pile. The photograph was gone. Bruno walked over to the counter and asked the librarian if she or any of her assistants had removed any photographs from the box. She assured him they had done nothing of the sort. He demanded that she check the library database. She turned the computer screen towards him. To his surprise, all photographs in the Leblon family archive were marked "In process."

"We are in the process of updating all photographs in the family archive," she explained.

"Updating them?"

"There have been some questions about the photographs' provenance. Most of them are now undergoing a process of re-attribution in light of recent findings."

"I don't understand. It's been widely accepted that these are photographs of my family."

"I thought you said your name was Fontaine," she said coldly.

Retreat, a voice in his head said. Yes, indeed, his name was Fontaine, he told her, mumbling an apology, something about being under a lot of stress, academic obligations, tenure review coming up, and so on. He couldn't stop himself. Fortunately she did.

"If you'll excuse me, Monsieur Fontaine, I have a lot of work to do."

He had to force himself to be slightly more apologetic than he was constitutionally capable of being.

"Of course, you're busy. If you don't mind, one last question. . . ."

He saw the window of opportunity—circumscribed by her low level of tolerance for any amateur questions concerning archival methods—closing fast in his face.

"You mentioned that the decision to re-attribute the photographs arose in response to recent findings. What might those be?"

"We're in the process of identifying the people in the background of each photograph. The bit players, so to speak."

He asked her if Monsieur Leblon would need the photographs today or he could have them for a while. She informed him that Monsieur Leblon usually came in the afternoon, after his shift at the museum was over. Bruno remembered that on several occasions the impostor had come to the library wearing what looked like a uniform, which, Bruno now knew, bore the insignia of one of the major museums in the city. He closed his eyes and tried to visualize the uniform. MDI. Museum of Domestic Interior.

The Museum of Domestic Interior occupied a beautifully restored 19TH century building on the corner of Rue Molière and Rue Charlemagne. It turned out to be a rather popular destination, although Bruno suspected this had more to do with the despondent meteorological state of affairs that morning—which had prompted many people who would not normally consider themselves art lovers to seek shelter in the warm, brightly lit museum halls—than with people's enthusiasm for historical bric-à-brac. He checked in his coat, picked up a free museum guide, and sat in a chair near the exit.

Bruno had always found museums and art galleries reassuring. He had a soft spot for museum cafés in particular. The minimalist furniture, the overpriced pastries bearing mellifluous French names melting on his tongue, the strong smell of espresso and ultra-dark chocolate, the Bossa Nova music playing seductively in the background, the soft whisper of museum patrons discussing anything else but art: as far as he was concerned all that was enough to calm the nerves of the worst-case neurasthenic.

The permanent exhibit was spread over five floors and ranged from ancient times to the 21ST century. According to the museum brochure this was the most comprehensive display of its kind in the world. A collection of home accessories was currently on tour from MOMA. Bruno walked through a series of identical square rooms, each devoted to a particular home accessory: one room featured vases, another one candlesticks, yet another one ceramic figurines of kittens, dogs, girls and boys. A single museum guard was assigned to every room. They were mostly men and women past their prime, who had retired a long time ago—the museum was keeping them out of pity, that is, gratitude for years of service. Afraid to spend their halcyon retirement days in the frightening privacy of their basement studio apartments, they were relieved, indeed delighted, to stand still four to six hours per day, silently watching museum patrons go slightly berserk at the sight of a 12TH century toilet bowl or an 18TH century baby cot made entirely of gold.

The vase exposition was especially crowded. The guard, a woman around sixty, short and plump, stood in the corner with her back to the window. Bruno followed the direction of her look: she was staring at the opposite wall. Once in a while she would incline her head to the left as though she had noticed something on the wall and wanted to see if it would still be there if she changed slightly her point of view. Then she would straighten herself up again and resume staring. Although she managed to keep her head straight, her eyes would gradually begin to droop. Seconds later she would open her eyes and look around, startled, confused about where she was. Assuming her previous neutral expression she would cross her arms behind her back and stroll through the room, glancing at the display cases with a slightly proprietary look, as though she herself had placed the objects inside them and had granted museum patrons permission to view them, but only on her watch.

In the next room a male guard in his early seventies sat in the special chair reserved for him, keeping a watchful eye on the patrons crowding around display cases that provided a historical overview of inkwells, fountain pens, cigar cases and other manly accouterments. Presently he stood up, walked over to one of the display cases, and looked carefully at the cigar cases inside. It wasn't immediately clear if he was trying to trick himself into believing that he had never seen these items before, or if this was part of the numerous routine check-ups he was supposed to do on the hour. Bruno approached the glass case and stood right next to the guard who was surprisingly well preserved for his age. *Must be the pleasantly constant temperature in the museum,* Bruno decided. The guard stepped back but Bruno saw, out of the corner of his eye, that the man was still watching him. Bruno stood there for a long time before walking over to the opposite side of the display case, feigning interest in one of the cigar cases while secretly savoring the guard's mounting irritation. Finally, he looked up, pretending to notice the guard for the first time.

"Is there a problem?" Bruno asked.

The guard furrowed his brows and uncrossed his arms.

"Monsieur?" he said, without a trace of the expected obsequiousness in his baritone voice.

"Is there a limit to the amount of time patrons are allowed to spend viewing each individual display?" Bruno inquired.

The guard stared at Bruno with unconcealed resentment.

"There is no limit. However, the recommended amount of time is two to three minutes per individual display. Our prerogative is to avoid crowding and to ensure that every patron has equal access to all display cases and sufficient time to view all of them."

The guard spoke in a self-important tone, a familiar strategy used by those not in a position of power to cover up their powerlessness.

"I don't think you need to be worried about crowds. Still, if it is your *prerogative. . . .*"

Bruno emphasized the last word. The guard bit his lip and straightened his uniform, which he seemed to believe the only appropriate response under the circumstances. Bruno returned to watching the cigar cases. The guard crossed his arms in front of his chest and stood on the opposite side of the case. The battle of wills continued for several minutes, during which the guard kept glancing longingly at his chair. Finally, he walked away from the display case and sat down. Bruno waited a few more minutes, savoring his victory, before slowly walking out of the room, hands behind his back. He waited a few seconds before quietly retracing his steps and peering back into the room: the guard was standing by the display case, face glued to the glass, staring at the objects inside. He was trying to re-appropriate for himself that which Bruno had 'stolen' from him in the last ten minutes. Bruno let him.

He walked up to the third floor, which housed the museum's main attraction: a series of meticulously recreated domestic interiors. To recreate the feeling of 'what life was like back then' each simulated environment was populated with wax figures dressed in period costumes and engaged in various activities representative of this or that historical era. The result: a series of surrealistic 'scenes of daily life', including intimate scenes from an 18TH century brothel, a 17TH century baby in a crib extravagantly decorated with emeralds, sapphires and diamonds, and an old man making dubious use of a representative medieval toilet. Most elderly art lovers perked up right around the Renaissance, which awakened the 'inner artist' in all of them, prompting them to snap numerous pictures of the different displays, of course always from 'creative angles'. They had found a way to fill the void of their post-retirement existence with frequent trips to museums and galleries where they discussed what they had learned in their evening Arts Appreciation class by playing the 'guess which artist and guess which year' game with other feeble-minded men and women. What would they do with themselves, Bruno wondered, if it were not for French and Italian for Beginners, French Impressionism and, last but not least, Advanced French Baking.

In the middle of the 19TH century Bruno stopped in front of an impressive display recounting the story of photography's invention. The wall behind the museum guard—an obese woman with a small head and a short haircut that further intensified the visual incongruity between head and torso—was covered with original photographs from the period, representative of the dominant genres at the time, travel photography and family portraits. The guard sighed in her sleep and as she repositioned her body in the tiny chair her right shoulder moved a bit to the side, revealing another photograph, of which only the upper left corner had been visible until now. It was a photograph of an aristocratic couple: the man and the woman stood very close to each other, without touching. The man, holding a cane in his right hand and wearing a pince-nez, looked sternly at the camera. The woman, her hair collected in a small bun hanging low at the back of her neck, looked slightly to the side, as if she had heard the photographer's instructions a second too late.

Bruno studied the photograph for a long time, much longer than a photograph of this kind would warrant. Nothing distinguished it from the other photographs on the wall, nothing, that is, except the woman in the photograph. He had seen that face before: the long alabaster neck, the small earlobes, the hair tied in a bun at the back of the head, the eyes staring, with a look of resignation, at something beyond the edges of the frame. She was the young woman in the library photograph, Mrs. Leblon. She was wearing a different dress and she looked slightly younger in the museum photograph but there was no doubt it was the same woman.

Bruno walked forward, stepping into the second part of the 19TH century represented here by a sitting room in a typical French chateau. The room looked vaguely familiar. Perhaps he had seen a photograph of it in the museum guide. He leafed through the brochure but couldn't find a photograph of the room. Most of the room was dark on account of the heavy curtains, drawn together, allowing only a tiny ray of light to fall across the center of the room. The piece of furniture closest to the do-not-cross line was an elegant settee with curved legs. Behind it

stood a writing desk covered with sheets of paper, among them
an unfinished letter. Tea and biscuits were served on a little table
in the middle of the room, behind the settee. Bruno stared at the
little pink flowers hand-drawn on the teacups and plates. Could
that be a coincidence? He recognized the room now: it was the
same room described in the handwritten note attached to the
photograph of Mrs. Leblon in the family archive at the Public
Library. The room in the photograph had been meticulously
recreated—from the burgundy settee and the unfinished letter on
the writing desk, to the tea tray and the drawn plush curtains
sinking the room into almost complete darkness—with the added
bonus that the whole thing was now rendered in color. The only
thing missing from the museum display was Mrs. Leblon. This had
once been the room where she entertained guests, served tea,
wrote letters (that she never finished) and spent long hours lost in
reverie on the burgundy settee, her body sinking further and further into it. To whom was her unfinished letter addressed? Why
didn't she finish it? Who was she expecting for tea that afternoon?
Did they ever come? Bruno tried to recreate in his mind Mrs.
Leblon's habitual movements: sitting at the writing desk, standing
up abruptly, anxiously pacing back and forth, pouring tea, walking to the window, looking out through the tiny opening in the
curtains, forgetting the tea, pacing across the floor, restless, biting
her lips, sitting down, lying down, trying to fall asleep, failing, sitting up again, ordering her body to remain still, stilling her
thoughts, eventually sinking into a pleasingly numb state, free of
the anxiety of waiting anymore for anything, anyone. Bruno
leaned over the do-not-cross line to take a closer look at the settee. Was that the imprint of Mrs. Leblon's body on the soft,
impressionable texture? He instinctively looked at the corner of
the room, where the curtains fell heavily to the floor into a stagnant burgundy pool of plush. The little boy playing with marbles
that he expected to find was not there.

But there was something else there, or rather someone else.
At first Bruno thought the man sitting in the chair was part of the
exhibit, one of the many wax figures that populated the painfully reconstructed 19TH century. Perhaps he was the master of the
house, a late 19TH century dandy shown here in his typical milieu.

Almost immediately he realized he was wrong or, rather, he *rea-soned* he must be wrong: instead of an elegant waistcoat the man was wearing the museum guard uniform with the letters MDI embroidered, in gold, on his front pocket. It was only the discrep-ancy in period clothing styles, rather than any obvious difference between a live human being and a wax figure, that convinced Bruno the man before him was a human being of flesh and blood. The guard was asleep. The color of his uniform, the same color as that of the curtains falling behind him and around him, made him virtually invisible: it was almost inevitable to mistake him for an element of the room's interior décor. A single ray of light fell across his head. *He was bald.*

6

When he returned to the library Bruno opened his laptop and logged into the Museum of Domestic Interior official website. It seemed the only real skill a museum guard was expected to have was the ability to withstand physical exhaustion and mental numbness, that is, to sit or stand in one place for a long period of time (four to six hours) without falling asleep. What made the danger of falling asleep so real was not only the great amount of time one was expected to remain still yet fully alert (to potential disruptions) but also the crushing lack of change in the guard's immediate environment, not to mention its artificiality. The museum management must have been aware of the negative psychological side effects this type of occupation might have, particularly on a sensitive personality, because museum regulations stipulated that guards be assigned to different parts of the museum every week to vary their surroundings. Bruno scrolled to the bottom of the screen and checked room assignments over the last several months. X was hired eight months ago, in April 2012. The records showed that in the first few weeks he had switched rooms every other day like everyone else; however, for the last two months he had been consistently assigned to the same late 19TH century sitting room.

Bruno sat back in his chair and stared at the bright screen of his laptop. Over time, he thought, X must have gotten so used to the 19TH century sitting room he was guarding that his habitual relationship to the room transformed it into a second home for him. He is allotted a small place in the corner, where he sits in a simple wooden chair, from 9AM to 3PM every day, Tuesday to Saturday, surrounded by 19TH century relics. Upon being hired he is given a uniform, which he is supposed to keep in a locker and change into every morning. As the days go by X begins forgetting to change out of his uniform at the end of his shift. Instead of having it cleaned together with the uniforms of the rest of the museum staff, he takes it to the cleaners himself and then irons it carefully at home before putting it on again the following morning. No one notices anything: all that matters is that X is always on time, his uniform always clean and perfectly pressed. Eventually they stop noticing that he is wearing the uniform *all the time*.

When he is first led into the 19TH century room where he will spend one fourth of every day, his chair is in one corner of the room, close to the exit, well concealed by the heavy curtains. With every passing day, however, his chair begins turning, ever so slightly, inward, and move, ever so slightly, closer to the curtain, until one day it no longer faces the little space in front of the exhibit, on the other side of the do-not-cross line, but instead faces the 19TH century room, of which it seems to have become a part. The curtains now conceal X from view and it is only by a special effort that museum patrons can see that there is a real man sitting in the corner of the room.

The first couple of weeks X stares at the furniture in the room simply because there is nothing else to do. The museum is usually empty in the morning except for the occasional high school student tour. X sits in his chair, focusing his attention on one specific part of the display. He observes it carefully, studying every feature of its design, feeling its texture with his eyes, sometimes walking over to touch it to see if it feels exactly as he has imagined it would feel. Then he moves on to the next object. At first he thinks a single day will be sufficient to do an inventory of all objects on display. Soon he realizes that he needs an entire day to get to know a single object. Something is slowing him down. As he stares at any given object his perception of it expands further and further. He becomes aware not only of the material properties of the object—what it is made of, for example—but also of its uses and functions, and the second he starts thinking about those his mind, until then tranquil and still, is abuzz with sounds and images, entire scenes of the object's past playing themselves out before his eyes. He imagines the men and women who have once sat in the room on an overcast December day, just like this one, the young woman waking up from her afternoon nap and beginning to write a letter, which she will never finish, the tea getting cold, the clouds moving sluggishly above the patches of frozen ground outside. X watches the dust accumulate—minute-by-minute, hour-by-hour, day-by-day—and then watches it disappear the following week when all rooms in the exhibit are vacuum-cleaned.

One day X gives the cleaning lady one hundred euros in exchange for her cleaning supplies. He dusts off the small pillows tastefully arranged on the settee, cleans the thick layer of dust on top of the writing desk and the tea table, and vacuums the carpet. The following week he boils some tea at home and brings it to work in a small thermos. At the end of his shift he pours it carefully in the teacups on display and places a few small biscuits he has baked himself on the tea plates. At the Sunday flea market he buys a beautiful antique inkwell and a fountain pen. Every afternoon before he leaves work he takes them out and adds a word or two to the unfinished letter on top of the writing desk, carefully copying the unknown author's handwriting. As time goes by, words become sentences, sentences swell into paragraphs, until one day he purchases 19TH century letter paper on eBay and brings it to work so he can continue writing the woman's unfinished letter.

When one morning a couple of elderly museum patrons enter the room they find X standing by the window, looking out. There is nothing to look at: no rolling green hills and valleys, not even the museum's parking lot. Just a brick wall. The patrons are too polite to ask him what he is doing there, behind the do-not-cross line, but also self-righteous enough not to let him think that he can get away without explaining himself. He tells them he is inspecting the curtains for any possible damage from yesterday's unruly teenagers (another high school tour gone amok). The woman notices the imprint of X's body on the settee, next to the "Do not touch!" sign. Indeed, X has spent the previous night in the room, sleeping on the settee. He mumbles something about museum renovations and annual checks of the historical accuracy of the display. They buy his story. He never repeats his mistake, not because he is afraid he would be caught, and very likely dismissed, but because he realizes he doesn't need to: he doesn't need to touch the objects, to lie down on the settee, to pretend to be drinking tea from the teacups on display. He understands that the less interactive his relationship with the room, the more the room opens itself up to him, until one day it *belongs* to him.

After months of sitting in the same chair, surrounded by the same objects, he stops *seeing* them. He begins *recognizing* them and, eventually, *remembering* them. Every object is now transformed into a repository of memories—memories of his earlier perceptions of the object and therefore memories of himself as well, of his past selves in this or that moment. On rare occasions he even experiences a déjà vu: his memory of a particular object is not false because he has never seen it before (this is impossible for he has seen every single object in the room multiple times); rather, it is false only in the sense that he attributes his present perception to an earlier memory but not to the right one. He can distinguish his present perception from his memories of previous perceptions, but since his previous perceptions are so numerous and fairly similar—he is, after all, limited to perceiving the same objects over and over again—they begin to dissolve into one another. Eventually, he finds it difficult to say for sure if he is remembering a past perception from the point of view of a more recently remembered perception, or he is remembering forward, that is, remembering a more recently remembered perception from the point of view of an older one.

The clock struck 7. Bruno opened his eyes. The screen of his laptop had frozen into an abstract shape resembling a bald man's face. He turned off the reading lamp and put all photographs back in the box. As he was leaving the librarian called after him.

"Monsieur Fontaine!" she repeated, more insistently. He realized she was calling him.

"You forgot your library card," she said and handed him the card with a name that was not his.

Outside the lights of the passing cars formed luminous abstract shapes that hung in the air for a split second before disintegrating back into new abstractions. Bruno tried to get a pack of cigarettes at the corner kiosk but realized his wallet was empty. All he wanted was a shot of whiskey. Several shots. The red neon sign of the Grand Casino flashed across the street.

He spent the night at the roulette table. In the beginning of the evening he had a lucky streak, amassing a respectable amount of money in a short period of time. He spent almost all of it on expensive drinks, which he consumed quickly and without any enjoyment. When things started to wind down he insisted on playing another game, then another one, and another one. He kept losing but did not feel disappointed or angry. Neither was he determined to win. After spending all his cash he started betting his savings. He responded to every losing turn of the roulette by betting twice the amount the next time around.

When he finally stumbled back home the door to Mrs. Damier's apartment was open. He heard her voice coming from the apartment opposite hers where another old woman, exactly like Mrs. Damier but for some reason bearing a different name, lived. Every once in a while the two of them paid each other a visit to catch up on the little that was going on in their lives. Now they were discussing the decline of proper manners among grocery store owners. They were naming names. Through the crack in the door Bruno could see a bottle of sherry sitting on a little table in the hallway. Mrs. Damier had a sweet tooth. He had never been a fan of desert wines but he was desperate for another drink.

Sudden bankruptcy pushes people to the edge, he thought as he climbed up the stairs to his apartment, bottle in hand. It was difficult to imagine what he might be capable of but under the present circumstances he thought it would be prudent to expect nothing less than *anything* from himself.

7

Bruno lifted up his head and looked around: he was lying on his kitchen floor. He checked his back pocket: his wallet was still there. But what good was it if all it contained were maxed out credit cards. After three cups of coffee he was able to think clearly again, which is not to say that he remembered anything from the night before. He tried to call his bank's toll free number but his cell phone was dead. He walked downstairs and reluctantly knocked on Girard's door. Bruno mumbled something he himself did not understand and was surprised when Girard showed him into his living room and pointed to the phone.

"Could you give me a minute please? It's a private matter."

Bruno dialed the number and leaned back in the chair, expecting to be put on hold. Shockingly, the next available agent answered his call after the first ring. She informed him cheerfully that his checking account balance was $409 and then wanted to know if there was anything else she could do for him. He hung up.

"Money problems?"

Bruno turned around. Girard knocked on the wall.

"Thin walls," he explained. "Listen, if you have any financial difficulties . . ."

Bruno assured him he didn't need any help. Girard smiled: he only meant to say that if Bruno had any financial difficulties he should inform Girard right away so that Girard can look for another tenant. Bruno had already reached the bottom of the stairs when he heard Girard's falsetto voice: "Just a friendly reminder: rent is due this Sunday."

As soon as he arrived at the library and sat down at his usual table a husky male voice on the intercom informed everyone that they were testing the library's alarm system. The test was going to continue for another hour and the man sincerely hoped it would not be too disruptive. Bruno stopped his ears and bent over a photograph of a young seminarian wearing a wooden plaque hung from his neck. He was positioned at the very edge of the frame, his face almost completely cut off, except for parts of his neck and one of his ears.

The young seminarians lined up in the dining hall to take their simple meal: a bowl of soup, porridge and a piece of bread. Father Charles walked around the tables, reading out loud passages from Feller's Philosophical Catechism. *Gaspard stared at the seminarians sitting across from him. Their hands moved up to their mouths and down to their plates in nauseating unison. Father Charles's stentorian voice echoed through the hall.*

"Our knowledge of our Lord, the supreme master and creator of this world, is the first principle and the end of everything that exists. What is the basis of such a profound and magnificent truth? It is based on reason's illuminating light, on the sentiments most natural to the human heart, and on the testimony of our senses through which we know the beauty, the order, and the innumerable wonders of this world."

Gaspard emptied his glass of watered down red wine and switched his empty glass with that of the seminarian sitting next to him. He drank his wine slowly, savoring every sip.

Father Charles stopped beside him and raised his hand prophetically.

"I will now demonstrate to you the existence of our Lord. . . ."

When the last students left the dining hall Gaspard stood, alone, before Father Charles and the Prefect. The Prefect held up the wooden plaque he was holding in his hands. Father Charles looked pleased.

"Do you understand the nature of your transgression, my son?" the Prefect asked.

Gaspard said nothing. Father Charles observed him coldly. He took the wooden plaque from the Prefect's hands and hanged it around Gaspard's neck.

"You shall wear the signum for the remainder of the day and think about what you did during lunch. If you happen to catch another student in violation of some rule, you must pass the signum to him. You may not, under any circumstances, pass it off to a friend if he is stupid enough to offer to relieve you of your punishment."

The young Gaspard Leblon came off as a boy-man of few words, an introvert, intelligent, somewhat affectless and aloof. Although he was not explicitly insubordinate and one could even feel pity for him—especially given his non-relationship with his emotionally impotent father—Bruno could not shake the feeling that deep down the boy was not a meek one at all but quite the opposite.

The next photograph—a large mansion in the middle of a wind-swept valley—didn't feature any people at all. Surprisingly, the written account accompanying it was several pages long and included a great deal of dialogue. The mansion in the photograph seemed to have been part of the landscape forever. The inevitable traces of decay were already visible in the paint peeling off of the once yellow walls and in the dark stains defacing the grand staircase leading up to the main entrance. Bruno held the magnifying glass over the photograph. The curtains in all the windows were drawn, except for one. He thought he saw a woman's face behind the window but he wasn't sure. The only other object in the photograph was a horse carriage in the upper right corner. Judging from the size and the direction of the horses' bodies it was leaving the mansion. The accompanying written account opened with a passage in Latin.

Doctus quisque his ipsis studiis suum animum alere debet. Illi fortunati olim suam patriam dilexerant nam ea multa bona capita creabat et divitias eorum alebat.

Father Charles was leading the class in Latin translation. Gaspard turned another page in the volume of Baudelaire's poems he was hiding in his lap.

> *In a rich fertile loam where snails recess*
> *I wish to dig my own deep roomy grave*
> *There to stretch out my old bones, motionless*
> *Snug in death's sleep as sharks are in the wave.*

Gaspard looked out the window at the lush seminary grounds and the sunken graves of the priests buried right next to the chapel. One of the older seminarians peered into the room.

"Gaspard Leblon, your father is here."

Father Charles looked at Gaspard's frock coat disapprovingly.

"Button up."

Out in the courtyard the Duke was pacing nervously. He smiled awkwardly when he saw his son.

"Your mother is not feeling well. She sends her love."

He moved his cane from one hand to the other and looked down at the burned grass.

"The Prefect tells me you are making progress in Latin but you seem to show no aptitude for living languages."

The Duke looked around, as if searching for help. Seeing none, he wiped the sweat from his forehead with a silk handkerchief.

"Well, I'm on my way to Paris. I am glad you are doing well. Your teachers seem pleased with you."

He patted his son on the shoulder and climbed back into the carriage. This time Gaspard did not wait for him to leave.

Bruno put down the sheet of paper and examined the photograph again. The longer he looked at it the more sure he was that this was not a photograph of the Jesuit seminary as he had originally thought. Although Gaspard Leblon's memories of his seminary days were not exactly pleasant, the simplicity and austerity of the seminary had nothing to do with the atmosphere of decadent decay surrounding the mansion-in-ruins in this photograph.

Bruno realized the chronology of events in X's written account of Gaspard Leblon's life did not necessarily correspond to the dates written on each photograph. Memories belonging to different time periods could be (and probably often were) attached to the same photograph, making the memory/photograph even less reliable than it already was. For instance, there were four dates listed on the back of the mansion photograph. Three of them were scratched out. The one left standing was *1888*. However, there was no way of knowing what that date signified. The construction of the house? The destruction of the house? The sale of the house? Bruno resumed reading.

Gaspard was sitting alone in the library. He felt someone's hand on his shoulder and turned around. The Prefect placed an envelope on the desk and left without a word. The letter began: 'Dear son, I am afraid I have some bad news. Last night your mother . . .'

Gaspard stopped reading and looked out the window. Two young seminarians were fencing in the deserted courtyard.

'. . . There was nothing we could do for her. Doctor Bauchet is of the opinion that exhaustion was the cause of death. I have arranged . . .'

The next paragraph was crossed out. Bruno tried to decipher the words but every individual letter was smudged beyond recognition. Frustrated that he was probably missing an important part of the story he had to resign himself to skipping ahead.

Father Charles's words sounded muffled through the black curtain separating his side of the confessional from Gaspard's.

"My son, I know it's your grief speaking, not you. The death of a loved one is never easy but it's easier to forbear when the Lord is with you. Son, forsake thyself and thou shalt find me. Stand without choice and without all manner of self and thou shalt win. Forsake thyself, resign of thyself and thou shalt enjoy great peace. Give all for all, seek nothing, ask nothing . . ."

At this point several lines were crossed out again.

The sky was overcast. A carriage waited in front of the seminary gates. The Father Rector and the Duke shook hands. The Father Rector approached Gaspard, who stepped back instinctively though not fast enough to prevent the Father Rector from embracing him.

"God be with you, my son."

Gaspard and his father climbed into the carriage. As the carriage pulled out of the courtyard Gaspard lifted the curtain and looked back: the seminary grew smaller and smaller in the distance. For a while father and son travelled in silence. The Duke checked his watch and settled back in his seat.

"We're invited to dinner tomorrow night. Your uncles have been asking about you."

Gaspard stared at the bleak landscape unrolling outside.

"I am not in the mood," he said.

"If your mother could hear how you speak to me. . . ."

"My mother?"

Gaspard quickly collected himself.

"My mother is dead," he said.

The Duke crossed his legs and pretended to ignore his son's moodiness.

"Tomorrow night at dinner," he began matter-of-factly, "I want you to—"

"Spend a crushingly dull evening listening to my uncles and aunts babble about their ailing bones while my mother's bones rot—"

"Enough!" the Duke blurted out. He wrapped himself in his coat and closed his eyes, signaling that this was the end of the conversation.

Back at Chateau de Lourps Gaspard wandered through the rooms, studying the furniture and the paintings hanging on the walls as though he was doing an inventory of his family home. His mother's bedroom was at the end of the hallway. He stood in front of the big round mirror and smelled, one by one, his mother's numerous boxes of make-up. He picked up her hairbrush and raised it against the light: his mother's hairs were still stuck in it.

In the evening he stepped out on the terrace for a smoke. The cloudless sky was full of stars. There was a knock on the glass door behind him. It was the maid.

"Monsieur, dinner is served. Shall I call your father?"

"I will," he said without turning back.

When he finally climbed the stairs to the Duke's study he found him sitting in his armchair with his back to the door. His right hand, holding a fountain pen, hung over the side of the chair.

"Dinner is served," Gaspard said coldly.

There was no response. Gaspard stepped forward and bent over his father. He was not breathing. There was a big ink stain on the letter before him. Gaspard was able to decipher only the first few words: "My dear Antoinette, I am finally free to . . ."

Gaspard opened his dead father's cold hand, removed the fountain pen and placed it back on the desk. There was a black ink stain on the carpet. He walked back downstairs and sat at the head of the dining table.

"Will the Duke be joining you for dinner, Monsieur?" the maid asked.

Gaspard motioned to her to pour him a glass of wine.

"It seems he has suddenly lost his appetite. Incidentally, the carpet in the study looks like it hasn't been cleaned in a long time."

The maid blushed and assured him she would clean it tomorrow.

"I have decided to move to Paris," he informed her. "You and the rest of the servants will, of course, receive your pay and a small amount to carry you through while you are looking for other suitable employment."

A week after his father's funeral Gaspard climbed into his carriage and watched his family home recede in the distance. The servants had lined up in front of the castle to see him off. The older ones, those who had come into the family when he was still a baby, were trying to hide their tears. Gaspard put down the curtain and ordered the carriage man to go faster.

Bruno put down the paper and looked at the photograph once again. Now he knew it was a record of Leblon's departure from his family home. He was sitting in the carriage, in the upper right corner of the photograph, determined not to turn back. The family cemetery behind the house had received two new additions. As Gaspard's getaway carriage was getting closer and closer to Paris, the meat was falling off his freshly dead father's bones, falling away from his severe cheekbones, digging up two empty black wells on either side of his aristocratic nose.

The next photograph in X's chronology of events was of a crowded opera house. A handsome young dandy was looking through a pair of binoculars at the women in the opposite box, his face turned away from the camera. The only feature that identified him as Gaspard Leblon was the barely glimpsed sharp cheekbone, the dark hair falling over his marble forehead, and, of course, the name "Gaspard Leblon" written on the back, next to the date "1888."

The carriage flew past Faubourg Saint Germaine and Rue de la Paix. The shops in this area carried the most expensive perfumes, silks, jewels, furs, hats and lingerie, all lavishly displayed in the store windows. In Rue Charlemagne Gaspard stepped out of the carriage and checked his reflection in the shop window. He took off one of his pale pink gloves and smoothed down his pointed beard. His long waistcoat was fastened very high by means of twelve buttons and negligently gaping lower down to reveal a fine white shirt with pleated cuffs. His tight trousers were fastened under patent-leather shoes. He walked down the street, smiling confidently at the women passing by and entered a store on the corner. Inside, a dozen tailors and boot makers were waiting for him, sitting in church pews

Gaspard had bought the week before. He climbed the magisterial pulpit and addressed his 'congregation' of tailors.

"To do the job I have hired you to do properly, that is, to my satisfaction, you must understand one thing: you are not only tailors, you are artists. Therefore, you must study art."

He surveyed his audience skeptically.

"I ask that you listen carefully to my directives in all matters of style. If you fail to follow to the letter the instructions contained in my monitories, you will suffer pecuniary excommunication. All tailors: come with me. I will see the boots men tomorrow."

The next several paragraphs were crossed out. The text continued on the next page.

Chappelle Notre-Dame de la Medaille Miraculeuse was almost empty. After reverencing the altar the priest began the Mass. Gaspard sat in the last row, next to Emile and Alfonse. He opened his copy of La Mode to Balzac's "Treatise on the Elegant Life" but not before making a note of Emile's ridiculous waistcoat. The priest's voice echoed throughout the church.

"My God, I do not know what must come to me today, but I am certain that nothing can happen to me that you have not foreseen, decreed, and ordained from all eternity."

Gaspard moved his finger down the page.

THERE ARE THREE CLASSES OF MODERN BEINGS:
The man who works
The man who thinks
The man who does nothing.
THEY HAVE, RESPECTIVELY, THREE FORMS OF EXISTENCE:
The busy life
The artistic life
The elegant life.

"Amen. The grace of our Lord Jesus Christ and the love of God and the fellowship of the Holy Spirit be with you all."

"And also with you," everyone responded in unison.

After Mass Gaspard walked across the square and stood opposite the chapel. Moments later Alfonse and Emile came out of the chapel. Gaspard considered walking away but was too lazy to move.

"Did you like the service?" Alfonse inquired in a falsely sincere voice. "I hope I didn't disturb your reading with my singing."

Slightly bored, and irritated at being bored, Gaspard began putting on his gloves.

"I don't understand why you get so excited over a fake Mass. Don't you know that they make the host out of potato starch? Gentlemen, do you really expect God to manifest himself in potato starch?"

Gaspard could tell from their faces that his words had made an impression. Alfonse pursed his lips. He had somehow gotten the impression that doing that made him appear more authoritative.

"No one would believe you spent four years at the seminary."

"I should count myself lucky if this is the impression I produce," Gaspard grinned. "Good day, gentlemen."

Gaspard walked back to his apartment to change. He had made it a habit to change three times a day: it was his firm belief that every occasion, no matter how insignificant, called for a different outfit. When he emerged from behind the divider in his bedroom, he was wearing an elegant velvet tunic and green gloves. He checked his reflection in the mirror, swept back his sleek hair into a little wave, took off the green gloves, put on a red cravat, and rearranged the pleats in his coat several times. He had explicitly told his tailor, Monsieur Ricard, to put in more pleats but the man had clearly ignored his instructions. Perhaps it was time to find a replacement for him.

He walked down Rue Charlemagne until he found a small café with an advantageous look over the street. In the evenings he enjoyed sitting outside and watching the beautiful women passing by. As each one of them walked in front of his table he focused his attention on a particular part of her anatomy—the wrist, the neck, the ankle, the knee, the elbow—freezing it for an instant before his gaze so he could admire its radiance. The warm evening breeze tickled his skin. He half-closed his eyes and imagined himself crossing a grand hall, wine glass in hand. Two brunettes, dressed in striking though not entirely accurate foreign costumes, approached him. They looked at him coyly but he barely acknowledged them. At the end of a long hallway he came to a door. He opened it: a dozen women sat around a table, drinking tea, talking, showing off their jewelry to one another, playing the piano, embroidering. One of them, a delicate young girl with red hair stood up and walked out of the room. He *followed her. Suddenly he was walking on the beach, his shoes filling up with sand. The young girl walked ahead of him along the embankment, the long streamers of her seaside hat flapping around in the wind. She turned around and noticed him. Embarrassed, she looked away, but then turned around again. He was now walking down a hotel hallway. At the end of it he stopped in front of a door, slowly took off his gloves, and opened the door. The girl with the red hair was standing by the window. She turned around to face him. Time passed. He opened the hotel room door and stepped out in the hallway. The girl stood behind him, half-naked, framed by the open door. He put on his gloves and walked down the hallway without turning back.*

"Would Monsieur like another coffee?"

Gaspard opened his eyes. The waiter was standing by his side. He paid quickly and rushed back home to change. He had to be at the opera at seven.

Gaspard Leblon's visual biography continued with a small erotic photograph. It was slightly more damaged than the other photographs (which was to be expected). Bruno examined it under a magnifying glass, hoping that this new character in Gaspard's story might tell him something about Gaspard's life of sexual abandon in Paris. Alas, while the woman's body was in focus—soft and voluptuous—her head remained out of frame. As always, all Bruno had to go on was the text accompanying the photograph.

Gaspard surveyed the women sitting in the opposite opera box. He lingered over a voluptuous brunette, who was similarly inspecting the men in the audience through her opera glasses. Their eyes locked. There was not a trace of embarrassment or false modesty in her look, two things that had begun to irritate Gaspard in young girls. Later that evening Madame Menard lay naked in his bed.

The walls in his bedroom were lined up with mirrors of different sizes, all in gilded frames. Every part of Madame Menard's naked body was reflected in a different mirror. Gaspard walked around the room, touching the mirrors. Every time he touched the reflection of a particular part of her body, the corresponding real part of her body responded to his distant touch. He lit a cigarette and blew out the smoke into one of the mirrors: the reflection of Madame Menard's body vanished in the smoke. He spent a whole week with her before his interest began to fade away.

On Sunday they were lying in the grass in Bois de Boulogne. She was trying to caress and kiss him while he struggled to suppress his boredom and irritation at her earnestness. A carriage stopped in front of them. A woman's naked arm, wearing several bracelets, appeared through the curtains. The hand gestured to two young men passing by to approach the carriage. One of them slipped money into the woman's hand and stepped back. The other one climbed into the carriage. The carriage pulled out but stopped again a little further down the path. After some time the man emerged from the carriage, his tailcoat slightly ruffled. Gaspard overheard him say goodbye to "Madame Laure."

Gaspard spent a passionate night with Madame Menard. He was uncharacteristically tender and generous: he knew this was the last time he was going to see her. The following night he was lounging in Madame Laure's lavishly decorated brothel, surrounded by prostitutes whose only wish was to please him. He chose three girls and retired to a private room in the back, where they began undressing him slowly and rubbing their young bodies against his. Gaspard struggled against the familiar sense of ennui creeping over him. He threw himself even more passionately at the girls, kissing them on the mouth, wrapping his arms around their small backs, breathing in the scent of their warm hair. But he felt nothing, nothing except the insufficiency of his passion, the absurdity of his despair. He told them to stop talking. They looked at him incomprehensibly. He now realized it was not their seductive young voices that he was hearing but a high-pitched male voice that he couldn't place, though it sounded terribly familiar. The voice was droning on, something about "the darkness of soul, disturbance in it, movement to things low and earthly, the unquiet of different agitations and temptations." To silence the voice Gaspard violently kissed one of the girls, then pushed her away. As she stepped back the girl 'morphed' into Madame Menard, who 'morphed' into another prostitute before 'morphing' back into Madame Menard. Now he was dancing with Madame Menard. They turned faster and faster until she began to disintegrate into a series of overlapping images of fragmented mirror reflections of different parts of her body. All the while the voice *in his head droned on: ". . . when one finds oneself all lazy, tepid, sad, and as if separated from . . ."*

Gaspard spent the next few months indulging his carnal desires and drinking absinthe in his favorite café, which had been taken over, to his greatest displeasure, by plebeians and anarchists, disheveled young men of questionable origin who practically lived there, indistinguishable from the smoky atmosphere, always arguing about some political issue or other and of course always smoking furiously, like tonight. One of them was reading aloud Joseph Déjacque's letter to Proudhon.

"I would like to see the question of the emancipation of women treated by a woman of proletarian stock, for she is more likely to see through the secret life of a noble lady than a woman of the salon is capable of fathoming the life of a daughter of the people. But in the absence of this anarchic daughter, I—a member of the male sex—shall stand up against you, Proudhon, the ass. . . ."

The others raised their glasses and toasted to "The ass! The ass!" The one reading waved his hand to silence them and continued reading.

"Your intelligence, virile and complete when it comes to men, is as if castrated—castrated—when it comes to women . . ."

Gaspard got up and put on his gloves.

"Are you leaving?" one of them addressed him with a tone of over-familiarity Gaspard despised.

"Perhaps he doesn't find the subject of women interesting!" another one laughed.

"I'd rather enjoy women than discuss their social status," Gaspard said scornfully. "Now, if you'll excuse me, my mistress—I mean, one of them—is waiting for me."

If he was hoping for them to respond with a mixture of envy, resentment and respect, he got everything he had hoped for.

Although Gaspard's face was not visible in the next photograph, the cut of his coat was sufficiently similar to that of the coats Bruno had seen him wear in other photographs to warrant the assumption that this was indeed Gaspard. His hand, holding a cigarette, stood out in the foreground, the rest of his body enveloped by the darkness that had descended over a narrow street illuminated by a single street lamp. Judging from the position of his hand and the direction of the cigarette smoke his body seemed to be turned to the right and so, Bruno assumed, was his gaze. He focused on the lower right corner of the photograph: there was something, or someone, at the end of the street. Holding a magnifying glass over the photograph Bruno was able to discern the contours of a man's silhouette. He was wearing an accountant's suit. His face was entirely in the shadows. As usual the only name on the back of the photograph was that of Gaspard Leblon. Two other words were scribbled right under the name: Laurent & Moreau.

Gaspard stood outside the café, smoking. Well-fed middle-aged men and women, with self-content grins on their faces, strutted past him, smelling of onion, soup and cabbage. Gaspard observed with disgust the men coming out of the trade and bank offices on the opposite side of the street. The sign over the most imposing trade office read: "Laurent & Moreau." Presently, a young man came out of the building and walked down the street. Judging from his poor taste in clothes Gaspard guessed he was an accountant. He was walking fast, occasionally turning back to look over his shoulder as if he was afraid of being followed. There was nothing extraordinary about him, nothing that would stir Gaspard's curiosity and make him follow the man. Nothing except the fact that Gaspard had no other plans for the evening except the desire to get away from the insouciances of Parisian café society.

At first it seemed that the man had a specific destination in mind: he walked purposefully, his head bent down. However, Gaspard soon realized that the man was walking in circles. He didn't seem to have lost his way; neither was he worried or surprised to come across the same houses and the same forks in the road. He gave the impression of someone walking just so that he wouldn't have to stand still. His movements were automatic and precise, as though he had rehearsed them numerous times and was now taking them for a test run.

They came to a cul-de-sac. The man stopped and took out a cigarette. He tried to light it but the paper had split. Gaspard approached him. Startled by the sound of his steps, the man turned around abruptly. He had a face that one would have difficulty describing: flat and expressionless, as if it hadn't been fully formed yet. Gaspard offered him a light. After some hesitation the man accepted. He had just gotten off work, he said. He was a bookkeeper at the firm of Laurent & Moreau.

"Do you want to have some fun tonight?" Gaspard said. "I'm paying."

An hour later he pushed the man into Madame Laure's open arms.

"Monsieur Gaspard!" she squeaked with pleasure. "We thought you had forgotten us!"

Gaspard casually slipped a few bills in her revealing décolleté.

"Monsieur is very generous," she smiled.

The bookkeeper stopped in the middle of the room, embarrassed by two half-naked women lounging on the sofa. Blanche, a striking brunette wearing turquoise earrings and a hat decorated with green feathers—and nothing else—stood up and lazily extended her hand toward the young man's crotch. Gaspard and Madame Laure watched from the hallway.

"Where the devil did you pick him up?" she exclaimed.

"In the street."

"You like to have them young, don't you?"

"That's not it at all," Gaspard said, distracted.

They left the brothel at sunrise, faces flushed, shirts unbuttoned.

"Did you enjoy that?" Gaspard asked.

The bookkeeper nodded. Gaspard stepped up closer to him.

"You can come back here every week. You don't have to pay a sou to Madame Laure. I've taken care of everything."

He took out a few bills from his pocket and slipped them in the man's hand.

"Do me a favor. Buy yourself a nice shirt and a cravat. And remember: do unto others what you wouldn't want them to do unto you."

Just before the man turned the corner Gaspard called out to him.

"And don't be ungrateful! Let me hear news of you in the newspaper crime reports!"

It occurred to him that he didn't know the bookkeeper's name.

The following evening he broke his self-declared abstinence from Parisian café society and sat down at his regular table for a game of baccarat with Francois.

"You gave him five hundred francs?!" Francois exclaimed after hearing the whole story.

"I didn't give it to him. I paid Madame Laure," Gaspard corrected him.

"Why?" Francois insisted.

Gaspard smiled at him through the cigarette smoke.

"I am simply trying to train a murderer," he explained. "The boy's a virgin. He could have run after the little girls of his neighborhood, amusing himself but remaining decent, content with his little share in the monotonous happiness reserved for the poor. I want him to get accustomed to pleasures he cannot afford to enjoy. I want the thought of a regular life, working in an office for his daily bread, to start to oppress him. According to my calculations, it will take three months for these pleasures to become indispensible to him. At the end of the third month I'll cut off the little allowance I gave Madame Laure. And then . . ."

He made a dramatic pause, enjoying the look of anticipation on Francois's face.

"I bet the boy will go to any lengths—steal, even kill—to roll on Madame's sofa again."

"Diabolical!" Francois said approvingly. "How much are you willing to bet?"

"Let's finish the game first," Gaspard said.

Later that night he found himself, against his better judgment, in Madame Menard's bedroom. After some lukewarm lovemaking he lay in bed, naked, silent. She raised her hand to touch him.

"You are in a strange mood tonight."

He felt a strong urge to be cruel to her despite the fact that she did not deserve it or, rather, precisely because of it.

"Tell me what you want. Anything . . ." she whispered.

He stared at her coldly, resentful that she was arrogant enough to assume she had something to do with his mood and, worse, that she could do something to improve it.

"Le secret d'être ennuyeux, c'est de tout dire," he said, pushing her away. His face twisted into a painful grimace.

"What are you wearing?"

She looked down at her nightgown.

"Do you like it?"

"I can't stand to touch it!"

She took off her nightgown and embraced him. Gaspard responded mechanically to her advances. He caught a glimpse of his face in the mirror and was surprised how determined it looked. He pushed her down and kissed her violently. Mistaking his disgust for passion she whispered in his ear:

"I will do anything. Anything . . ."

He pushed her away. As he ran down the stairs he imagined her sitting up in bed, on the verge of crying, studying the reflection of her naked body in the mirror, trying to identify the part of her body that was responsible for his sudden departure. Back in his apartment he lay in bed, naked, and set in motion the little silver cage hanging over it. He watched the bird in the cage endlessly reflected in the play of mirrors until it seemed to his dazed eyes that it was not the cage that was moving but that the whole room was reeling and turning.

8

Bruno woke up with a fever, made himself a pot of tea and stood by the window, blowing the steam against the cold glass. Through the small circle formed by the steam he saw a patch of sparkling blue: the indoor public swimming pool across the street.

The sauna was bursting with melting human flesh. In the main swimming pool the daily diving lesson for octogenarians was well under way. Bruno's only option was the kids' pool. While he was undressing he felt something in the inside pocket of his jacket. It was a photograph of Le Grand Palais, seemingly indistinguishable from any vintage 19TH century postcard of Le Grand Palais except for the fallen man in the lower right corner. His face was not visible but judging by his hat and tailcoat he was an aristocrat. A group of aristocrats stood around his prostrate body. Several women had turned their heads away from the intolerable sight; one was holding a handkerchief to her mouth.

What was it doing in his pocket? Had someone slipped it in the last time he was at the library? Bruno stepped into the kids' pool and unfolded the written account attached with a paperclip to the back of the photograph.

Gaspard dropped the towel he had wrapped around his body and lied down in the tub. His hands sank in the water on either side of his body. He felt his face twitching. Powerful jets of water slapped against his spinal column. He clasped his hands together under the water, trying to control the shaking. After a while he dozed off or fainted: he couldn't tell which when he finally came to his senses.

On the corner of rue Castiglione and rue Seville he ran into Francois and Gilbert. The three of them stood at the edge of the embankment, staring at the muddy Seine. Gilbert was telling them about an incident that had happened earlier that morning.

"And just like that he collapsed. Right in front of the Grand Palais!"

"The risk in the city is especially high," Francois observed. "Our vital energy is depleted. Everything we do requires an effort of the nervous system. Every line we read or write, every face we see, every conversation we have sets in activity our sensory nerves and brain centers. You can change a normal man into a hysteric simply by tiring him."

Gaspard made his shaking hands into fists and plunged them deep inside his pockets.

"In that case I must be insane," he mumbled.

Francois and Gilbert laughed.

Gaspard spent the next two weeks in bed trying to recover from a condition he suspected he was suffering from, but which he could not identify. Finally, he mustered the little energy he had left and wrote a letter to his lawyer, Monsieur Bassett. Bassett arrived the day after, bringing with him all documents pertaining to Gaspard's family estate. When he saw Gaspard's pale face Bassett shook his head.

"If you don't mind me saying this, Monsieur, you don't look well. Have you been sleeping at all?"

His hand shaking, Gaspard put a cigarette in his mouth and leaned forward. Bassett reluctantly gave him a light.

"Bassett, while I am touched by your concern for my health this is not the reason I asked you to come tonight."

Bassett put on his default obsequious face and assumed a businesslike posture.

"I read your letter, Monsieur. I understand you are thinking of leaving Paris. Unfortunately, I've drawn up an account of your finances and, frankly, I don't think you'd be shocked to hear that you've spent the greater part of your patrimony."

Gaspard bit his lips.

"I was under the impression I had money invested in some lands somewhere."

"The amount of money these investments are bringing you is, alas, negligible," Bassett informed him.

Gaspard walked over to the window. He remained silent for a long time, staring at the dead-end street his window was facing.

"Sell the chateau," he finally said.

"Sell Chateau de Lourps?! Monsieur, please be reasonable. . . ."

"If you sell the chateau and all my other assets and then buy government stocks, what will that do for me?"

Gaspard turned around. Bassett was calculating on a piece of paper.

"Fifty thousand francs annually, give or take, and an additional lump sum."

"Fine. Sell the chateau and buy a small villa just outside Paris."

He sat down, put his feet up on the table and closed his eyes.

"Now leave me alone."

Two weeks later Gaspard walked through a little garden at the back of his new home. The painting contractor, Boucher, followed him into the sitting room, where he took out a folder and showed Gaspard the different color options for the walls.

"I would suggest going with some gentle pink or light green: either one will bring out the expressiveness of the colors," Boucher said.

Gaspard interrupted him.

"I spend most of my waking life at night. I don't care if the colors look insipid or crude in the daylight."

He walked up to the window.

"Fournier, when does a man like you usually go to bed?" he asked.

"With all due respect, Monsieur, my name is Boucher. . . ." the contractor mumbled.

Gaspard ignored him.

"Nothing compares to the experience of being in a well-illuminated room, the only person up and about, surrounded by the shadows of the neighboring houses. There is nothing quite like drawing the curtain aside and realizing that everything around you is dark, silent, dead."

Gaspard glanced at the color display Boucher was holding.

"Are you familiar with Goethe's theory of colors?"

Boucher's puzzled face suggested he was not. Gaspard pointed to the orange strip.

"What do you think of this color?" he asked.

"Too bright. It will irritate your eyes, Monsieur," Boucher said.

Gaspard looked at him triumphantly.

"Orange it is! I want the whole room painted orange!"

In the kitchen, Morel, the servant Gaspard had hired, was already waiting for him. Gaspard handed him a piece of paper. Morel looked at it incomprehensibly.

"I've developed a system of bell rings," Gaspard explained. "You'll find the meanings of the different chimes recorded here—according to their number, their brevity, or their length. I expect you to memorize them."

Gaspard placed a second sheet of paper on the kitchen counter.

"This is the timetable for meals. I would appreciate it if you do not deviate from it."

Bruno leaned back, propped his head against the edge of the pool, and placed his hands behind his back, right against the stream of hot water flowing into the pool. Gaspard Leblon was beginning to take shape in his mind. What did he know about him so far? His father sends him away to a Jesuit seminary not because he is concerned about the moral and spiritual education of his son, but simply because the boy is a nuisance to him. While he is a student at the seminary his mother dies, most likely as a result of some potent combination of hysteria, melancholy, ennui and neurasthenia, with a broken heart on the side. Gaspard leaves the seminary and returns home for the funeral of his mother. Soon after—just a few days later—his father dies as well. Gaspard is the one who discovers his father's body. What does he do? He doesn't call a doctor. Instead, he goes downstairs and has dinner alone.

The written accounts attached to the photographs from that period of Gaspard's life did not contain a single word about his father's funeral, which he must have attended if only for the sake of propriety. Instead, Gaspard provided an exhaustive account of the new clothes and boots he purchased once he moved to Paris and an equally detailed account of his (enviable) brothel experiences. Dozens and dozens of pages describing the color of a new tailcoat or the musky smell of an old prostitute, yet not a single word about the color of his father's coffin or the smell of cyanide (possibly) wafting through his mother's bedroom.

What did all of this tell him about Gaspard? Not the sharing type? Not sentimental? Not one to dwell on the past? Cold and aloof like his father, with the added bonus of being revengeful and cruel? His father might have been incapable of feeling, he might have been a lousy husband, cheating on his wife and never bothering to conceal his transgressions, but he was weak. His son was anything but weak. A weak man does not sell his family home a few days after the death of his parents and transform himself, overnight, from a humble Jesuit seminarian into a Parisian dandy.

Gaspard's description of his father's death left a lot of unanswered questions. On the surface it looked like the Duke died of a heart attack that unfortunately interrupted his love letter writing (not to his dead wife, most likely to a young prostitute—men of his kind always fall for a prostitute). Nevertheless, Gaspard's memories of his relationship with his father over the years, not to mention his peculiar reaction to discovering the Duke's dead body, suggested that he certainly did not lack reasons for hating the man. Perhaps the Duke committed suicide? This seemed unlikely. In his preliminary research on suicide statistics in late 19TH century France Bruno had already established that the two most common methods of suicide were drowning and charcoal. The Duke did not fit the statistical profile for a French suicide.

Bruno exhaled and looked around. Flabby, wrinkled limbs crisscrossed by varicose veins floated gracelessly on the intensely blue surface of the water in the main pool. Suddenly he noticed a familiar figure. X was sitting on one of the benches lined up against the wall. Bruno had not spotted him until now on account of the two octogenarians in front of him, who were busy performing a powerful stretching routine that would have left most men half their age utterly incapacitated. X was watching the men lift up their short legs and shake them so that the flabby skin folded up and down their knees, while their brittle, curled up toenails threatened to break into tiny yellowish pieces. The little hairs sticking out from under their rotting armpits glistened with perspiration and their bellies swelled like balloons. Their greasy white hair was stuck to their aging temples shiny from the layers of sweat produced by needlessly excessive physical exertion. Having reached the end of their stretching routine, the two old men stood up, bent down one more time, raising their soft buttocks up in the air, came up, faces red, trunks vanishing into the cornucopia of flesh, ran unsteadily towards the pool and jumped, or rather collapsed, into the water.

As X watched the old men his face did not register disgust with the inevitable signs of aging or shock at the absurd incongruity between the invisible vitality of these old bodies and their explicit proximity to death. No, what Bruno read on X's face was something akin to admiration bordering on envy.

X lifted up his right arm and waved it around, all the while observing with great curiosity the shaking of his upper arm's loose skin. He did the same with his left arm, and then with both legs. That didn't seem to satisfy him. He raised his hands in front of his face and moved his fingers in all directions. Perhaps he was warming up before going into the water? No, Bruno reasoned, the level of attentiveness with which X performed these movements was not typical of a warm up. A warm up is, precisely, a routine. One performs certain movements with the expectation—confirmed by prior experience—that they would produce a certain result. On the contrary, X's every single movement was shot through with an unmistakable skepticism concerning the reliability and validity of the movement, as though he felt there was no guarantee he would complete the movement, as though he didn't believe the movement would produce any effect or even register in the first place. His arms fell, lifeless, into his lap. X took his left wrist with his right hand. Was he measuring his pulse? Bruno checked the clock on the wall. Five seconds. Ten seconds. Fifteen. Twenty. Thirty. Forty. X was now breathing faster and faster. Was he having a panic attack? The octogenarians were doing laps. Bruno was about to call for help when X stood up from the bench and walked over to the pool. He stood at the edge and stared at the water. Then he jumped. His body sank to the bottom. The lifeguard blew the whistle and jumped into the water. A few of the octogenarians swam towards X, pulled him out of the water and started performing mouth-to-mouth.

A museum guard is a damaged man, Bruno thought. Of course, there is nothing inherently damaging about this kind of occupation. Every job has it psychological hazards and its benefits. Still . . . the museum guard spends a considerable amount of time doing nothing while remaining on guard, that is, trying to meet two conflicting demands at once: he is expected to be, at one and the same time, passive *and* active, indeed more than active insofar as *anticipating acting* produces higher levels of anxiety than simply *acting*. His state of mind is best characterized by a feeling of numbness or acute ennui (which accompanies any experience of 'doing nothing') mixed in with nervousness and anxiety (which accompanies the performance of any kind of duty, of which 'guarding' is one example). The act of standing on guard, protecting something or someone, is oriented towards the future by virtue of its preventive character. The guard does not live in the present; he is expected to be always one step ahead, looking at the present moment from the privileged point of view of the future and doing everything in his power—which, in his case, paradoxically means 'doing nothing'—to maintain the status quo, that is, to extend the present moment into the future without any radical changes to it. However, the job's orientation towards the future is in conflict—an unresolvable one—with the object of his job, which is firmly rooted in the past: after all, what he guards is the past. Thus, he finds himself schizophrenically torn between the past and the future, between numbness and anxiety.

Thousands of years, in concentrated form, are perched on elegant pedestals all around the museum guard, dramatically lit by strategically positioned lights that remain unseen, meticulously categorized in beautiful printed words on tiny pieces of white paper: "3000 bc", "500 ad". Suspended amidst these time capsules, made to look harmless enough even as they spell out the fate that awaits us all, the guard slowly begins to turn into a time capsule himself. He is supposed to be immune to time: after all, the time inside the time capsules he guards has stopped; it is frozen and thus immune to further decay. But outside these time capsules time continues to flow, layers of dust gathering casually over this frozen time, revealing its ultimate vulnerability to itself: it cannot escape decay, which is to say it cannot escape itself. With every second passing the decay of time decays itself. Tiny specs of temporal dust gather on the guard's forehead and eyebrows, stick to his eyelashes, fall on the epaulettes of his crisp museum uniform and on his polished shoes, turning them—turning *him*—into another item in the museum's permanent exhibit. What patrons see when they walk into a room and spot, to their great displeasure, a museum guard, is not just a man in uniform but a *representation of a man in uniform*. The man *is*, and, at the same time, he *represents who he is*. He is himself a display item in the virtual museum of the history of museums. In short, he enjoys a special relationship with history: he guards public history, represents the very concept of history, and is part of the virtual history of history, a museum item of the first order.

Most professions require people to spend their working hours either in the company of other human beings (however undesirable they might find it) or alone. The museum guard spends his time or, rather, his *shift*, in the company of dead things—a commonly used euphemism is 'relics'—in various stages of ruin. He stands in the vortex of temporal decay, surrounded by abandoned things that have lost their purpose and use, whose value is now reduced to *storing time, storing the decay of time*, and *representing the decay of time*. He guards things from a particular time long gone, but he also guards the decay of time these things embody, and, on yet another level, he guards—and makes visible—the decay of time these already decayed things participate in right now, as items in a museum collection, a decay to which he, too, is subject. In short, he guards his own mortality, his own future death. And the longer he guards it, the more he becomes it . . . his own death. Until one day he begins to believe he is already dead.

Bruno recalled chapter XVI—"Of Reverie, or Absence of Mind"—of Benjamin Rush's last book *Medical Inquiries and Observations upon the Diseases of the Mind* [XIV] where Rush described madness in terms of *inattentiveness*, a certain predisposition to reverie or distractedness. The 'disease' of absent-mindedness, he argued, could be induced by two possible causes, "By the stimulus of ideas of absent subjects being so powerful as to destroy the perception of present objects; and, By a torpor of mind so great as not to feel the impressions of surrounding objects upon the senses." Not surprisingly, Rush compared madness to dreaming. Dreaming, he wrote, "is always induced by morbid or irregular action in the blood-vessels of the brain, and hence it is accompanied by the same erroneous train, or the same incoherence of thought, which takes place in delirium. This is so much the case that a dream may be considered as a transient paroxysm of delirium, and delirium as a permanent dream. It differs from madness in not being attended with muscular action." In his 1845 study *Mental Maladies: A Treatise on Insanity*[XV] J. E. D. Esquirol, following Rush, described insanity as "a cerebral affection, ordinarily chronic, and without fever; characterized by disorders of sensibility, understanding, intelligence and will. Among the insane, sensibility is exalted or perverted; and *their sensations are no longer in relation with external or internal impressions. They seem to be the sport of the errors of their sense, and of their illusions.*"

The essential feature of insanity was, therefore, *the loss of attention* and of the ability to reason, which was apparently *not a property natural to us*: "We are not naturally reasoning beings; that is to say, *our ideas are not conformed to objects, our comparisons exact, our reasonings just, but by a succession of effort of the attention,* which supposes in its turn, an active state of the organ of thought."

Max Nordau, a prolific writer of Austro-Hungarian Jewish origins who studied and practiced medicine in Paris under Jean-Martin Charcot, also drew the line between normality and insanity in terms of *attention*, more specifically in terms of a *gap* between the input of external stimuli and the subject's motor response to those stimuli (the transformation of idea into action). In *Degeneration* he located madness or degeneracy in the realm of ideation, specifically in *the separation of the realm of ideation from the realm of action.*[XVI] Degeneracy, he believed, was a form of *inattentiveness*, a break or gap in the psychic-motor apparatus of stimulation and response, which resulted from malfunctioning association of ideas: "To put it popularly, the cell is able to remember its impressions. If now a new, although it may be a weaker, disturbance, reach this cell, it rouses in it an image of similar stimuli which had previously reached it. Memory is therefore the first condition of normal brain activity. Every stimulus that reaches a cell will take the line of least resistance, and this will be set out for it along those nerve-tracks, which it has already traversed. Thus a definite path is formed for the course of a stimulus-wave, a customary line of march; it is always the same nerve cells which exchange mutually their stimulus-waves." The four laws according to which ideas are associated are similarity, contrast, simultaneity and contiguity (occurrence in the same place). When the association of ideas works properly, "the perception of a ray of light, of a tone, is sufficient in order instantly to produce the presentation of the object. To the brain without association of ideas that perception would only convey the presentation of having something bright or sonant in front of it. In addition, presentations would be aroused which had nothing in common with this bright or sonant something."

The 'degenerate' brain does not work efficiently: instead of taking the path of least resistance, it allows presentations that have nothing to do with the present stimulus and it fails to match past perceptions with present ones based on the four laws of association. The longer X sat in that museum chair, looking at the relics he was guarding the less clearly he saw them, until one day he became blind to them. From that moment on his sensations lost any relationship to external or internal impressions.

The museum guard doesn't have a personal history, burdened as he is with an intensely symbolic and philosophical function: representing the decay of time/history *and* participating in it at the same time. As the specks of time gather over his unblinking eyes his personal time stops circulating and, instead, coagulates. He suffers an existential thrombosis. Before the specks of time gathering in his eyelashes grow too heavy and force his eyes to close forever he has one last chance to reclaim (or invent) a particular speck of dust as the beginning of *his* story and choose another one as its end, one last chance to determine the limits of his own private existence lest he drowns in the uniformity and anonymity of universal time.

How does he determine those limits? By pointing to records of it. Records are discreet, unique, and perishable. But this is exactly what the museum guard wants—and needs. The only way to free himself from the wall of universal time, to set himself apart from the dead things that surround him, is to preserve his own perishability, his own *capacity to die*. Not just preserve it: flaunt it.

How does one construct a personal history? Through the family album of course. Although the belief that one is dead is, of course, a symptom of depression, it also functions as a self-defense mechanism i.e. it is a sign of resistance. One of the sub-beliefs supporting the main belief structuring the museum guard's world—the belief that he is already dead—is that if he is now dead there must have been a time when he was alive. The further back in the past he projects himself as *having been alive*, the better protected he is from the present, in which he feels always already dead.

Bruno now understood the nature of X's 'library research': X was indeed writing his own family history, that is, he was constructing it from the bits and pieces he found around him, in the Museum of Domestic Interior and at the Public Library. In the absence of a real personal history he had resorted to the next best option: a Frankensteinian history made up of dead bits and pieces of other people's histories. He had identified the mise en scène for his private history—the 19TH century sitting room he was hired to guard—and, filled with the enthusiasm of a first time film director—an auteur!—he began populating it with characters, including himself. He projected himself back into the past, inventing a whole life for himself under the name of Gaspard Leblon.

In short, the man was mad! Bruno now recalled the sentence scribbled in the lower left corner of Mrs. Leblon's photograph: *The scene depicted in the photograph might be helpful in establishing an early symptomatology of the psychopathology currently under investigation.* What else could this mean except that X and his fictional alter-ego Gaspard Leblon shared the same psychopathology that made them deny their own existence: one of was forgotten by his own mother, who exiled him, from a very young age, to the edge of her consciousness, and the other one suffered the side-effects of an occupation that deprived him of a personal history and transformed him into one of the dead objects he was forced to guard against time.

X's 'choice' of the Leblon family was not a deliberate one then; rather, it was dictated by the peculiarities of X's job as a guard in a late 19TH century museum exhibit. Once the head librarian at the Public Library handed him a box of photographs dating back to the period he was *guarding*, that is *living*, X set to work. He employed the methods of appropriation and falsification (he must have thought of the latter as 'creative attribution') and 'cast' the people in the photographs as characters in his own personal drama. He had to select and match photographs of different people to create his own story. To this end, he had to 1) choose photographs that were not taken head on but always from an oblique angle that would make it impossible to verify the identity of the person in the photograph, and 2) arrange these completely unrelated photographs in a way that would be dramatically satisfying, telling a story with a clear beginning, middle, and end.

The need to believe that one comes from somewhere is a symptom of a certain lack of belief that one comes from somewhere, that one 'comes' at all. People's experience of themselves is always an awareness of themselves as existing in time, that is, as characters in a story. The sense of time is just another name for fiction, a structuring of raw experience into past, present, and future. Not having a past or a future is a frightening experience one would do anything to avoid. Once X had selected the right photographs it probably took him no more than a few weeks to arrange them into a coherent story, one in which he could begin to believe himself.

Perhaps X didn't think of photography right away. It might have happened by accident. One day, on his way back from the bathroom, he walks through the adjacent room in the 19TH century exhibit, dedicated to the birth and early history of photography. He has walked through it many times, of course, but he has never stopped to look at it until now. Most of the photographs on the wall are family portraits featuring men, women and children of all ages staring dutifully at the camera. One photograph of a young couple attracts his attention: the man stares directly at the camera but the young woman standing by his side looks at something beyond the frame. He walks back to his room and sits in his chair. All of a sudden, he has a strange feeling of absolute certainty. He doesn't know what the object of the feeling is—what it is that he is certain about—or why he feels so certain about it. But he knows that it concerns him in some way. He simply has to wait for the object of the feeling to reveal itself.

It does so the following day. He is sitting, as usual, in his chair, recollecting some of the objects on display and reminiscing about others. A middle-aged tourist wearing purple tights, sneakers, a professional looking camera hanging conspicuously from her thick neck, walks into the room. She starts taking pictures of every single object on display, from multiple angles. She is particularly taken by the tea set. She asks X if she is allowed to take pictures. He assures her that she is and encourages her to do so, because, he tells her, "This is a room with a very interesting story." She is surprised to hear that: the museum brochure does not mention anything special about the room. That is because the story is rather morbid, he explains to her. That gets her attention. He asks her if she has seen the exhibit in the previous room, and if she has taken any pictures of it. They go through her pictures. When they get to the picture of the wall of late 19TH century photographs he zooms into the photograph of the aristocratic couple and points at the young woman:

"This is the woman who lived in the room you are in now. Her name is Laetitia Leblon, wife of Duke Phillip Leblon."

The woman asks if they had any children. At first he is surprised: that question has never occurred to him before. Then the answer presents itself to him.

"A son," he says.

Bruno now remembered the first written note he had read, the one attached to Mrs. Leblon's photograph. The note had said she was not alone. Was the invisible boy playing with marbles in the corner, behind the heavy curtains, Gaspard Leblon, Laetitia's son, the man mysteriously absent from the family's official records and from its photographic memory, a fictional being conjured into existence by a madman out of thin air, out of the film grain of old photographs?

He slipped. His mouth filled up with water. Two flabby arms grabbed him by the shoulders and pulled him out of the water. Bruno opened his eyes: a pair of octogenarian eyes stared back at him. He signaled to his savior that he didn't need any help getting up. Yes, he did.

9

The sound of rain beating against the window woke him up. He turned on his side, ran his finger over the edge of the bed and looked at it: his finger was not covered with dust. Alarmed, he sat up in bed and looked around. For a while he couldn't put his finger on what was wrong. Then it hit him. The room was larger, significantly larger. But how could that be? He walked up to the window and parted the heavy curtains to let in more light. To his surprise the curtains felt lighter than he remembered. He looked at them more closely: they were beige, not burgundy. He turned around and reached for the bell. Morel better have an explanation for this. He had explicitly ordered Morel not to interfere with any element of the interior decor, and that certainly included the curtains.

The silver tray with the bell was not there, and neither was the side table on which it usually stood. He gasped. Now he understood why the room felt bigger: with the exception of a simple bed and a side table, the room was empty. He circled around several times as if he hoped that by changing the direction in which he was walking he would see a different version of the room, the one he expected to see. The writing desk was gone, and so were the burgundy settee, the bookshelves, the armchair, the tea table with the teapot and four teacups. He ran his finger over the floor where all of these objects once stood and brought it up to his nose. His face convulsed and his body twitched as he waited to sneeze. But he didn't sneeze: his finger was *not* covered with dust. He sat down on the edge of the unfamiliar, dustless bed in which he had woken up. The house was silent. He fell back in bed and closed his eyes. And just then he suddenly felt the familiar tingling inside his nostrils, as if he had leaned forward and breathed in the dust covering the bookshelf. He took a deep breath and . . .

Bruno sneezed. The covers had fallen off the bed. He reached out, pulled them back up to his chin and closed his eyes. A memory image of a random library photograph floated slowly into his field of vision. It was a long shot of a man lying in bed. A doctor stood by the side of the bed, measuring the man's pulse. Although the man's face was not visible Bruno had no difficulty recognizing the contours of Gaspard Leblon's body under the covers. Gaspard's right arm hung from the edge of the bed. On the back of the photograph X had written "Gaspard Leblon con-valescing." Bruno looked through the remaining unattributed written accounts: it was easy to find the only one matching the photograph's mood.

The first few days in Gaspard's new home passed slowly. Despite years of experience with demanding employers Morel needed some extra training. Gaspard spent countless hours explaining to him basic rules. On the second morning in the' house Gaspard woke up early. There was an odd smell in the air. He stayed in bed for a few minutes, trying to identi-fy the source of the nauseating smell. He inhaled deeply several times and nearly choked. He rang the bell. Morel, who had finally learned to iden-tify correctly the meanings of different rings, appeared at the door. Gaspard asked him if he smelled anything. Morel stuck his formless, long nose up in the air, inhaled deeply, shook his head disapprovingly, walked over to the window and opened it wide.

"Some fresh air will do you good," he proclaimed.

Gaspard stumbled toward the window, coughing uncontrollably.

"Close it! I can't breathe!" he gasped.

Morel helped him get back in bed and closed the window. Still cough-ing Gaspard pointed to a side table.

"Jasmine. . . ." he whispered.

Morel looked at the little bottle Gaspard was pointing at.

"Monsieur wants perfume?"

Gaspard stared at him with unconcealed hatred. Morel picked up the bottle and brought it right under Gaspard's nose. Gaspard inhaled sever-al times. His face relaxed. His servant observed Gaspard's swift transfor-mation with an incredulous look on his face.

Over the next few days, however, Gaspard's condition got worse. In clear violation of his master's instructions, Morel began preparing nourishing meals, which Gaspard refused to touch. His hunger strike lasted for about a week, over the course of which his stomach shrank down to the size of a tastefully small perfume bag. He stayed in bed all day, drifting in and out of consciousness, a state of mind he would have continued to enjoy—though enjoy was probably too strong a word for someone who had lost all capacity to feel pleasure or pain—if Morel had not called doctor Gautier, thereby violating yet another one of Gaspard's commands. Gautier measured Gaspard's pulse and checked his tongue. Morel entered the room, carrying a small jar filled with a yellowish liquid. Gautier examined it carefully.

"See these white stripes?" he pointed to the jar. "This is one of the indicators."

"What does it indicate?" Gaspard heard himself saying although he did not recognize his own voice; rather, he felt the muscles around his mouth contract, from which he inferred that he had said something.

"Neurosis," Gautier informed him.

He wrote something on a piece of paper and gave it to Morel.

"Give him a nourishing peptone enema for a week. Repeat the procedure three times every twenty-four hours."

Morel nodded. Gautier took off his glasses and looked at Gaspard.

"Monsieur, the enema I prescribed will improve your physical condition. However, I must warn you: only distraction and amusement can make an impression on your illness now. Go back to Paris. You cannot afford to continue living in self-exile."

Gaspard made a concerted effort to look away emphatically in demonstration of his utter indifference to what Gautier had to say about his patient's condition. Gautier stood up and began packing.

"I'm giving you my professional opinion. Of course, you are free to disregard it at your own risk. One thing is certain: a radical change in lifestyle is a question of health or insanity followed shortly by tuberculosis."

A week later Gaspard returned to Paris. He made a point of not announcing his return to anyone. The last thing he wanted was to spend his evenings answering dull dinner invitations. The enemas had done their magic, though he still had to apply a bit of rouge to his cheeks to disguise their deathlike paleness. He had gotten so accustomed to his yellowish, sickly skin tone that the rosy-cheeked, healthy-looking masks he *created for himself—different masks for different parts of the day—struck him as too alive to be credible.*

On his first evening in Paris he finally settled on a believable face, believable enough to take out for a walk by the river. The Seine's muddy embankment was covered with decomposing leaves, whose wretched smell tickled his nostrils pleasantly. He almost tripped over the body of a homeless man sleeping on the ground, hugging a torn piece of paper from which protruded large pieces of unidentifiable meat ravished by maggots.

Gaspard left the embankment and crossed the bridge. There was not a single soul in the street except for a young woman standing awkwardly in front of a dilapidated house. When she saw him, she raised her torn skirt above her dirty knees and twisted her lips into what she believed to be a seductive smile. Gaspard followed her into a dimly lit, cheaply furnished room. A child was crying upstairs. The woman, whose name, he learned, was Albertine, let her long hair down: it looked like it hadn't been washed for a while. Gaspard pushed her onto the kitchen table and lifted up her dress. In the broken mirror he saw himself mechanically slide his hand over her thin leg, as if he was rubbing a metal pole. She grabbed his hand and placed it on top of her flat chest. Gaspard looked at her with indifference. Unsure what to do, she tried to kiss him. Her mouth was dry.

"Does Monsieur have any special requests?" she whispered.

"Bring me some absinthe," he said.

She seemed relieved to have been given a task that required her to leave the room. Gaspard waited a few moments, grabbed his coat and ran outside. As he approached Rue Venezia his ears were assaulted by horses neighing, drunken screams, women's vulgar laughter, and the shrill, numbingly repetitive cries of street vendors. Big-bellied, bewhiskered bourgeois with an obnoxious learned air about them walked past him, every once in a while stopping to check their reflection in a shop window. He leaned against a wall and vomited.

"Looking for love, Monsieur?"

He turned around. A young girl with a worn out, apathetic face stepped out of the shadows. She was practically a child. Gaspard put up his collar and trudged through the mud without turning back. As he walked past the Bourse he was almost knocked over by a newspaper boy yelling at the top of his lungs:

"Le Figaro! All the latest crime stories! First-hand witness accounts! The Phantom Killer strikes again!"

Gaspard turned the corner and found himself in front of an imposing building. The sign on the wall read SALPÊTRIÈRE PSYCHIATRIC WARD.

Bruno opened his eyes. He was sitting at one of the reading tables in the library. He did not recall getting out of bed, leaving his apartment and arriving at the library. Entrances, exits and transitions had somehow lost their significance: his brain had simply decided they were not worth keeping a record of.

A hand entered his field of vision. He looked up. The librarian was standing in front of him.

"I am sorry to interrupt your work but I wanted to give you this. It must have fallen out of the box."

Bruno glanced at the photograph and returned it to her.

"It's not part of this collection."

She assured him that it was. There was no need to examine the photograph carefully. He had seen it numerous times. It was a photograph of a lithograph by Eugene Pirodon after Andrew Brouillet's famous 1887 painting "Une Leçon du Docteur Charcot a la Salpêtrière." So far all photographs in the box had been 'unattributed': they figured men and women that had not yet been identified. The reliability of the fake personal history X was constructing from photographs depended precisely on the unverifiability of the photographs' provenance, as well as on the ultimate unknowability of the people in the photographs. As long as X could randomly put together photographs of anonymous people to whom he could attribute the identity of specific characters in his own personal drama, his story was internally consistent in its fakeness. That he could manipulate all photographs meant that they were all equally unreliable, which, paradoxically, made Bruno's investigation of X's psychopathology easier. Bruno could assume they were all 'fake' and concentrate on examining the *particular connections* X was drawing between them and through which the truth of his psychopathology would reveal itself, because even though the *materials he was working with were fake*, his sick mind was drawing *real connections* between them. In short, if Bruno had any hope of identifying X's psychopathology it hinged on his analysis of the *real connections* X was drawing between *fake elements.*

However, if even one of the photographs in the collection turned out to be real—for instance featuring a historically well-established figure or event—it would discredit Bruno's main premise that the personal history X was constructing was entirely fictional. If the famous Charcot photograph really belonged in the collection—if historical truth was introduced in the midst of a fictional personal history—Bruno would have to seriously consider the possibility that other photographs in the collection might also be real, and that the personal history he had considered fictional might actually be historically true. In historical research if one element is found to be fake, the rest of the research is thrown into doubt. Bruno was facing the opposite problem, however: his whole research into X's alleged past, which he had originally assumed to be pure fiction, was now threatened to be exposed—by a single piece of historical fact, Charcot's photograph—as historically true. It suddenly seemed possible that the men in the library photographs—whom Bruno had thought to be identifiable as the same man, Gaspard Leblon, *only by a great leap of X's imagination*—could, in fact, be photographs of the *same man*, and *a real man* at that!

Up until now Bruno had proceeded from the assumption that the only justification for attributing the same name to all photographs was a certain visual consistency across all photographs i.e. that what held them all together was not the name itself but *an aesthetic* feature many of them shared—a matter of composition (Gaspard Leblon always appearing at the edge of the frame, in the back, or out of focus) or of Gaspard's consistently eccentric sartorial taste. Now, however, as the introduction of truth was beginning to undermine the fictional nature of Gaspard Leblon's past, the name 'Gaspard Leblon' assumed a new potency, threatening to exist on its own, providing the unquestionable provenance for all photographs, regardless of how *dissimilar from himself* Gaspard Leblon looked across different photographs.

But if Gaspard Leblon was real, it stood to reason that the house in which he grew up must be too.

Bruno motioned to one of the library assistants to approach him and showed her the photograph of Chateau de Lourps. He explained to her that he wanted to find out who had lived in that mansion in the last several decades of the 19TH century. What he really had in mind—he did not want to share with her his whole plan—was to visit the house, or whatever remained of it. The librarian asked him for the house's location. Embarrassed that he hadn't considered this obvious question at all Bruno excused himself and went back to his seat. For all he knew the mansion could be anywhere in France.

The man sitting at the next table leaned back and lifted up the book he was reading: *Architecture in Late 19TH Century France*. Bruno stared at the title. What if he could find out the architectural style of the mansion in the photograph? He could then check which styles were most prominent in which parts of France during the last three decades of the 19TH century.

In less than an hour another library assistant, whose skin tone suggested she rarely left the confines of the building, parked a cart stacked with books on late 19TH century architecture next to Bruno's table. He went through all of them, decade by decade, holding the photograph of the mansion next to every illustration, looking for the perfect fit. After a long, useless search all houses started to look the same to him. Just when he was about to give up he came upon a detailed pencil drawing of a chateau with a grand staircase leading up to the main entrance. Although the stains of decay were not yet visible in the walls there was no question about it: this *was* the house. It was a perfect copy of the photograph, from the woman's face barely visible behind the curtains on one of the second floor windows, right down to the horse carriage disappearing in the upper right corner. The caption under the drawing read "Second Empire, 1870s." Bruno flipped back to the beginning of the book chapter and skimmed the first couple of pages. The chapter was an extensive account of the architectural styles typical of the region just west of Paris, featuring numerous illustrations, photographs and drawings. Using the illustrations in the book as a visual map of architectural styles Bruno was able to pinpoint the location of Chateau de Lourps, which turned out to be not very far from Paris, near Cedille. There were trains from Paris to Cedille every two hours. The next one was leaving Gare du Nord in an hour and a half. He had just enough time to go home and change.

Half an hour later, after a quick, invigorating shower Bruno stepped out of his apartment. Mrs. Damiers' door was open. A policeman stood in the hallway, filling out a form. Bruno tried to sneak behind him but when he heard Bruno's steps the man looked up.

"Monsieur . . . ?"

He checked his notes to verify the name.

"Monsieur Leblon?"

Bruno nodded.

"I am sorry but I am in a hurry."

The policeman gestured to him to wait and picked up the coffee cup Mrs. Damiers had been holding for him. He took a few sips, commended Mrs. Damiers on the quality of the coffee grain, closed his notebook and turned phlegmatically towards Bruno.

"We are investigating a little incident, breaking and entering," he informed Bruno. "Were you home last night?"

Bruno confirmed he had been in his apartment but he had had a bit too much sherry and had fallen asleep rather early.

"Did you say sherry?"

The policeman wrote something down in his notebook. Without looking up he said casually:

"Do you mind if I take a look at that sherry bottle?"

He closed his notebook and stepped up closer to Bruno, a little too close.

"You see, one of the things missing from Mrs. Damiers' apartment is a sherry bottle."

Bruno unlocked the door to his apartment.

"I am sorry for the inconvenience. I am just being thorough. Standard procedure," the policeman said in a falsely apologetic voice.

Bruno showed him the empty bottle of sherry. The policeman held it up against the light, turning it around slowly. Then he wrote a short report based on his observations. Finally, he signaled to Bruno to follow him back to Mrs. Damiers' apartment where he showed her the bottle and asked her if she recognized it. No, this was not her sherry bottle. Yes, she was sure of it. Bruno said goodbye to both and was about to leave when the policeman called out after him.

"Where are you off to this morning?"

Bruno explained that he was trying to catch a train to Cedille. The policeman was familiar with the little town and the surrounding area.

"Beautiful countryside," he said. "Not much to do there though."

"I am considering buying some property there," Bruno said.

The policeman looked at him as if he didn't quite believe him, but then wished him luck and went back into Mrs. Damiers' apartment. Outside in the street Bruno hailed a cab. The leather seat smelled of vomit. In less than ten minutes he was in front of Gare du Nord. The train was already on the platform. The trip to Cedille was a little over an hour. He pulled out the book he had brought with him, a heavily illustrated guidebook to late 19TH century architectural styles in France. Every time the train passed by a small village or chateau he flipped through the book searching for the image that most closely resembled it but the real houses were so schematic and abstract that Bruno had to use his imagination to fill in the gaps and make reality and representation snap into a single image. Once they left Paris and its suburbs the landscape outside the window was reduced to a series of monotonous horizontal lines. Bruno flipped through the book until he found an illustration of Chateau de Lourps. He took out a blank sheet of paper and began drawing its outlines, using the illustration in the book as a model. Soon, however, the warm air, the smell of soup drifting from the restaurant car, and the rhythmic sound of the train engine lulled him to sleep.

When he woke up the train had stopped. His drawing had fallen on the floor. He looked out the window. There was no train station in sight.

Right then he saw it. The mansion stood in the middle of a small valley whose monotonous contours could put to sleep even the most arduous heart. It was an exact reproduction of his drawing and of the illustration in the library book: he recognized the shape of the roof, the turrets, and the color of the walls. One of the train attendants walked past him.

"Why are we stopping?"

"Waiting for another train that's been delayed," the man told him.

"How long do we have to wait?"

The man shrugged.

"Could be ten minutes, could be two hours."

Bruno grabbed his coat and walked down to the next exit. He jumped just as the train was starting to move.

He walked ahead, parting the tall grass with both hands to create a narrow tunnel. The wind had died down. The overcast sky hung low over his head. It looked like it had rained recently. With every step his shoes sank deeper and deeper in the mud. He kept losing his balance and reaching out to hold on to something but there was nothing to hold on to. The grass before him seemed to grow higher and higher. He could no longer see the mansion. Up ahead of him there was a little hill. He climbed on top of it and looked ahead. No trace of the house. He turned left, then right. Nothing. Had he imagined it?

A flock of crows flew above his head and disappeared behind him. He turned around and followed them with his eyes. Now he saw it: the house was immediately behind him, no more than five hundred meters away. The grand staircase leading up to the main entrance was overgrown with weeds, the steps preserving the imprints of different feet—maids', dukes', counts', viscounts', cooks', and the young Gaspard Leblon's feet, assuming he ever left the house where he kept his mother company while she slipped further and further into her world of sighs, swoons, and warm baths, oblivious to her son's presence.

Bruno walked around the house and came back to the main entrance. The wind ruffled the last leaves on the trees. He waited and listened. Nothing. There was a big rusty lock on the front door but when he pressed the door lightly he found, to his surprise, that it was open. He checked the lock: there were no traces of breaking and entering. The house had, likely, remained unlocked for decades. As he stepped into the hallway Bruno squeezed his nose with his fingers, preparing himself for the usual smell of human excrements mixed in with the stench of time sitting still for a long time. In the middle of the impressive circular foyer he let go of his nose and looked around: no excrements, no blades of grass sprouting from the sunken floors of ghostly rooms, no broken chandeliers on the floor. In the bedroom he stopped in front of a grand mirror in a golden frame, picked up one of the objects lying in front of it and blew off the dust, revealing a woman's hairbrush underneath. A *dead woman's* hairbrush. Bruno held it up against the light: several light brown hairs were still stuck in it.

He lay down on the burgundy settee with curved legs and closed his eyes. He noted, surprised but also calm, that he didn't have the uncanny sensation of stepping back in time. He didn't feel the urge to 'transport' himself back in time and imagine what the house might have looked back then. The past was not dead. It was right here, right now, disguised unsuccessfully by several layers of dust, which, oddly enough, did not feel like a natural record of time. He had the feeling (or was it a suspicion?) that someone had manufactured the dust, transported it here, and spread it over the furniture to create the impression of time past, to trick him into thinking that what he now saw around him was not the present. Space is everlasting and indestructible, he thought. We apprehend space not through the senses but through a sort of bastard reasoning. On the other hand, inasmuch as time is always 'becoming' it's merely an object of belief. The past, the present and the future do not exist. The only things that exist are the present of things past (memory), the present of things present (sight), and the present of things future (expectation). What remains fixed and allows us to measure time is the impression a thing leaves in memory. Only the memory of a thing can be present.

He wondered if there are disciplinary-specific modes of thinking about time, if there were certain *types* of questions about time that were specific to philosophy, for example, but not to physics, history, aesthetics, literature, and cinema. In physics the question of time was usually posed as one of origin (the origin of time), relation (the temporal determination of things in their relation to one another; temporal paradoxes), direction (cause and effect) or measurement (point of reference). Philosophy approached the question of time in terms of existence, being, and the subject's relationship to reality. In literature, the question of time was often translated into that of point of view, narrative, and the constitution of subjectivity through language. While Proust's *Remembrance of Things Past* was the privileged example of the importance of memory to narrative, memory was the condition of possibility of any narrative, not just ones explicitly dealing with the past. Since living does not coincide with telling, the telling of events always takes the form of remembrance, (re)construction. Thus, in literature time was inevitably tied to problems of truth, falseness, and interpretation. In aesthetics the question of time underlay the ongoing debates about what constitutes art, how the arts differ from one another, and which particular art best expresses the 'essence' of art.

Yes, the hierarchy of the arts in different historical periods had always been determined by their relationship to temporality. Earlier works on aesthetics (Baumgarten, Schelling, Lessing, Nietzsche) privileged music and the verbal arts—which give us things in the process of being created, that is, as the work of spirit—over the plastic or formative arts, which present things as already given, purely material, 'dead'. The twentieth century turned this hierarchy of the arts upside down, with Merleau Ponty writing on Cezanne and Jean-Francois Lyotard on the ontology of non-representational painting. However, the experience and representation of time remained the criterion by which the arts are judged. The increasing influence of philosophies of becoming on aesthetic theory could clearly be traced back to a fundamental premise of aesthetic theory: the 'essence' of art is to be sought in its treatment of time. In film the question of time was, from the very beginning, integrally connected to the problem of perception and of the realism of representation. In considering the relationship between time and the perception of movement one could draw a clear line from Muybridge's experiments with photographing movement (analyzing time into segments or, as Bergson puts it, spatializing time) and the technique of bullet-time photography used in *The Matrix* (compositing live-action footage with simulated or virtual movements).

Bruno stood up. His body had left an impression on the dusty settee. It seemed to him that the present impression of his body was the first element of time passing through this house where the layers of dust-past had frozen into a permanent, infinite present. The intrusion of his body, and with that, of the present, had broken through the house's insulation, the impression of his body suddenly spawning the impression of chronology, a retrospective chronology whereby the past had stopped passing and coagulated into an infinite, unchanging present while, at the same time, his present—and presence—was creating the past. He walked around the house, running his hand over this or that piece of furniture, picking up random objects, involuntarily inscribing himself in the history of Chateau de Lourps.

He stopped in front of a small room on the second floor. Judging by the way it was furnished he guessed it must have been a study. He pulled out a random book from the top bookshelf. The dust that had accumulated between the pages flew up into his nose and eyes. The covers had grown soft: the book split into two parts, both of which slipped from his hands and fell on the floor, the dust gathered between the pages mingling with the dust on the floor. Bruno stood motionless in this vortex of dust, particles of time swirling around him, wrapping him up, mummy-like, for posterity.

Suddenly he saw himself through the eyes of a visitor to the Museum of Domestic Interior: a wax figure rendered in hyper-realist detail sitting at a late 19TH century dinner table, part of the permanent exhibit. Museum patrons circled around him, visibly impressed by how realistic he looked, although they knew he was hollow inside, his organs having been scooped out so that his torso could be filled with preserving fluids. His skin was painted over to give it a believable, lived-in texture and appearance. His lips were pursed not just to suggest his character—a man of few words—but also to conceal from the public the unsightly sight of his mouth, from which all teeth had been knocked out, the gums having been soaked in formaldehyde. His eyes had been pulled out of their sockets and carefully transferred to a little jar from where they now looked out at the world without ever having the freedom to close. In his empty sockets the museum curators had placed a pair of artificial eyes that resembled too closely the simple marbles he used to play with when he was a little boy. The skin on his fingertips, around his eyes, and on the back of his palms was appropriately wrinkled to suggest that he had aged to a particular moment in time, that he had a history of his own. The hair sticking out of his skull looked soft and natural, as if he had just washed it and treated it with a conditioner, but upon touch it was dry and bristling, since it was made of long plastic sticks which, upon close inspection, revealed themselves to stand, unnaturally, separate from one another, all exactly the same length. The clothes he was dressed in were draped over his hollow body in such a way that the material formed natural looking wrinkles in certain parts to imitate the way a real body's habitual movements leave an imprint on the fabric over time. What if there was a hole in his tastefully stitched body, a hole through which all the preserving fluids that were keeping him alive would flow out and evaporate?

He looked down at his feet and saw it right away: a big ink stain on the beige carpet. It was exactly where it was supposed to be: behind the desk, next to the chair. Bruno recalled the drops of ink trickling down from the fountain pen in the dead man's hand hanging lifelessly from the side of the desk piled up with unfinished letters of lust and marital treason.

The door to the terrace, which wrapped around the back of the house, was closed but not locked. Bruno stepped out for a cigarette. The valley sprawled before him all the way to the horizon. The only variation in the monotonous landscape were the subtle changes in the color of the tall grass whenever the cold December sun broke through the clouds illuminating one part of the valley and throwing it into relief before letting it recede once again into a homogenous mass of brownish green.

The only passage from the house to the cemetery was through the kitchen. Right next to the little fence surrounding the cemetery he came upon a small vegetable garden. Here the soil was darker than in the rest of the cemetery, as if it had been watered recently. He walked around the cemetery. Near the southern side he stopped in front of three graves, the only ones with tombstones. He knelt down and brushed off the dead leaves and dirt piled up on top of the tombstone on the left. The title 'Duke' followed by the initials 'P.L.' were engraved in the stone. There was no date. He cleaned the other tombstone: this one bore the initials 'L.L., his loving wife'. There was no name on the third tombstone.

Bruno walked back into the house through the kitchen entrance. Like the rest of the house the kitchen lay under layers of dust, except for one part of the counter on which there was a plate with bread and a few ripe garden tomatoes. The fork was propped up against the plate, as if the person had left in a hurry without finishing his meal. Bruno took a bite of the bread and ate one of the tomatoes. The bread was a little stale, perhaps a day old, but the tomatoes were fresh, as if they had just been picked up from the garden.

Bruno had always assumed that correspondences are located along two separate axes: 1) past and present (something in the past corresponds to something in the present) and 2) fiction and reality (certain fictional things turn out to be true while certain other things, which one has supposed to be true, turn out to be fictional). He was beginning to doubt that this was the case. In the case of X—or, rather, in the case of X's history of Gaspard Leblon—there seemed to be four distinct possibilities. It was still unclear to Bruno whether he should approach X's history of Gaspard Leblon 1) as a case of an element of a fictional past reverberating in the present as something true, 2) as a case of a factual element of the past being appropriated in the present as part of a fictional story, 3) as a case of an element of a fictional story (or a delusion) in the present resuscitating something factual about the past, or 4) as a case of a factual element of the present being projected back into the past to construct a memory or a history that never happened.

His search for Chateau de Lourps had originated in the assumption that by adopting X's method—constructing a past through clues in the present, that is, 'reconstructing' Gaspard Leblon's family house as described in various written accounts and photographs—he could, perhaps, understand X better. What Bruno had *not* expected to find was *the real* Chateau de Lourps. Yet how else could he explain the names of Duke Phillip Leblon and his wife Laetitia Leblon on the tombstones in the cemetery behind the chateau?

And the third tombstone? *Who was buried there?*

10

The head librarian was in an inexplicably excellent mood. Before Bruno had even sat down she rushed to his desk with the two boxes of photographs and wished him a 'productive day'. The correspondence between the very first photographs he had examined and the written accounts accompanying them had not been that difficult to establish as it was mostly visual in nature: every written account was simply a description of what anyone could see 'happening' in the corresponding photograph. However, he was beginning to notice a growing separation between image and text: the only thing that seemed to hold them together was *a particular mood, motif, or idea*.

Gaspard stood by the door craning his neck to get a better view of the stage. The poster on the door read: Professeur Charcot. Leçons du Mardi. Grand Auditorium. *The podium in the middle of the auditorium was brightly illuminated as if for a theatrical performance. Charcot rolled up his sleeves as he walked toward the patient sitting in a chair in the middle of the stage.*

"Shut your eyes," Charcot ordered him. "Imagine you are extending and flexing your left hand and playing the piano with your right hand. It's a very complicated piece of music."

The patient extended his hands forward.

"Now, do you feel your left hand?" Charcot asked.

"I don't feel it."

Charcot turned around, facing the audience.

"Gentlemen, the idea of movement, in the course of being executed, is already movement; the idea of the absence of movement, if strong, is already the realization of motor-paralysis. The only conclusion we can draw is that hysteria is a mental, not an organic disorder."

Charcot made a pause, observing the effect of his statement on the audience. He rubbed his beard and smiled mischievously.

"Let me tell you a little story. One of my patients, a traveler by rail, was imprudent enough to attempt changing carriages while the train was still in motion. While he was on the step outside the train, he noticed the train was about to enter a tunnel. Hanging on with his right hand and foot, he expected that his left side would be crushed against the arch of the tunnel. He fainted, but was hauled in, uninjured, by his traveling companions."

Charcot crossed the stage and stopped in front of Gaspard. He stared at him for a few seconds before he resumed talking. Gaspard had the strange feeling Charcot was addressing him.

"Yet in due course he developed a paralysis of the entire left side of his body. Here we have a case of a hysterical symptom developed subsequent to a purely psychic trauma, but in accordance with the specific injury the patient expected to receive but which, in fact, he escaped. Gentlemen, note the lapse of time between the original trauma and the emergence of the hysterical symptom. It took two weeks—fourteen days!—of mental elaboration for this particular trauma to be worked up! In some cases it takes even longer."

Charcot turned on a bright light and directed it at the patient's face.

"Now, it's well known that in certain circumstances an idea may produce a paralysis. Conversely, an idea may cause it to disappear. This leads me to the second subject of my lecture today: the use of hypnosis in treating hysteria. Focus on the bright light."

The patient did. Using his fingers Charcot applied pressure on his eyeballs.

"Ten, nine, eight . . . four, three, two, one."

The patient fell under hypnosis. Using his fingers Charcot opened his eyes.

"The patient has now entered the cataleptic phase. If I place his arms in a position of prayer, and I let them stay for a certain time, he will think only of praying. Where are you right now?"

"In church," the patient said.

Charcot was pleased with the answer.

"Indeed! If I incline his head forward and bend his arms, he will feel his spirit invaded by ideas of humility and contrition; if I tilt his head high, he will have feelings of pride. An initial stimulus, such as putting the hands into a position of prayer, activates a reflex system so that other

muscles are drawn into the praying attitude. Monsieur Duchenne has explained all of this brilliantly, as you will see at his lecture next week. I will now put the patient into somnambulism."

Charcot touched the patient's shoulder.

"Your shoulder is paralyzed," he said.

"No, it's not," the patient objected.

The audience laughed. Charcot ignored them.

"Yes, it is," he insisted.

"I am telling you it isn't," the patient repeated.

Charcot pushed his shoulder a little harder: it was completely stiff.

"Your shoulder is paralyzed," Charcot concluded. "The shoulder joint is now completely immobile. However, you are still able to move elbow, wrist and fingers quite freely."

The patient moved each corresponding body part. Charcot took out a pin, showed it to the audience, then turned to the patient and pricked his shoulder, chest, and, finally, his upper arm.

"I am now going to induce paralysis of the elbow," he announced.

He touched the patient's elbow to demonstrate its immobility.

"Finally, the wrist. Note that the fingers retain voluntary mobility."

The audience applauded.

"And now, gentlemen, compare this patient's symptoms, produced, as you all saw, artificially, with the hysterical symptoms of the next patient."

Charcot's assistant brought forward another patient, whose right hand, arm, shoulder and part of the chest were paralyzed.

"As you can see, the symptoms are in all respects identical," Charcot announced.

He then undid the first man's symptoms, proceeding by segments upward from the patient's hand and verifying at each stage the corresponding retreat of the anesthesia.

Gaspard stumbled toward the exit. The ground under his feet opened up and he began falling. The last thing he remembered was the red face of a nurse bending over him.

He woke up in his apartment. Doctor Gautier was standing by his bedside, watching him.

"I didn't write to you."

"You didn't," Gautier confirmed.

Gaspard tried to sit up. Gautier pushed him back down.

"How do you like Paris?" he asked.

"A real bore . . . until yesterday."

Gaspard told him about Charcot's demonstration. Gautier frowned.

"I can't decide if the man is a genius scientist or a magician," Gaspard said. "What do you call a man who can manipulate your feelings and thoughts simply by manipulating your posture?"

"A charlatan!" Gautier said scornfully.

"Imagine the possibilities!"

"And what might those be?" Gautier asked, visibly irritated by Gaspard's infatuation with Charcot. "Do you know where Charcot finds his so called 'case studies'? Jail or the vaudeville house! That's right. His 'patients' are murderers and actors! They are certainly not insane!"

"That's brilliant!" Gaspard exclaimed. "Successfully feigning insanity under close medical supervision is no slight achievement. Who is to say that after feigning insanity for so long nature doesn't lend some assistance to art?"

Gautier put away his stethoscope and crossed his arms in front of his chest.

"There is nothing medically wrong with you. How do you feel?"

"Empty."

"Don't we all?" Gautier sighed.

"I don't mean metaphorically empty. It's not my mind that is empty. On the contrary: it's constantly occupied with some thought or other. The chattering never stops. But I feel as if all my internal organs have been scooped out of me."

"I see," Gautier said. "You need to rest."

"I thought you recommended distraction and amusement," Gaspard reminded him.

"Sadly, they don't seem to agree with you," Gautier said in all seriousness.

Bruno closed his eyes and rubbed them until a few abstract shapes began flashing on the inside of his eyelids. He opened his eyes and looked up. One of the clerks was shelving books. When she turned around to pick up the next book Bruno saw that this was not the clerk from the Salpêtrière archives. It was one of the library assistants he had seen working every morning in the Public Library Reading Room. What was she doing here? Bruno looked around. He was sitting in the Reading Room at the Public Library, not in the Salpêtrière Archives, where he (thought he) arrived early this morning. He looked down: he was holding a photograph of a man standing in the shadows. The tip of the man's cigarette glowed in the dark, illuminating his diamond cufflinks. There was no doubt about it: the man was Gaspard Leblon. He was standing in front of a building, under a big sign: 'Hotel L'Etoile'. Attached to the back of the photograph was an excerpt from a newspaper article (dated 1892) titled "Who is the Phantom Killer?" and the usual written account.

After Gautier's departure Gaspard got up. He took out a cigarette from the bedside table and looked for matches but couldn't find any. He slowly began to get dressed.

The streets were deserted and dark except for the light coming from a building across the street: Hotel L'Etoile. The hotel receptionist, a very old man who seemed to be aging fast right in front of Gaspard's eyes, was reading a newspaper article. Gaspard squinted, trying to make out the title: "Who Is the Phantom Killer?"

"Do you have a light?" he asked casually.

The hotel receptionist looked up from the paper, smiled pleasantly, and offered him a few matches. Then he placed a hotel key on the counter.

"At what time would Monsieur like his breakfast tomorrow? Ten o'clock as usual?"

Gaspard hesitated. Finally, he picked up the key.

"As usual," he said.

"Does Monsieur like his new job?" the receptionist asked.

Mistaking the confusion on Gaspard's face for irritation he immediately apologized.

"I don't mean to pry. It's just that Monsieur mentioned he had started a new job at one of the biggest accounting firms in town. Laurent & Moreau, was it?"

"I am pleased with the job," Gaspard said.

The receptionist stared at his tailcoat, white gloves, pink cravat and tall hat. Gaspard smiled awkwardly.

"I am in an amateur drama society. They cast me as a Duke. Imagine that!"

The receptionist nodded.

"I love theatre," he said without any love. "Good night, Monsieur Blanc."

Room 12 was on the third floor. Gaspard looked out the window. To his surprise, the room faced his own apartment, now completely dark. There were no personal belongings except for a nondescript pair of shoes. Inside the dresser there were three pairs of suits, the kind an accountant might wear, all identical. He quickly changed into one of them, folded up his own clothes and put them in the bottom drawer, which was empty except for a small notebook filled with names, addresses, dates and times. The first entry read "November 17, corner of Rue du Saint Elois and Rue du Saint Sacrement. 7 o'clock."

The head librarian's voice came over the intercom informing everyone that the library was closing two hours earlier on account of the Fiction Reading that was going to take place at 7PM. Bruno collected his things and got up. The door to the lobby seemed far away, at the end of a narrow tunnel made of tightly packed words.

After walking around aimlessly for an hour, overwhelmed by the evening crowd, he stopped and leaned against the glass door of a building. The doorman motioned to him to step aside: he was blocking the hotel entrance. The sign above the entrance read *Hôtel Dauphine*. He went in and walked around the reception area with the confidence of a returning guest who always stays in the same suite. He then sat in the lobby and pretended to read a paper before finally moving to the hotel bar. Outside, the fog was hanging in various irregular shapes from the bare tree branches and the constant drizzle maintained a consistently dreary mood.

Bruno paid for his whiskey and climbed up to the third floor. A wheeled table with cleaning supplies was parked on the right. Bruno walked past the first room. Through the half-opened door he caught a glimpse of the maid pushing a vacuum cleaner, like some pre-historic beast twice her size. Her small, sleepy face looked relaxed: she did not seem to register the horrendous noise the machine produced. Bruno stopped in front of the second room on the left. The door was wide open. The bed was unmade. A large pillow was propped up against the wall, as if someone had been watching TV all day and night. The TV was on, but the volume was turned down. The fog streamed through the open window and hung over the bed like a weightless mosquito curtain. Bruno walked into the room and closed the window. A pair of men's pants hung over the back of the chair. On the floor, at the foot of the bed, there was an open suitcase. Inside Bruno found clothes arranged neatly in piles and several books whose titles he could not make out. There was something sharp at the bottom of the suitcase, under the shirts and pants: a vintage 19TH century woman's hairbrush.

The TV weather forecast filled the room with the hypnotic sounds of world natural disasters represented on the screen with tiny cute symbols. Across the globe hurricanes and tornadoes with exotic sounding names ravished cities and towns while he was sitting here, in the warm hotel room, safe.

Or was he?

The room, he now realized, resembled a crime scene. There was no guarantee the hotel guest would ever come back. He had gotten up this morning, taken a quick shower, gotten dressed, watched some TV and finally descended to the hotel restaurant for breakfast. He had left without putting things into their proper places, without taking one final look at the room. He assumed he would be back in the evening. Bruno threw the cover off the bed, lied down, turned off the night lamp and stared at the images moving across the TV screen. The silhouette of a woman, dragging something bulky behind her, appeared in the doorway. She flicked the light switch and screamed when she saw Bruno in bed. It was the sleepy-faced maid.

"I am sorry, Monsieur," she said in a plaintive voice. "I didn't realize you were here. I will come back later."

Bruno looked around: he couldn't quite recall how he ended up in this bed. Before his body could reposition itself in this unfamiliar environment the maid had already disappeared. She came back in a second and waved something in front of him: a "Do not disturb" sign.

"I'll hang it on the door," she said.

Bruno threw the bed covers aside and got out of bed. The white bed sheets preserved the imprint of a body. Was it his body or the body of the hotel guest under whose name this room was booked? He turned on the lamp: the imprint of his body was superimposed over that of the previous body, whose legs and arms, he now saw, were longer than his. Bruno walked over to the balcony door but did not open it. All he could see was the reflection of his own face in the glass. The guest staying in this room must have stood in exactly this spot, looking out the window, just like Bruno. He paced across the room, trying to imagine where the guest might have stopped, what part of the furniture he might have touched, what phone numbers he might have dialed, what conversations he might have had. But it didn't stop there, did it? Hundreds of guests had pulled aside the curtains to check the weather, enjoy the view, complain about the view, or open the balcony door to jump. Bruno was conjuring them all back into existence but freezing them individually in one particular moment, in one particular place: one was hiding behind the balcony door, another one was sitting up in bed, a third one was writing at the desk. Before too long the room was crowded. He undressed quickly and jumped in the shower, pulling the shower curtain around him so as not to see the others. Only they were everywhere. He closed his eyes—something he did whenever he was trying to be rational—but that didn't prevent him from seeing the water trickle down numerous naked limbs and torsos other than his. When he got out of the shower he opened one of the little whiskey bottles in the fridge and poured it down his throat.

11

He woke up the following morning with a hangover. On the night table next to him seven mini whiskey bottles formed a perfectly straight line. As he was getting dressed it occurred to him that the room's occupant had not come back last night.

The hotel lobby was crowded. Several tour groups, heavily equipped with photographic devices, had surrounded their respective leaders, who were waving brightly colored flags with the name of the tour operator. A man standing at the reception desk put something in his pocket, mumbled "Thank you" and walked toward the hotel exit. Bruno recognized the bald head, the slightly slouched figure, and the nondescript jacket. Bruno followed X up the stairs and was not really surprised when X stopped in front of the room in which Bruno had spent the night. Quick! Think! Had he moved anything around? Had he turned off the TV before leaving?

"Good morning, Monsieur."

Bruno turned around and found himself face to face with the maid from the night before.

"May I go in and clean the room?" she asked.

"I am not staying here. I was just visiting a friend." He looked at her conspiratorially. "It's a private matter," he added.

She smiled. Bruno wasn't entirely sure she understood but pressing the point further would only make her more suspicious. At that moment he heard the key in the door. He turned around with his back to the door, hoping X, who was now leaving his room, would not recognize him. He waited for X to get in the elevator and ran down the stairs.

He spent the rest of the day at the library, trying out new 'research methods'. He turned off the reading lamp on his desk, and the reading lamps on the neighboring tables, and picked up a photograph from the box at random. The more he stared at it the darker it got until all he could see were a series of overlapping dark circles, one blacker than the other. Two human figures began to come into focus, one lying face down on the ground, the other one, with his back to the camera, bent over the body, arms behind his back. The V shape the second man's arms formed was enough to identify him as Gaspard Leblon. The following text was attached to the photograph.

Gaspard walked up and down the deserted Rue du Saint Elois. When he reached the corner of Rue du Saint Elois and Rue du Saint Sacrement the clock struck 7. Suddenly, there was a gunshot, followed by a scream. Somewhere, a window was shut closed. He caught a glimpse of a man turning around the corner at the opposite end of the street. Gaspard turned around: in the little dark alley behind him another man slumped to the ground. The dead man was dressed modestly, like an accountant. Gaspard searched the body. The identification papers belonged to one 'Theodore Blanc', the man in whose hotel room he had just moved in, the man he was pretending to be. Hearing steps behind him, Gaspard bent over the body and picked up the gun lying next it. He was holding it behind his back when Captain Boileau ran up to him, his puffy face red and sweaty.

"Are you the only witness?" the Captain asked, breathing heavily. Gaspard showed him the gun.

"No one saw me," he said.

An hour later Gaspard found himself sitting across Poiccard, head of precinct. An authoritative male voice came from behind the white screen separating Poiccard's office from the other half of the room:

"Kleptomania and exhibitionism: seven cases. Sexual perversions, alcoholism, and drug addiction: twenty-three cases. Psychosis: two cases. Persecution delirium: one case. Hysteria: thirty-two cases. The alcoholics and the drug addicts go to Bicêtre, the rest to Salpêtrière."

Gaspard glanced at the pile of paperwork scattered all over Poiccard's desk. On top of the pile was a list of names in alphabetical order.

"Name?" Captain Boileau barked.

Gaspard randomly picked one of the names on the list.

"Polgar. Jacques Polgar."

"Occupation?"

"None at the moment," Gaspard said nonchalantly. "I do have some preoccupations if you'd care to hear them."

Boileau bared his teeth.

"Monsieur, may I remind you that you are a suspect in a murder case. Earlier this evening you were walking along Rue du Saint Elois and Rue du Saint Sacrement. Is that correct?"

"Yes," Gaspard confirmed.

"Upon being apprehended you confessed to murdering a man near the corner of these two streets, a little before midnight."

"Correct."

"Did anyone force you to confess?"

"Do I look like a man who can be forced into doing something?"

Boileau's face turned red.

"Do I look like a man who gives a damn about how you look?"

Poiccard signaled to Boileau to calm down and turned to Gaspard.

"Monsieur Polgar, I urge you to take a little more interest in the proceeding. Your own life is at stake. What is your relationship to the victim?"

"I never saw him before."

"Why did you murder a stranger?"

Gaspard raised his right hand to his mouth to conceal a yawn.

"Dozens of crimes are being committed in Paris as we speak," he said. "Instead of dispatching your people to all four corners of the city, you ask me inane questions in spite of the fact that I already confessed and assumed full responsibility for the crime. I have told you the time, the day, the circumstances. I've described in great detail how I murdered the victim yet for some unfathomable reason you deem all of this insufficient or irrelevant. Frankly, I find that disrespectful. What would it take to convince you that things are exactly as they appear to be?"

"We do not need to be 'convinced' of anything, Monsieur. I strongly advise you to reconsider your attitude. For the last time, why did you murder that man?"

Gaspard looked out the window as if he was really thinking about the question.

"His sartorial taste offended me," he said in a mock-confessional voice.

Gaspard's trial was set for the following week. He was looking forward to it like a young debutante anticipating her first ball and was disappointed when they finally led him into an almost empty court-room. Apparently the Paris high society had better sources of entertainment. The Judge could conceal neither his indifference to the proceedings nor his tendency to doze off during slightly longer speeches.

The Investigating Magistrate adjusted his glasses and stood up to read out the indictment.

"Your Honor," he began. "The defendant is Jacques Polgar, age thirty-seven, occupation unknown, residence unknown. On the night of November seventeen the defendant attacked and murdered the victim, Theodore Blanc. The bullet that killed Blanc matches the gun found on the defendant. Your Honor would be interested to know that the bullets that killed the last two victims of the "Phantom Killer" came from the same gun. Doctor Girard will present his medico-legal report."

The magistrate returned to his seat. Doctor Girard put on his glasses and stood up. He was a peripatetic thinker. Gaspard grew dizzy watching him pace back and forth, gesticulate wildly and regularly point at Gaspard, as if he thought it necessary to remind the judge and the jury who the criminal in the room was.

"Your Honor! Gentlemen of the jury! I found the defendant to be a vain, idle man of a brooding temper, given over to unwholesome and dangerous introspection, and prone to analyzing his feelings to a confusing and unnecessary extent. He exhibits strong flat affect, possibly a reaction to the crime he committed. During the initial interrogation he alternated between a calm, rational state and an irritable, narcissistic one, answering my questions with a subtle but unmistakable whiff of superiority. When I mentioned to him the lack of witnesses might work in his favor he anxiously claimed full responsibility for the crime. He seemed almost desperate at the prospect of being found non-guilty. It remains to be seen whether he is dissimulating for the purpose of mocking us or there is a real reason for his behavior, possibly a lesion of the brain."

Girard paused to wipe the sweat off his forehead. Gaspard was content with his psychological portrait. Gaspard, it turned out, was a man with specific qualities, a man of a particular temperament, a man who related to others in a particular way, a man capable of feeling "almost desperate." It all sounded quite promising. He felt an unexpected outburst of warmth and bonhomie towards Girard and would have gladly shaken the doctor's hand.

"There is no evidence of a disequilibrium of his mental faculties," Girard went on. "I have no doubt that the defendant is intellectually capable of perceiving the difference between right and wrong. I trust no further comment is necessary to establish his high degree of moral imbecility."

Girard returned to his seat. Someone in the back opened a bottle of champagne. The judge brought his fist down.

"Silence! May I remind you that the court is not a theatre and the popping of champagne corks is incompatible with the sobriety of a legal proceeding."

He turned to Gaspard.

"Why did you murder that man? To rob him?"

"Certainly not!" Gaspard replied resentfully.

"Were you seeking revenge?"

"Perhaps," Gaspard grinned.

The judge made no attempt to hide his irritation.

"Monsieur, it is in your interest to enlighten us!"

The attorney stood up.

"If I may, your Honor, the defendant has already confessed to the crime, indicating his desire to be sentenced."

The judge frowned.

"The defendant has indicated a desire to be sentenced, not a desire to be judged. His refusal to participate in the interrogation can be interpreted as contempt of court."

He furrowed his brows to lend his small, sleepy face some degree of authority.

"Monsieur, do not destroy the goodwill the jury may be disposed to show towards you. For the last time, why did you murder this man?"

"I wanted to experience the sensations of an assassin in order to analyze them," Gaspard said.

After a short break, during which everyone in the courtroom stared at Gaspard as if he was a rare exotic beast, the trial continued. The judge addressed the jury.

"Gentlemen, you will now hear the prosecutor's and the defense counsel's closing statements. I urge you all to consult your conscience and consider only the facts of the case."

Gaspard leaned back, basking in the warm light of legal rhetoric. The prosecutor stood up and looked around to make sure all eyes were on him.

He walked back and forth in front of the defendant's box, occasionally glancing at the jury, the judge and, finally, at Gaspard. It wasn't clear if this carefully choreographed barrage of significant looks was part of his closing statement or just a prelude to it. Finally, he spoke.

"Gentlemen of the jury, born criminals are easily recognizable by certain physical traits—asymmetrical face, prominent ears, abnormally long arms, insensibility to pity, lack of affect. They are destined by their innate qualities to a life of crime. As you can see, Jacques Polgar exhibits all of these characteristics."

The jury members craned their necks to get a good look of Gaspard.

"Born criminals represent a case of atavism, a throwback to an earlier stage of primitive human development. There is no other way to account for the defendant's appalling moral insensibility, in which he seems to take a perverse pleasure. There is only one 'treatment' for a man of his kind: the guillotine."

Gaspard signaled to the prosecutor to approach him.

"Very impressive: succinct and eloquent!" he congratulated him.

The prosecutor looked at Gaspard with a mixture of resentment and embarrassment before returning to his seat. The attorney stood up and adjusted his wig, which was too big for his head.

"Gentlemen, the prosecution's account of criminality makes the idea of individual moral responsibility seem irrelevant and the idea of punishment outmoded. If offenders were predestined to a life of crime, well, it would be meaningless to speak of punishment. The social milieu is the mother culture of criminality; the microbe is the criminal, an element, which gains significance only at the moment when it finds the broth that makes it ferment."

Gaspard closed his eyes and appeared to doze off. The attorney paused, embarrassed by his client's indifference toward his own fate.

"Jacques Polgar committed this crime under the influence of extreme cerebral excitement. His reason was temporarily affected by the action of acute mental distress on a highly sensitive temperament. The defendant belongs in a mental asylum, not in jail."

The judge reluctantly turned towards the defendant's box. It was obvious that he found the mere sight of Gaspard prohibitive.

"Monsieur, is there anything you'd like to say in your defense?" he asked wearily.

"Nothing comes to mind, your Honor," Gaspard said calmly as he clasped his hands and invited Boileau to cuff him.

Bruno put away the underexposed photograph. As he got closer to the bottom of the box he was finding more and more imageless memories, written accounts not based on photographs, seemingly existing independently of any indexical material. He wasn't sure if the lack of visual evidence meant that the memories were getting stronger or was it the other way around, that is, as memories faded away they had to be elaborated over and over again verbally?

At this point any further attempts to match up photographs with written accounts struck him as useless. He picked up one of the folded sheets of paper that was *not* accompanied by a photograph, not even an underexposed or overexposed one. The paper smelled of mold and felt more brittle and fragile than the others, as if it had been stored under different physical conditions.

The warden locked the door behind the prison chaplain.

"I am not here to judge you. Only the Lord can do that," the chaplain began cautiously.

Gaspard pretended to be intrigued by his words.

"My son, you have committed a sin. You have taken another man's life."

The chaplain smiled sorrowfully and clasped his hands together.

"What is sin? Sin is an offense against reason, truth, and right conscience. It is a revolt against God through the will to become like gods, knowing and determining good and evil. Sin is love of oneself even to contempt of God."

Gaspard began counting the bricks in the opposite wall. The chaplain's inflated words continued to roll off his tongue somewhere behind him.

"Do not despair, my son. Let him who is in desolation consider how the Lord has left him in trial in his natural powers, in order to resist the different agitations and temptations of the enemy."

"Six, seven, eight, nine . . ." Gaspard counted out loud.

"Since he can with the Divine help, which always remains to him, though he does not clearly perceive it: because the Lord has taken from him his great fervor, great love and intense grace, leaving him, however, grace enough for eternal salvation. Let us pray."

"*Eighteen, nineteen . . . I don't remember how . . . twenty . . .*"

The chaplain moved closer to Gaspard and took his hands in his.

"*Put your hands together like this. Incline your head forward. Can you not feel your soul invaded by ideas of humility and contrition? Repeat after me: I believe in God, the Father Almighty, Creator of heaven and earth, and in Jesus Christ, His only Son, our Lord, who was conceived by the Holy Spirit, born of the Virgin Mary, suffered under Pontius Pilate . . . was crucified, died, was buried and—*"

"Monsieur?"

Bruno shook his head.

"Monsieur, are you alright?" the same voice said.

"Descended into hell," he mumbled.

The head librarian was staring at him with a concerned look on her face. He assured her he was feeling well, waited for her to walk away, and picked up another photograph. This one was different from the rest in one important respect: it did not feature any human beings. Or perhaps they were there but the photograph was so overexposed that the only thing that had registered was the horizon. The rest was pure, milky white. Twelve(!) pages were attached to the photograph.

The day after the trial Captain Boileau escorted Gaspard to Poiccard's office.

"*Good news,*" *Poiccard exclaimed when he saw Gaspard.* "*You have received a full pardon!*"

Boileau, who obviously didn't think this was good news, could not restrain himself any longer.

"*Monsieur Blanc, you have made a mockery of the court, the police and the church!*"

Poiccard gave him a stern look and turned back to Gaspard.

"*Several witnesses, including the receptionist at your hotel, have come forward to testify that you are, in fact, Theodore Blanc, bookkeeper, currently residing at Hotel L'Etoile. Now, I do not claim to understand why you decided to assume a different name or to claim responsibility for a murder you did not commit. All I know is that since Theodore Blanc is not . . . I mean you are not . . . dead, we are left with no other choice but to release you immediately. This case is closed.*"

"With all due respect, you seem to be forgetting that you still have a corpse in the morgue," Gaspard said anxiously.

Poiccard sighed.

"You are a free man, Monsieur Blanc. Try to see this as a good thing."

Gaspard returned to the hotel. When he entered the lobby the receptionist was reading a newspaper article titled "The Phantom Killer . . . Remains a Phantom." He waved his hand magnanimously.

"There is no need to thank me, Monsieur Blanc. I only did what anyone else in my place would have done."

Gaspard ignored him and walked up the stairs. Up in his room he opened Blanc's notebook with the list of names and addresses. The next entry on the list was "Corner of Rue d'Orsel and Rue de Ronsard, August 11, 8 o'clock, evening." He checked the clock: he had four hours. Everything went as planned. This time his trip from the crime scene to the courtroom was slightly delayed by a new procedure the criminal court had recently adopted as part of the preliminary criminal examination: all criminals had now to be photographed at the Salpêtrière Photo Lab. When Gaspard was finally escorted into the same courtroom the judge (the same one) observed him with curiosity.

"It seems to me the defendant was already tried by this court."

The prosecutor stood up and flung his long arms dramatically.

"Your Honor, the defendant confessed to another crime of the same nature as the one for which he was earlier tried and acquitted."

The judge turned to the attorney.

"Have you spoken to your client and advised him of the best course of action?"

The attorney reviewed his notes.

"Your Honor, my client insists that he committed the murder." He checked his notes again, but they appeared to confuse him even more. "He says I must, I quote, 'protect his right to claim responsibility for his own acts,' and that, I quote again, 'it is my duty to prove he is as guilty as he claims to be'."

"Your Honor," the prosecutor interjected. "As we discovered during his first trial, the defendant is a pathological liar! I believe his confession is part of an elaborate delusional system of belief that requires further medical investigation."

He turned to the audience and announced that, with the help of a new and exciting scientific method, Doctor Girard would now demonstrate that the defendant's confession was utterly unfounded. The announcement was greeted with enthusiastic applause: Girard had already proven himself an entertaining speaker. He came out from behind his desk and began pacing across the floor, gesticulating and spitting involuntarily every time he reached the end of a sentence.

"Your Honor, we have recently adopted a reliable method for eliciting the principal types of insanity by methods of optical superimposition of the portraits of the insane. The composite portrait enables us to obtain with mechanical precision a generalized picture that represents no man in particular but portrays an imaginary figure possessing the average features of any given group of men, whether epileptics, hysterics, or what have you. It is mathematically true that deviations from the average man are indistinguishable from error—"

"The average man?" the judge interrupted him.

Girard opened a folder lying on his desk and took out a number of portrait photographs. He spread them out in front of the judge as if they were cards and pointed to the men in two of them.

"The average man is in society the analogue of the center of gravity in matter. He is a fictional being in regard to which all things happen in accordance with average results obtained for society."

The judge seemed impressed. Girard picked up one of the photographs.

"Here we have an example of a composite portrait of hysterical and delusional patients. In the last year we have seen an inordinate increase in the number of such cases. This portrait was obtained from the photographs of all patients in this class, including the defendant."

Girard walked over to Gaspard and held up the photograph next to his face.

"You will no doubt notice the portrait bears a striking resemblance to the defendant. Now, to verify our results we conducted another, parallel study."

Girard took out another set of photographs and showed them to the judge.

"This is a composite portrait of an average murderer produced from individual photographs of all murderers currently serving their sentence in Paris."

Girard walked over to the defendant's box and held up the composite portrait next to Gaspard's face.

"Note that the defendant's face represents a significant deviation from the portrait."

He turned around, facing the courtroom.

"Ladies and gentlemen, on the basis of the scientific evidence presented here, as well as on the results of the defendant's first trial, I conclude that the defendant is innocent of the crime he has confessed to. I believe Theodore Blanc suffers from an unknown kind of mental disturbance that forces him to claim responsibility for random acts that cannot, in fact, be attributed to him."

The courtroom doors shut behind Gaspard. He was free. Again.

He walked around aimlessly all day. Just before sunset he found himself on the Left Bank. The water stretched out before him, grey and smooth. He lit a cigarette. It had become a habit, something to do when there was nothing else to do. An old man stood on the opposite side of the bridge, with his back toward Gaspard. Gaspard inhaled slowly. His head was empty. The old man leaned over the railing and spat in the water. Gaspard dropped the cigarette butt on the ground and pressed down on it with the sole of his shoe. He took his hands out of his pockets and walked forward at a leisurely pace. Somewhere in the middle of the bridge he wondered why he had decided to cross the bridge. When he finally got to the opposite side he understood what the motive for this action must have been. He raised his arm, extended it forward and pushed the old man into the river. The water opened up to receive his body and closed over it. Everything was smooth and grey again. Gaspard lit another cigarette and waited.

"Murderer! Murderer!"

Finally.

Gaspard's route from the bridge to the courtroom was swift and painless. He sat down in the defendant's box and looked calmly ahead of him, ignoring the prosecutor's intense stare. Although Gaspard prided himself on being an excellent judge of character he had difficulty deciding if the prosecutor was angry, indignant, resentful, jealous, or just sleep-deprived. His stare was obviously a part of his statement so he milked it for as long as he could, that is, around three minutes. Finally, he seemed to have found the strength to overcome his resentment towards Gaspard—or at least he put up a very good show of doing that—and to address the judge.

"Your Honor, the defendant is painfully familiar to us: Theodore Blanc, two prior murder convictions, acquitted twice. Last night he was apprehended after allegedly committing another criminal act of the same nature."

The prosecutor smoothed down the unruly hairs sticking out of his wig and adjusted the pleats of his gown.

"Monsieur Blanc, please describe what happened on the evening of August nineteen."

"I was standing on the bridge. On the opposite side of the bridge I noticed a man. He appeared to be homeless."

The prosecutor grinned smugly.

"What was he doing?"

"Nothing. He was staring at the water."

"What happened then?"

"I walked over to him and pushed him in the river."

"What was your motive?"

He emphasized the word "motive" as if to suggest the ludicrousness of even bringing it up.

Gaspard took his time. The prosecutor's self-satisfied grin began to fade.

"He was obstructing my view," Gaspard said.

"Monsieur Blanc," the judge interrupted. "I'm warning you: you will be held in contempt of court if you continue in this manner."

"What I say is true," Gaspard protested.

The prosecutor raised his bony finger.

"But is it statistically true?! Your Honor, I call to the stand Doctor Girard."

Girard, even perkier than usual, jumped from his seat and walked quickly to the front of the room. His hands were shaking but Gaspard knew it was excitement, not stage fever.

"Your Honor, esteemed members of the jury!" He made a dramatic pause. "Did you know that in Paris, in ordinary times, the number of letters at the Dead Letter Office is remarkably stable from one year to the next?"

The judge was confused yet intrigued by this piece of information.

"What does this tell us? It tells us that every year, all other things being equal, the same number of deaths are registered in Paris. Every year we witness the same crimes reproduced in the same order and bringing with them the same penalties in the same proportions. We can enumerate in advance how many individuals will stain their hands with the blood of their fellow creatures, how many will be forgers, how many prisoners, pretty nearly as one can enumerate in advance the births and deaths which must take place."

Girard stopped and looked around triumphantly.

"To understand crime," he continued, "we have to understand the laws and customs of society, not the caprices of individuals. Individuals are too variable and inconsistent to serve as the basis of the moral sciences. Often we do not understand why they do what they do. But the average man we can understand. In the average everything exceptional balances out. Once we adopt the statistical approach and seek causes whose effects can be discerned in large numbers, it becomes immediately clear to us that the moral order falls within the domain of statistics."

A few people in the audience applauded. Girard had now entered full-blown explanatory mode.

"The first thing to be established in a case like this is the defendant's propensity to crime. Supposing men are placed in like circumstances, the propensity for crime is the greater or lesser probability of committing a crime. After considering a large enough number of cases, I devised an empirical formula, which can be used to calculate the propensity for crime, taking into consideration the specific information available in the defendant's record:

$$Y = (1 - \sin X)\, \frac{1}{1+m} \quad \text{supposing } m = \frac{1}{2x - 18}$$

"The degree of the propensity for crime Y is expressed as a function of age X. It is necessary to take for the axis of the abscissas the quarter of the circumference rectified and divided according to decimal division. Using this formula I was able to establish a statistical profile for murderer. I then compared the defendant's profile to the murderer's profile."

Girard took out a sheet of paper from his folder and waved it around as if he was waving a flag to signal the end of a victorious war.

"*This table shows the defendant's propensity to crime to be close to zero. Taking into consideration his education, marital status, age, birth place, time of the crime, place of the crime etc., I concluded that all his claims to the contrary, the defendant did not, in fact, murder the victim.*"

Gaspard jumped from his seat.

"*What does statistics have to do with any of this? My actions are real, no matter how statistically improbable. A corpse is a corpse!*"

Captain Boileau pushed him back in his seat. Utterly oblivious to Gaspard's outburst Girard produced several sheets of paper containing tables and numbers and showed them to the judge.

"*Your Honor, this document shows the latest suicide statistics in Paris. As you can see, the two most common methods of Parisian suicide are drowning and charcoal. By contrast, Londoners prefer to hang themselves or use a gun. Our victim clearly fits the statistical profile for a Parisian suicide. Indeed, even without resorting to statistical tables, it is easy to see why a man in the victim's situation—miserable, poor, homeless, with no family, et cetera—would find death a welcome solution.*"

Girard paused to wipe the sweat off his brow.

"*It is a statistical law that a certain proportion of the people in Paris will commit suicide in a given year. Then it is not true of each Parisian that he or she is free not to commit suicide. If each person were free to do so, then it might have happened that none did so, and hence that would not have been a statistical law about the population, which is absurd!*"

Two days later, after careful consideration of the evidence presented in the case against Theodore Blanc, the court reached the conclusion that, while Gaspard's motivation for claiming responsibility for the homeless man's murder remained unclear, his propensity to crime was statistically negligible. He was, therefore, innocent.

Upon his release from prison Gaspard didn't go back to the hotel; instead he paid a visit to Madame Laure. Natalie, one of the new girls, poured him a glass of absinthe, sat next to him, and gently rubbed his thigh. He listened distractedly to a conversation between two other girls, who were busy putting on makeup.

"*When is Monsieur Gaspard coming again?*" *one of them asked.*

The other one giggled.

"*Isn't he the most handsome man you've ever seen? And a real gentleman!*"

When the girls left the room he asked Natalie whom they were talking about.

"Another client," Natalie said and leaned over to kiss him. He pushed her away.

Back in his hotel room he asked for a bottle of wine to be brought up to his room. He stood by the window, drinking. Madame Laure had not shown up the whole evening and none of the girls at the brothel had seemed to recognize him. He examined his reflection in the window: had he really changed that much while he was in prison?

A light flickered in one of the dark windows across the street.

There was nothing strange about lights in other people's windows. This light, however, was coming from Gaspard's own apartment window across the street. A hand emerged out of the dark and moved into the candlelight. Gaspard instinctively stepped back and hid behind the curtain. When he looked again the light was still there but the hand had vanished.

When he woke up—he had fallen asleep slouched in the chair next to the window—the curtains in his apartment across the street were slightly parted. He could now see the shadow of a man moving around his sitting room. The man was wearing Gaspard's blue tailcoat. As much as Gaspard strained his eyes he could not make out the stranger's face. The man picked up Gaspard's silver cane and walked out the room. ·

Gaspard waited for him in front of the hotel and followed him discreetly. The route seemed familiar but it was only when the man stopped in front of a small, smoked-filled café that Gaspard realized it was the same café where he used to meet Francois and Gilbert. Through the window he saw the stranger sit down at a table with Gilbert. The two of them ordered absinthe. The stranger began dealing cards.

The stranger left the café an hour later, alone. Gaspard followed him until he disappeared inside a little shop on rue Denis. Gaspard looked through the dusty window: his impostor stood in the middle of the room while Gaspard's personal tailor—whose name, Jacques Perrier, Gaspard suddenly remembered after years of never addressing the man by his name—waltzed nervously around him, making corrections to an elegant grey waistcoat.

Later that night Gaspard returned to the shop, broke one of the windows in the back and climbed inside. The grey waistcoat was draped over a headless male mannequin. A little note with the customer's name was pinned to the front pocket: 'Monsieur Gaspard Leblon.' Gaspard took off his town coat and tried on the grey waistcoat. It was too tight, the sleeves too short.

The following morning the impostor didn't leave Gaspard's apartment until the early afternoon. Gaspard followed him across town until they arrived at La Salpêtrière. Gaspard stopped at a distance from the entrance and watched the stranger exchange a few words with the doorman. The doorman returned to his post. Only now he noticed Gaspard.

"How many times do I have to tell you? Your entrance is at the back!" he yelled.

Gaspard found the back entrance with some difficulty. In the hallway a dozen men in white patient robes were waiting in line. An old nurse with a severe expression on her face handed him a white robe with the letters TB embroidered on the front. Gaspard changed in the bathroom and rejoined the other men in line. They were escorted to the center of a big stage inside the hospital auditorium. Charcot signaled to two of his assistants to bring Gaspard to the chair in the middle of the stage. He then turned to face his audience.

"Gentlemen, if I show a hypnotized subject an imaginary snake or lion on the completely empty floor, the subject will immediately display all the signs of terror, but if I tell him the next instant that it is a humming bird, he will admire and caress it."

A shadowy figure rose up from one of the seats in the back and walked towards the exit. Gaspard tried to stand up but Charcot bent over him, closed his eyes and pressed down on his eyelids. His deep voice seemed to come from far away.

"Once plunged into sleep the brain of the subject may be considered absolutely blank and incapable of any will . . ."

Gaspard didn't hear the rest.

Several hours later he was changing back into his clothes when one of Charcot's assistants approached him.

"Did you forget something?"

He handed Gaspard several bills and patted him on the shoulder.

"You earned it."

Back at the hotel Gaspard washed his face and arms and lay down, covering his burning face with the cold, crisp bed sheets. There was something square and hard under the sheets. He raised his body and pulled it out: Theodore Blanc's notebook. He found the page with the details of the two murders. At the bottom Blanc had scribbled the following: "Duchenne, La Salpêtrière, 6 o'clock."

Gaspard spent the next day keeping a watch on his apartment window. As soon as the impostor left, Gaspard grabbed his coat and hurried down the stairs. It was only when he entered the lobby of his apartment building that he remembered the concierge, an unpleasant old man with a secretive air. It was too late to turn back.

"Can I help you?" the concierge said.

Gaspard, who had already climbed up several steps, keeping his face turned away, faced the concierge reluctantly. To his surprise the concierge showed no signs that he recognized him.

"I am looking for Monsieur Gaspard Leblon," Gaspard said slowly. The concierge smiled obligingly.

"The Duke just left. Would you like to leave a message?"

"He is expecting me. He told me to wait for him upstairs," Gaspard said with conviction. "I'm with the firm of Laurent and Moreau. I am managing the Duke's accounts."

The concierge signaled to him to go up. The apartment looked exactly as Gaspard had left it, except for a pair of binoculars he found on the table by the window. When he brought them up to his eyes his hotel room across the street came into sharp focus.

12

The trip to Chateau de Lourps felt a lot shorter this time. Bruno walked around the house a few times. Everything was exactly as he had left it the last time. A sudden gust of wind swept through the cemetery pushing one of the kitchen windows open. Bruno looked back. The wind rushed from the opposite side of the house, pushing open another window on the opposite side of the house and creating a mise-en-abyme, the other window now framed by the kitchen window. In the center of this mise-en-abyme a tiny human figure was walking away from the house . . . or was it toward the house?

The plate with tomatoes was still on the kitchen counter. Why was he surprised? Of course it would still be there: he hadn't removed it the last time he was here and no one else could have. But there was something different about it this time. The week before the only things on the plate were a couple of tomatoes and a few slices of bread. Now there was a whole loaf of bread, tomatoes, several radishes and a piece of cheese. Bruno took a bite of the bread: it was fresh, most likely purchased the day before or even today.

"Good evening. You must be the owner."

Bruno turned around. X extended his right hand. Bruno hesitated for a moment before shaking it. For the first time he noticed how thin X was. His pants were held up by a leather belt, which had been folded twice because it was too long. If one were to blow on this face layers and layers of dust would rise up from the razor sharp cheekbones and the thin, chaste lips.

"Romain Goreaux, aspiring screenwriter and director," X introduced himself. "I know the area very well. I've passed through this valley dozens of times. I remember seeing the ruins from afar but never bothered to come closer. I thought the house was abandoned a hundred years ago."

X laughed. It was a good-natured, sincere laugh, but that didn't mean Bruno appreciated it more, or at all.

"Do you mind if I take a look around? I find places like this fascinating."

Bruno motioned to X to follow him. The heavy curtains in the sitting room were drawn, allowing only a tiny ray of light to reach the center of the room, just behind the settee, where a tray with exquisitely drawn teacups and tea plates, broken into pieces, sat on top of a mahogany table covered under thick layers of dust. X stopped in front of the burgundy settee.

"Do you live here?" He pointed to the imprint of a human body on the settee.

"Of course not," Bruno said coldly.

X pointed to the plate with the bread and tomatoes.

"Looks like I interrupted your lunch. I'm sorry."

"No, this is not—"

"The tomatoes look really good. Do you take care of the garden yourself or did you hire someone?"

Bruno pretended to be busy dusting off the table.

"I hired someone," he said with his back to X.

"What's the name of the estate?"

Bruno bent over and pulled out a blade of grass that had gotten stuck to the sole of his shoe.

"Chateau de Lourps," he said.

"Chateau de Lourps," X repeated. "That's strange."

"What do you say that?"

"Oh, it's nothing, Monsieur . . . I didn't get your name?"

"Leblon. Bruno Leblon."

X laughed.

"This is incredible! Simply incredible!"

"Monsieur, your behavior is most strange," Bruno smiled coldly.

"Please forgive me. I'll explain. As I mentioned I am an aspiring filmmaker. I've been working for some time now on a feature length screenplay for a drama set in late 19TH century Paris. The thing is, some of the action in my script takes place at my protagonist's family estate, Chateau de Lourps."

"I see," Bruno said after a long pause. "This is quite a coincidence indeed."

"Yes, an incredible coincidence," X repeated. "And an incredible space! I mean, just look at this! You wouldn't even have to hire a set designer!"

He noticed Bruno's lack of enthusiasm.

"As you might have guessed I am location scouting for my film."

"You are out of luck," Bruno said, not without content. "I am selling the chateau. I was just walking around the house one last time. So many memories . . ."

"Of course, of course," X nodded. "It's an emotional thing . . . selling your past," he added, looking at Bruno strangely.

They stopped in front of an antique clock, possibly dating back to the middle of the 19TH century. The heavy pendulum, barely visible under the spider webs, had frozen in the upper right corner of its trajectory.

"If you don't mind me asking, Monsieur Leblon, how long has this estate been in your family?"

Bruno sat down in one of the armchairs. The dust floated up in the air before falling back down and settling on his shoulders.

"My great-grandfather bought it."

X furrowed his brows as though he was trying to remember something.

"Don't tell me your great-grandfather is Duke Gaspard Leblon?"

"Yes, he is."

"Is that his grave out there? I mean the one without a name."

"Yes, it is. He is buried next to his parents, Phillip Leblon and Laetitia Leblon," Bruno said.

X stared at him for several seconds, as though he expected Bruno to say something more.

"Of course, Phillip and Laetitia. I've read about them a lot."

"Where did you read about them?"

"Here and there, mostly in the Public Library," X said casually. "Wait! Haven't I seen you there? Yes, I have! I knew you looked familiar when I first saw you."

"You look familiar too," Bruno said.

"You might have seen me at the library or at the Museum of Domestic Interior. I work as a guard there."

"Must be a difficult job. Most people would be crushed if they had to stand or sit still in one spot for so long," Bruno remarked.

"Actually, I don't mind it at all. It gives me plenty of time to think about my screenplay, tweak the story here and there. And it pays decently: that means a lot to a struggling filmmaker."

"Still, I imagine it must be difficult to have to spend so much time in the past, surrounded by relics, ruins, inanimate, dead things and then to have to go back to your normal life," Bruno insisted.

"I see you understand exactly what that's like. It's not really that different from living in a place like this." X pointed to the dusty furniture and the cobwebs hanging from the broken chandelier. "Some days you can't quite tell if the things around you are coming to life or you are slowly turning into a mummy yourself. They maintain a constant temperature in the museum, which, I am afraid, prevents it from ever becoming truly haunted. You, on the other hand, must be an expert at communicating with ghosts."

Bruno remained silent.

"Location scouting is a funny thing, Monsieur Leblon," X went on. "I would have never guessed I would run into a place that not only looks ideal but has the same name as my fictional location! Not to mention running into a descendant of 'the real Gaspard Leblon'! Talk about reality copying art!"

"Why did you use quotation marks just now?" Bruno asked.

X waved his hand.

"It's just a figure of speech. I didn't mean anything by it. And really, what could I have possibly meant?"

Bruno stood up and dusted off his pants.

"It's getting late," he said.

X stood up too.

"If you ever change your mind about selling the house. . . ."

Bruno watched him walk away through the tall grass until he disappeared from view. The wind blew more forcefully now. Bruno closed the kitchen window. His hand automatically pressed the little lever underneath to lock it, as though he had done this numerous times. He walked around the house and closed all windows. If he wanted to find his way back to the train station, which, by his calculations, could not be too far away, an hour walk at the most, he had to leave before dark. All of a sudden he felt terribly sleepy. He lied down on the burgundy settee and covered himself with his coat. The house was absolutely quiet but when he closed his eyes he heard a distant, booming, thunderous sound, drawing closer and closer. It seemed to fall from above towards the top of his head rather than reaching his ears from right or left. It was as if someone was dropping down, from a great height, enormous slabs of stone. He opened his eyes. Hundreds of dust specks twirled gracefully in the air above his head before settling gently on his cheeks and forehead. He would not let himself be deceived, however. He knew very well that every speck of dust was a portentous slab of time inexorably falling down.

He slept with his eyes open. When he finally closed his eyes and woke up the sun was setting. Somehow he managed to get himself on the last train from Cedille back to Paris and arrived home, exhausted, a little after midnight.

13

Ford Harder lit a cigarette and reached for the bottle of whiskey. It was empty. Mrs. Doyle appeared at the door.

"There is a man waiting outside," she informed him.

"There always is," Harder observed as he lifted the empty bottle against the light and shook it to see if there was a sip of bourbon left at the bottom.

"He says it's urgent," she warned him.

"A sense of urgency: now that's something to be envied," Harder noted wearily.

A tall man in a bright yellow raincoat walked in and sat down. Although his hat was soaking wet he did not remove it. They stared at each other in silence for a while.

"I like a man of few words," Harder finally said. "Leaves much to the imagination, I am told." He smiled. "I'm not the imaginative kind, though."

"I'm a writer," the man announced. "Detective novels, serpentine, baroque plots. You get the idea. A few months ago I began a new novel. I had the whole thing planned out in my head to the smallest detail: multiple murders, unexpected plot twists, etc. Last week I started writing the last chapter. All of a sudden I could not remember how the whole thing is supposed to end!"

Harder uncrossed his legs and checked the clock on the wall.

"I see," he said.

"All that's left are scattered clues," the writer went on. "I don't remember how they fit together. So here I am."

Harder made a concerted effort to redirect his look from the clock on the wall to the man's face.

"Look here, Mister . . ."

"Kratt."

"Mr. Kratt, I'm a detective. I follow people. I solve murders. That's what I do."

"And that's precisely what I'm asking you to do."

"You're asking me to help you remember a story you began writing."

"I'm asking you to solve a murder."

"A fictional murder!"

"Every murder is fictional . . . before someone commits it."

Bruno sat up straight. A low gurgling sound reached his ears. It seemed to be coming from below. He listened carefully. There it was again. It was coming from his stomach.

Kratt took out a little bottle, squeezed his finger inside, retrieved three pills and popped them in his mouth.

"What are these for?" Harder asked.

"An obscure psychological problem I might not have," Kratt said.

"If you keep taking them you might actually develop some obscure psychological problem," Harder observed.

"In that case I would have to start taking them," Kratt grinned. "So you see, I am one step ahead."

"Let's go back to the so called 'murder' you want me to investigate, do you at least remember the motive?"

Bruno pressed down on his growling stomach with both hands. He was distracted by a slight movement behind the curtain, stage left. One of the actors must be standing behind it, waiting for his turn.

"Nothing out of the ordinary," Kratt said. "Obscure psychological reasons."

Those kinds of reasons are always obscure, Bruno thought.

"Who's the victim?" he heard the actor playing Harder ask.

"I don't remember," the actor playing Kratt confessed.

The actor playing Harder laughed:

"Forgive the trivial question but who's the suspect?"

Kratt looked down, embarrassed.

"I don't remember," he said. "But I'm sure it's a murder case."

The actor playing Harder stood up and walked up to the mock up window. For some reason the set designer had decided to forego the curtains: the window faced a brick wall. Harder pretended to look pensively at the Insurance Company office that was supposed to stand across the street, according to the script.

"I realize the case is slightly unusual," Kratt admitted.

Bruno wondered if the actor playing Kratt was satisfied with the way he delivered his line. Bruno sure wasn't. But then again Bruno was feeling an excruciating physical pain in his abdomen that was very likely clouding his aesthetic judgment at the moment.

"In unusual cases like yours I find my usual methods most helpful," Harder said. "I'll need a copy of the manuscript, or at least the part you've actually written. It'll help me think. You know what else helps me think?"

Kratt took out a crisp white envelope, counted the money in it, and slid it across the table. Harder slipped it in his pocket.

"I'm already thinking," he assured Kratt.

Bruno stood up and walked toward the exit, stepping on people's feet. A tiny old woman kicked him in the shins. It was small revenge but still worth the trouble, she must have thought. When he came back from the bathroom twenty minutes later he had already missed the first part of Harder's investigation. The light in the detective's fake office was now dimmed to intensify the noir atmosphere. Kratt was anxiously examining the clues piled up on Harder's desk.

"Are you sure this is the original syntax? You haven't moved anything around?" he pointed at the clues.

Harder lit another cigarette. Bruno sniffed the air. Was that real cigarette smoke coming from the stage?

"Fuck syntax! There are more pressing problems we need to deal with," Harder said.

"Such as?"

"Such as the curious fact that apart from all this junk," Harder pointed at the clues, "I didn't come across a single decent corpse. *Everyone* I saw had *never* heard of a killer, or of a corpse for that matter. In fact, *no one* I saw had *ever* heard of a killer or a corpse."

"When you put it this way it does sound hopeless. But don't worry: there will be a body," Kratt reassured him.

"I like to worry. It keeps me motivated. And what do you mean 'there *will* be a body'? Don't expect me to do your dirty work. My job is to find the body. Yours is to put it there."

Harder picked up one of the plastic bags of evidence containing a black rotary phone. He took out the phone, plugged it in, and dialed a number. The phone rang off stage. Someone picked it up.

"Mrs. Doyle, has anyone been in my office while I was out? No? Thank you."

Harder hung up.

"I suppose this is what you call realism," he mumbled. "I almost believed this was my phone."

"It *is* your phone," Kratt said.

"Of course it is!" Harder grinned. "I brought it along just in case I wanted to call you long distance."

"It looks like you were not entirely able to suspend disbelief," Kratt shook his head.

Bruno checked the theatre bill. The title of the play was *The Space of the Novel*. A bit too clever, he thought.

He had made a habit of leaving films and theatre plays before their official ending. This time it was not only because he didn't care for the play: he had to be somewhere at 9 o'clock.

At 9PM sharp X came out of the Public Library and walked briskly down the stairs. Bruno followed him at a distance. Large snowflakes got stuck in his eyelashes but he didn't dare blink for fear of losing his target. When he turned around the corner the strong December wind blew into his eyes. He closed them for a second; when he opened them again X had disappeared. Had he turned around the corner? There were no corners: the street continued straight ahead for another five hundred meters before the next intersection. Bruno stopped. A cat crossed the street, glancing at him apathetically. The pale moonlight fell over the street sign: Rue du Saint Elois. He walked to the next intersection and looked up: Rue du Saint Sacrement.

A gunshot. Followed by a scream. They are shooting a film, Bruno thought. The scream sounded theatrical, like something real that had been reproduced so many times that it begins to sound theatrical. There was no use denying it. It was happening, right here, right now. He turned around frantically, trying to gauge the direction from which the gunshot had come. Around the corner! He got to the corner in a matter of seconds, just in time to catch a glimpse of a man's silhouette melting into the blackness squeezed in between the walls on either side of the back alley. He ran back to his initial spot, bumping into something soft on the ground. The broken bulb of the street lamp illuminated the back of a dead man's head. *A bald dead man's head.*

Bruno turned around and ran as fast as he could. In the distance he heard a police siren. It was drawing closer and closer. He ran in the opposite direction but the police siren—the same one?—drew nearer and nearer. On his right a bright red neon sign—*Cinema XXX*—painted the street in red. He slipped his last ten-euro bill to the cashier, anxiously grabbed the ticket, almost tearing it in half, and walked as calmly as he could into the darkened theatre. The film had already started. He tried to focus on the shapes and colors moving across the screen but all he could see were the wrinkles in the upper left corner of the screen. The shrill sound of a police siren reached his ears. Was it coming from the street or from the speakers behind him? He slouched down in his chair and turned up his collar.

When the lights came back on Bruno waited for everyone to leave before he ventured outside. The streets were empty. No police cars. The worst thing he could do right now was go back to Hôtel Dauphine: that was now a crime scene. Bruno remembered X's smug, mocking smile last night at the chateau, the not so hidden sarcasm with which he asked all those questions about Bruno's ancestors, about Gaspard Leblon and his parents. Well, X was dead now, wasn't he!

He started walking without direction. Before too long he realized he was walking towards Hôtel Dauphine. He was already in front of the main entrance. But where were the police cars? The coroner? The hotel security staff? He approached the entrance tentatively but didn't dare go inside. Several hotel guests were sitting in the lobby leather armchairs, reading newspapers. One of them brought down his newspaper, killed his cigarette in the ashtray, sat back comfortably, and raised his newspaper again. The top of his bald head remained visible above the page.

Bruno gasped. He had just seen X lying face down in the gutter. Dead. What was he doing here casually smoking a cigarette? No, this could not be! This was sheer madness. Bruno might be a murderer but he is certainly not mad! And if the only proof of his sanity is that he is a murderer . . . so be it! The man in the hotel lobby smoking a cigarette and reading a newspaper was clearly an impostor! Bruno observed the man's every gesture, the flick of the hand, the tilt of the head, the tapping of his foot on the floor, the length of the arms stretching the newspaper in front of the hidden face. The longer he studied them the more convinced he was that the man before him was not an amateur but a professional, that is, a professional actor. He imitated X's mannerisms so perfectly that they appeared more real than the real thing (which, ironically, belied their fakeness). Reality never insists upon itself so desperately. Only those imitating it do.

Surely when the police searched Bruno's apartment they would find sufficient evidence to prove Bruno's unquestionable guilt and, therefore, his sanity. Yes, if they only searched his apartment tomorrow any suspicion that he might be innocent, and thus mad, would be cleared up.

There was only one problem. Where was the gun with which he had shot X, that is, the *real* X? Think! Think fast! Had he thrown it away and already forgotten about it? It's possible. He was in shock after all. No need to panic! He could always buy one from the drug dealers that hang out in the underpass near Rue Charlotte. Buy? With what? He had squandered his last money at the roulette table.

He stopped. Dozens of tables covered with antiques and all kinds of bric-a-brac were lined up along the embankment for the weekly flea market. At one end of the market two hobos were trying out different poses of supplication and despondency. Suddenly Bruno recalled his surprisingly lucrative, unplanned 'begging performance' from several weeks ago. Why not repeat it and earn some much-needed cash? The two hobos watched in disbelief as Bruno sat quietly on a bench, indifferent to anything around him. As people left the market they passed by him and threw coins on the ground in front of him. Bruno didn't move. Only when they had gone would he stand up and collect the money, always leaving a few coins on the ground to attract new customers. He knew very well people were suspicious of unhappy types, including hobos. People didn't want to feel responsible. They resented it. But if he refused to give them any reason to suspect that he might be unhappy on account of his poverty, they would feel free to like him. If he acted gleeful and cheerful they would ask themselves whether he was not actually pretending to be happy and concealing his suffering, which they would interpret as a heroic gesture on his part, a gesture worthy of their pity . . . cash!

Several hours later Bruno counted his earnings: seventy-four dollars and thirty-eight cents. Not bad for a beginner. He strolled through the flea market, past Chinese baby shoes, Soviet style hats, medieval swords and old Moskvitch parts and stopped in front of a table near the exit that boasted an impressive selection of WWII machine guns and revolvers. He picked one up. It was scratched all over, but that made it even more unique and desirable, the old man who was selling it told him.

"Late nineteenth century," he said as he raised the revolver and aimed it at Bruno. "As good as new."

Bruno twirled the revolver between his fingers. The man rummaged through the pile of random gun parts and pulled out a small box of bullets. He showed it to Bruno seductively as if it was an expensive piece of jewelry.

"How much?" Bruno asked.

"A hundred."

Bruno put the revolver down. The man picked it up and shoved it back into Bruno's hands.

"Seventy-five," he said sadly.

He watched Bruno count his change.

"Looks like your last purchase," the man observed.

"Hopefully it's the best one," Bruno said.

The man wrapped the gun and the bullets in an old newspaper. Bruno sat down on a bench and lifted his face toward the cold sun. He caught himself daydreaming about hushed words, the smell of rotting paper, the cracking sound of new library books being opened for the first time, the monotonous sound of dozens of hands typing on laptops out of sync. Instead of penetrating his skin the sun's deceitful light seemed to bounce back, over and over again, leaving his cheeks frozen.

The Public Library Reading Room welcomed him back with the useless yet soothing industriousness of its patrons. He carefully placed the revolver wrapped in the newspaper under the table and pulled a sheet of paper from the remaining pile of handwritten notes.

Tuesday afternoon. Gaspard was sitting, again, in the middle of the hospital auditorium stage, searching the room for a trace of the impostor. Duchenne de Boulogne, a kind-looking man with long sideburns and unruly eyebrows, was in the middle of his lecture. Sitting in the first row, Charcot was taking notes. Outside, newspaper boys ran up and down the street screaming at the top of their lungs, "Le Figaro! The latest news! The Phantom Killer strikes again!"

"I will now produce the expression of glee by stimulating the greater zygomatic muscle with electric current," Duchenne announced. "To complete this expression, the muscles of both sides must be excited, in connection with the orbicular fibers of the lower eyelids, which contract in a horizontal depression beneath the eyes. Note that this is missing in a false or simulated mirthfulness."

Duchenne touched Gaspard's face. He signaled to his assistant to bring over a little wooden box and began attaching electrodes to Gaspard's face. He stepped away and pointed to Gaspard's face—stretched by the electrodes into a disturbing, gleeful grimace—like a magician at a freak fair.

"Similarly," he continued, "we can produce the expression of aggressive malignity by means of electric contractions of the pyramidalis nasi. What is interesting in the case of this patient is that the development of the pyramidal muscle is so full that its isolated contraction under the rheophores gives a dramatic play of cruel instincts, which his will has no power to evoke and which are only latent in his character. I have observed the same phenomenon in a great number of subjects, which leads me to the conclusion that the aggressive muscle of malignity is one

of those which least obey the will, and that it is put in action only by the instinct or mode of passion of which it is the essential agent of expression."

Duchenne finished molding Gaspard's face into a terrifying mask and faced the audience.

"Gentlemen, what is this but a foresight of Nature, forbidding us easily to dissemble or to mimic those expressive lines by which man can distinguish his friends from his enemies!"

One of his assistants handed him a photograph. Duchenne lifted it up so everyone could see it. It was a photograph of Gaspard taken at La Salpêtrière Photo Lab in between his first two trials.

"Gentlemen, this photograph renders the maximum of hatred and wickedness this patient's pyramidals are capable of expressing. This is all the more singular as he possesses extraordinary power over his eyebrow muscles. He can give his eyes varied expressions and move them in contrary directions. But his will does not exert the least action over his pyramidals. He cannot, by any effort, give to his countenance the expression of hardness, of aggression, or wickedness. This patient is of a very gentle character; had he become the prey of evil passions, their gymnastic exercise would have very soon developed his pyramidals, and changed the habitual expression of his countenance."

Duchenne removed the electrodes from Gaspard's face. The demonstration was not over, however. Charcot came up on stage, accompanied by the usual standing ovation from his loyal supporters.

"Allow me to draw your attention to an aspect of my studies that challenges Doctor Duchenne's theory. I should like to demonstrate the extent to which subjects can be compelled by the hypnotist to commit acts foreign to their natural inclinations in the waking state."

Charcot proceeded to put Gaspard into a state of somnambulism by rubbing the top of his head lightly with the palm of his hand and talking to him in a soothing voice. A few minutes passed. Gaspard opened his eyes. He looked around anxiously, like a wild animal that expected to be attacked. He ran across the stage, 'stabbing' the air with his arms, 'shooting' and 'poisoning' imaginary enemies. Then, just as suddenly, he collapsed on the floor. Duchenne pointed to the lifeless body before him.

"Gentlemen, although you can't see it, this room is littered with corpses!"

"*How can you be sure the patient is not dissimulating?*" someone yelled from one of the back rows.

Gaspard searched the audience but could not identify the speaker. Duchenne couldn't either: he faced the auditorium, addressing no one in particular.

"The desire to deceive without purpose," he began slowly, "by a kind of disinterested worship of art for art's sake, is a common enough experience, particularly in hysteria. But let me assure you, very few simulators have the intelligence to combine and display, with the object of deceit, all the symptoms that belong to the natural history of the illness, without taking from or adding in any way to this group of symptoms. They overelaborate. See you next week, gentlemen."

Duchenne's assistants escorted Gaspard and the other patients to the back stage where each of them received his pay. Gaspard counted the money: it was enough to live on for a week at the most. Then what? His only option was to wait for an opportune moment and sneak back into his apartment where he was sure to find money or at least some jewelry he could sell.

The opportunity presented itself on Sunday. He didn't even have to remind the concierge that he was the Duke's accountant. Alas, the apartment search produced no results, except for his mother's necklace. Back at the hotel he was surprised to find Captain Boileau and another policeman waiting for him.

"Theodore Blanc," Boileau said dramatically, "you are under arrest for murder, or should I say 'murders'!"

Gaspard stared at him coldly.

"I was acquitted on all counts. Surely you remember that."

Boileau grinned maliciously.

"A witness, who shall remain anonymous, has come forward and advised us to search these premises. Our witness believes we shall find something relevant to the most widely discussed murder case—or, rather, cases—of the year. I imagine you've heard of the Phantom Killer? I am a man of reason, Monsieur Blanc. I don't believe in phantoms."

Boileau handcuffed Gaspard and searched the room. When he came back he dangled Blanc's notebook in front of Gaspard.

"Perhaps you can tell us why your journal contains a list of the exact dates, times and locations not only for the first two murders for which you

*were tried—and mistakenly acquitted—but also for several other murders
still under investigation?"*

*"I am warning you: these insinuations directed at someone of my
rank might cost you dearly."*

"Someone of your rank?!" Boileau burst into laughter.

*"You might want to reconsider whether this is the proper way to
address a Duke," Gaspard said coldly.*

"A Duke?!"

"Duke Gaspard Leblon."

Boileau found this even more amusing.

*"I suppose there is no point hiding this from you any more. It was
indeed Monsieur Gaspard Leblon who led us to you."*

*"I am Gaspard Leblon. If someone else has been trying to pose as
me, that man is obviously an impostor."*

*One of the other policemen raised his hand: he was holding a hospi-
tal white robe with the initials "TB."*

*"An interesting story, Monsieur Theodore Blanc," Boileau smiled at
the sight of the patient's robe. "Nothing the mind of a madman could not
produce."*

When the library closed Bruno went straight to his apartment, where he waited for three hours until all his neighbors,
including the nosy Girard, went to bed. His apartment was cold:
he had left all the windows open the last time he was there. The
last time? When was that? No matter. No time to lose on this
now. He unwrapped the revolver, hesitated for a moment and
then put four more bullets inside. Where to hide it? The pillow?
Under the pillow? Inside the pillow? Yes, inside. Before putting
the revolver in he rubbed it between his hands as if it were a
magic lamp.

What if he stayed here and took a nap? Without taking off
his coat he lay down and closed his eyes. The sheets were cold and
smelled funny. It was the familiar smell of an old, decrepit man
rotting away the last hours of his life. This is how his father's bed
smelled hours after they had removed his corpse and packed it
away in a coffin lined with a warm blanket, as if they were concerned the corpse might catch a cold. He closed his eyes and saw,
once again, the imprint of X's body on the hotel bed sheets, the

imprint of the yet unidentified body on the burgundy settee in
Chateau de Lourps, and then another imprint, this one deeper, as
if the person had spent years pressed between the sheets like a fly
pressed between the pages of a book no one has ever read. The
longer that imprint stayed in front of his closed eyes the less it
resembled an imprint. Now it was a real man, arms, legs, head and
all, a man lying on his back, his unblinking eyes wide open.
Horrified, he shut his eyes and . . . woke up.

Only ten minutes had passed. The idea of spending the rest
of the night in his own bed, sinking further and further into the
imprint of his own body, did not appeal to him. Walking around
for hours under dim streetlights and starless skies did. He walked
to the train station and back four times, each time taking a different route. He had read somewhere that varying one's commute
route was emotionally and intellectually stimulating. Even if that
was true for commuters it was definitely not true for men wan-
dering aimlessly, waiting for time to pass. Around six o'clock the
first mournful commuters crawled out of their residencies, shoulders sinking under the identical burden of identical backpacks,
headed blindly towards their respective subway stations. For a
while he distracted himself by following a few of them, pretending to be curious about their daily routine. He tried to remember what his own routine had been a few months ago when he
was still going to the university every day, suited up like everyone
else, but this familiar image now struck him as absurd.

His mind was suddenly flooded with images of him walking
in different directions, in different seasons, wearing different suits,
from his apartment to the university, up and down the stairs, multiple images of him walking, sitting, thinking, pencil in hand,
writing, phoning, drinking, laughing, an endless parade of Brunos,
of moments in which Bruno had existed, breathed, thought, perhaps even felt something. All these past moments were superimposed over one another, existing—insisting—simultaneously in a
fractured 'now' that was neither here nor there. He didn't recognize himself in any of these images. They were all impostors pretending to be him, including the last one, the one standing now
in front of Hôtel Dauphine, checking his watch. Everything about

him was fake: he was standing on his left foot, drawing circles on the ground with his right one, something Bruno used to do when he was a child. The way he raised his right hand all the way to his eyes to check his watch, even though he was not nearsighted— this, too, the impostor had studied carefully and was now reproducing faithfully. Bruno ordered himself to stop moving, stop giving his impostor opportunities to imitate Bruno's involuntary gestures that he had memorized so well. If Bruno didn't move, the other one would not have anything to imitate. So he stood still. But keeping still was also a habit. He was acutely aware of standing still in a very particular, Brunoesque way that the other reproduced immediately.

The hotel lobby smelled of freshly brewed coffee and warm croissants. He chose one of the armchairs farthest from the reception desk. The receptionist, who must have recognized him, walked over to him and asked in a distastefully courteous voice if he was waiting for someone.

"I am," he said.

He did not bother looking up but he bothered enough to let her know that. She smiled resentfully and walked away swaying her hips in revenge. She did have nice hips.

Now it was just a matter of waiting. Sooner or later, they would come find him. He tried to imagine the police going into his apartment. Would they search the bed first? If they did, how long would it take them to find him? The more he thought about it, the more anxious he grew. Would they find the revolver inside the pillow? What if it didn't occur to them to look inside? How could he have been so naïve as to leave everything in their hands!

He picked up the newspaper lying on the side table and flipped through it. A short article on the last page caught his attention. "Homeless man murdered in cold blood." It was a brief police report from the previous night. Homeless man. Shot in the back. Back alley. The time and place of the murder were familiar, too familiar. The man was murdered in the same street and at exactly the same time Bruno had murdered X.

Copycat?

The hotel doors slid open. Bruno looked up. A uniformed policeman walked in. Any moment now! The policeman exchanged a few words with the receptionist, turned around, and walked out. Bruno followed him outside. The policeman was chatting with one of the taxi drivers. Bruno walked up to him casually and stood several feet away, occasionally glancing at him. Finally the policeman noticed him.

"Can I help you?"

"Have you caught him yet? The murderer?" Bruno asked.

At that moment X, or rather the man who was pretending to be X, for Bruno very well knew X was dead, came out of the hotel.

"Did you witness a murder, Monsieur?" the policeman asked but Bruno was already crossing the street, following X.

X walked fast. Bruno turned up his collar and trudged after him through the muddy snow. X turned the corner. Bruno ran after him, past another man walking in the middle of the street. Bruno pushed the man aside. When he reached the corner he saw X: he was not very far ahead. Bruno stopped. The man he had pushed aside now caught up with him. Bruno didn't dare look at him. He had already caught a glimpse of his face as he ran past him. The man walked past him and turned the corner. It was X. Bruno laughed out loud as if he was hoping the ludicrousness of the incident would automatically discredit its veracity. Then he laughed again, this time in the direction of another man who was just then crossing the street from the opposite side, and who, Bruno hoped, would confirm the absurdity of the situation. Alas, this other man was not a stranger either. He was X. Bruno spread his arms and fell back into the body of yet another stranger. He turned around. It was X. He closed his eyes and tried to focus only on the sounds around him. After a few seconds he heard a familiar noise. It was growing louder and louder. Finally, he was able to identify it: it was laptop keyboard muzak. The muzak grew louder. Now it was real music, not the sound of multiple keyboards being worked overtime. The hotel doors opened and two men in business suits walked in. He was still in the hotel lobby.

Gaspard could not tell how much time he spent in the psychiatric ward of La Salpêtrière. The other inmates complained that time dragged on but his experience was the opposite. Since he was obsessively thinking about the impostor living in his apartment he didn't have any time left on his hands. Sometimes he felt the days were too short.

One day two nurses came in, shaved his face, cleaned him up and escorted him to Charcot's office. Charcot pointed to a suitcase on the floor.

"All your belongings are inside."

There was another man in the office, sitting with his back to the door, dressed in Gaspard's extravagant lavender tailcoat, the one Gaspard used to wear to the opera. When Gaspard entered the man turned around. It was not the fact that the man was wearing Gaspard's clothes that shocked him: Gaspard had almost gotten used to seeing his own clothes on the impostor. No, what shocked him was the face, flat and expressionless, as if it hadn't been fully formed yet. He had seen that face a long time ago. He had even bet on it.

Charcot turned to Gaspard.

"Monsieur Blanc, please meet . . ." Charcot looked at the impostor.

"I apologize. I didn't introduce myself. Monsieur Gaspard Leblon," the stranger said.

Charcot stared at him.

"Monsieur Gaspard Leblon?" he asked again, as though he wasn't sure he had heard the name right. The stranger nodded.

Charcot approached Gaspard. Gaspard stepped back.

"Don't touch me! Who are you?"

Charcot glanced at the stranger.

"We've been through this twice this morning. You know who I am. I am Doctor Charcot."

"Liar!" Gaspard screamed. "What have you done with Doctor Charcot?"

Charcot took the stranger by the arm and walked with him to the other side of the room.

"He is quite the performer, isn't he?" Charcot whispered.

"What do you mean?" the stranger asked.

Charcot lowered his voice even more.

"Some of the criminals I work with become—how should I put it— 'over-invested' in the role of the patient they happen to be playing."

"What kind of patient did he play last?"

"It's a new type of paranoia," Charcot explained. "We know very little about it. As in all other cases of paranoia the patient believes someone is after him. What's original, I mean different, in his case is that he is convinced his pursuer assumes different identities. He believes everyone else except him is an impostor."

"How do you treat him?"

Charcot sighed.

"How do you run away from a phantom unless you become a phantom yourself?" he said mysteriously.

Charcot called in one of the nurses and asked her to escort Gaspard out of the room and wait with him outside. The nurse left Gaspard alone and walked briskly toward a group of rowdy inmates at the opposite end of the hallway. Gaspard listened through the door.

"I assume once you heard about him you were curious to meet him," Charcot was saying.

"Wouldn't you be curious about someone who's been trying to impersonate you?"

"Fair enough," Charcot said. "Bear in mind that he is not simply trying to pass himself off as you. He actually believes he is you. Which, according to his logic, makes you an impostor."

"Does he have any family?" the stranger asked.

"None that we're aware of. His parents are both dead," Charcot replied. "It seems that he used to be a bookkeeper, before becoming a criminal, that is. You know how it is with men like him. Once they get a taste of the good life . . ."

"They would go to any lengths, steal, even kill," the stranger said. "Monsieur Charcot, curiosity is not the only reason that brought me here. I've been following your work and I must say I find it truly fascinating. In fact, you've inspired me to design an experiment of my own."

"What kind of experiment?" Charcot asked, visibly flattered.

"I've been wondering about something for a while now. What would happen, I wonder, if a delusional man, like Monsieur Theodore Blanc, for instance, were forced to live with the subject of his delusion, in this case me? I suspect that as a criminal who really believes himself to be a Duke his delusional belief system must be quite elaborate. I am curious how long *it would continue to function before it implodes. How long would he be able to hold on to the delusional belief that he is me if he is faced with the truth every single day?"*

Charcot was listening attentively.

"Fascinating, truly fascinating!" he exclaimed.

"To conduct my experiment I would need to have Monsieur Blanc at my disposal. I've come here to ask that he be released."

Charcot assumed a pedantic, self-important attitude.

"Monsieur, although I am flattered that you hold my work in such high esteem, I am sorry to say that existing protocols do not allow me to release Monsieur Blanc, or indeed any other patient to anyone who just happens to come in. . . ."

"Monsieur Charcot, surely I don't need to remind you that you are the head of this ward. You make the protocols!"

Charcot tried to say something but the stranger interrupted him.

"I suppose your hospital wouldn't be interested in a fairly substantial donation . . . for research purposes?"

Charcot pretended to be shocked by the proposition.

"Monsieur Leblon, if I didn't know better, I would think you were trying to buy my patient!"

The stranger did not try to deny that.

"You realize you are putting me in an awkward position," Charcot said nervously, fiddling with the papers on his desk. "How much do you suppose such a, eh, donation would—"

"Ten thousand francs. Cash."

Charcot took out a handkerchief and wiped the sweat off his face. He nodded. The stranger stood up and extended his hand.

"It's a pleasure doing business with you."

Charcot opened the door and signaled to Gaspard to come back in.

"Monsieur Blanc, you'll be happy to know that you are leaving us. Monsieur Gaspard Leblon has been generous enough to offer to be your . . ."

He searched for the right word.

"Benefactor," the stranger said with a smile.

The following day Morel received a letter: "I arrive tomorrow evening. I shall be accompanied by my friend Monsieur Theodore Blanc. Signed: Duke Gaspard Leblon."

In the morning Gaspard climbed into the carriage waiting for him in front of the hospital gates. The stranger was already inside, dressed in Gaspard's blue velvet waistcoat and a cream shirt. They rode in silence for a while.

"Are you familiar with the countryside?" the stranger asked.

Gaspard didn't respond.

"I like to leave this infested city regularly," the stranger went on. "Anywhere you go in the city you simply can't escape this new breed of man with his dull, provincial mind, his mind-numbing work ethic, his bookkeeper sensibility, counting his francs, stuffing himself with bread, cabbage and herrings."

After a long journey the carriage stopped in front of Chateau de Lourps. Gaspard stared incomprehensibly at the familiar staircase leading up to the main entrance. The stranger climbed down from the carriage and stood behind him.

"Beautiful, isn't it? I spent my entire childhood here. Would you believe there was a time when I briefly considered selling it?"

Gaspard stumbled back, falling against the carriage door. The horse lazily looked back at him and continued chewing hay. Gaspard felt the blood drain from his fingertips. When he came to, he was on the ground, his back propped up against the carriage door, which was covered with vomit. The stranger was standing over him, looking concerned.

"Are you feeling better? Must be the fresh air. You are not used to it after spending all your days amidst nauseating hospital smells."

Gaspard unbuttoned his shirt. The stranger smoothed down his hair.

"Morel, when you are finished unloading the bags, escort Monsieur Blanc to his room. I am afraid he is too weak to walk on his own."

The stranger walked into the house. Gaspard watched Morel unload the bags. When would he finally recognize him?

"How was the trip, Monsieur Blanc?" Morel asked dutifully.

"Long," Gaspard said. "As usual," he added.

"Monsieur has travelled in these parts before?"

Gaspard studied his face carefully. No, Morel was not pretending.

"How do you like working here? I imagine the Duke is a difficult man to please."

Morel was embarrassed by the direct question.

"Some might find his tastes eccentric but he is a fair man. If you'll excuse me, I have to start preparing dinner."

Gaspard got up and walked unsteadily toward the house. To his surprise the marble staircase, which he had seen for the last time a long time ago, was not overgrown with weeds or stained by the passage of time. It looked freshly painted and clean. He placed his hand on the cold marble and closed his eyes, expecting to be overwhelmed by memories. Nothing. Finally the darkness behind his eyelids began to dissolve into silhouettes with vague, trembling contours that threatened to dissolve back into darkness. He let go of the staircase and pressed his eyes with his fists in a vain attempt to keep the memory images from vanishing. The pressure he was applying on his eyes threw the vanishing images into relief one last time and only now he realized that these were not memory images at all but merely formless, abstract shapes produced by the pressure he was applying to his eyes.

The house was quiet. He thought everything looked exactly as he had left it years ago but this observation struck him as meaningless since none of the objects around him stirred up any memories. They all looked familiar but it was a kind of empty familiarity that had nothing to do with him. He ran his fingers over the mantelpiece, the bookshelves and the writing desk, expecting to see layers of dust accumulate on his fingertips. There was no dust. The furniture was smooth, as if it had been recently polished. He sat down on the burgundy settee and looked around the room. His look was caught between the folds of the tightly drawn curtains that left only a narrow opening through which he could see the repulsively whitish sky outside. He stood up and walked over to the window. His feet got tangled up in the curtains, which fell heavily to the floor into a stagnant pool of plush. As he was falling he looked back at the room. Every part of his body thrust itself forward, desperately trying to hold on to the sensory memory of something in the room—the tea things on the table, the chandelier, the writing desk, the seductive fabric of the burgundy settee—to soften the fall, but every single thought or feeling he thrust out slid, slime-like, down the object he was trying to grab onto, as if all the things in the room were just props made of reflecting glass, as if they were all conspiring against him. The room was smooth and self-contained, seemingly existing out of time. No trace of decay, of a passage of time in which he could re-inscribe himself.

"What happened?"

Gaspard looked up. The stranger stood in the doorway, Morel peeking over his shoulder.

"I fell," Gaspard said.

"Come upstairs. I want to show you something."

Gaspard followed him up the grand staircase. The door to one of the bedrooms was slightly open. Through the opening Gaspard could see a big mirror in a golden frame and in front of it little bottles of perfume and a woman's fan. He reached for the door. The stranger stopped him.

"I would appreciate it if you don't go in. It's my mother's bedroom."

As the stranger closed the door Gaspard felt a slight movement in the air and for a second the faint smell of a woman's perfume tickled his nostrils, before dissolving in the general anodyne smell of the house. The stranger led him into the study and pointed to a long shelf crowded with bottles of all sizes and shapes.

"Since you seem to appreciate perfumes . . ." the stranger said and he uncorked three of the bottles, poured the liquid in special measuring cups, and then mixed the precise proportions in a small glass. He invited Gaspard to smell it.

"To decipher the language of flowers, one must first master its grammar," the stranger said. "Can you guess what it is?"

"Sweet pea with a touch of jasmine," Gaspard said.

The stranger was surprised.

"Monsieur Blanc, I must say you have a wonderful nose for a bookkeeper. This reminds me: I still haven't told you why I've brought you here. Please come with me to the kitchen. Morel must be finished unloading our bags by now."

Morel was already preparing dinner. The stranger frowned when he saw the big cauldron of boiling water.

"What is this?" he demanded.

Morel hesitated.

"Soup," he said defensively. "I thought Monsieur might be hungry after the long trip. Fois gras would take too long."

The stranger shook his head violently.

"What does hunger have to do with it? Right now I am thinking of the fatty warmth spilling over my tongue. Do you want to take away the pleasure I am experiencing right now by filling my stomach with a bowl of soup!"

Morel seemed even more confused. The stranger continued his explanation in a deliberately neutral tone of voice, which further emphasized his mounting irritation.

"I must be exposed to nothing but the most exquisite food, the most subtle aromas and flavors until I reach a point where my mind begins to admit only highly-refined sensations and sensual torments. Tomorrow you shall receive detailed instructions about the kinds of meals I expect you to prepare. Under no circumstances will you prepare the same meal more than once. And you will certainly not serve wine made after 1880. Is that clear?"

"Yes, Monsieur," Morel said.

The stranger turned to Gaspard.

"Now, as I was saying earlier, I brought you here because I have something in mind for you. Morel has been working for me for a long time but as his responsibilities around the house keep growing he is finding it increasingly difficult to manage my accounts. The truth is he has never been especially good at managing my finances. I was told you used to be a bookkeeper for one of the bigger firms in Paris. Laurent & Moreau was it?"

Gaspard opened his mouth to say something but the stranger ignored him.

"I should think several hours per day would suffice. You will sit down with Morel, every day, and teach him everything you know. You will, of course, be paid for your work."

The stranger looked Gaspard up and down.

"Morel, did you lay out Monsieur Blanc's clothes in the study?"

Morel replied that he had. The study was small and dark. Gaspard opened the small window. It faced a brick wall.

"I thought it might remind you of the office where you used to work and make you feel more at home. I find that the absence of windows and the lack of direct sunlight increase productivity considerably. Rest assured: nothing will distract you from your work here."

Two pairs of pants, two frock coats, several shirts, a few cravats, and a hat were laid out on the writing desk, next to an inkwell, a fountain pen and two accounting ledger books. A beautiful white shirt with long, wide *sleeves and a tall collar stood out among the other shirts. Gaspard stepped forward and touched it. The stranger picked it up and showed it to Morel.*

"What is my shirt doing here?"

Morel apologized.

"Bring another one of his," the stranger said. "Try something on," he told Gaspard.

Gaspard changed into one of the outfits. Everything fit perfectly, as if it had all been specially tailored for him. The stranger walked around Gaspard, inspecting every little wrinkle in the fabric. He selected a cravat and tied it around Gaspard's neck.

"Doesn't it feel great to be yourself again?" the stranger exclaimed.

Gaspard looked him straight in the eyes.

"You wouldn't know," he said.

The stranger smiled pleasantly.

"Monsieur Blanc, why didn't anyone warn me about cryptic utterances?"

"I think you understand the meaning of my cryptic utterances very well," Gaspard said.

"I am glad we understand each other so well," the stranger smiled again.

Gaspard looked down. A few centimeters from his right shoe there was a little black stain on the beige carpet. He stared at it intensely, as though expecting it to answer a question he hadn't even formulated in his head yet.

"I remember this stain," he said.

The stranger laughed. His eyes did not.

"Monsieur Blanc, be reasonable. How can you remember something you've never seen before?"

"I have seen it before," Gaspard insisted as his eyes tried to penetrate the thick fabric. He shut his eyes. A whole procession of stains, of different size, shape and color stretched out in his mind as he feverishly tried to find a match for the one on the carpet. The stains in his mind bled into each other until they formed one enormous, irregularly shaped black stain that screened out all other images.

When he opened his eyes again Morel was on his knees, trying to rub out the stain with hot water and soap. Gaspard motioned to stop him but the stranger signaled to him to step away.

"Something happened here. I know it," Gaspard said vengefully.

"Yes, something happened. Morel was clumsy and spilled some ink on the carpet."

"My father . . ." Gaspard began.

"This was my father's study," the stranger said. "I'd rather not talk about him. Morel, show Monsieur Blanc the rest of the house."

As Gaspard followed Morel up the stairs he looked out the window. The stranger was walking around the house, picking up flowers. Intrigued, Gaspard excused himself and told Morel he would find him later.

He walked to the back of the house. There was a small cemetery, flanked on one side by a vegetable garden. In one corner of the cemetery the stranger was standing in front of a grave. A marble sculpture of an angel holding her head between her hands cast a shadow over the tombstone. The stranger bent down and left something on the grave. Gaspard stepped back and hid behind the wall. He waited for the stranger to leave and only then approached the tombstone. A bunch of wild flowers lay over the name engraved in the stone: Laetitia Leblon. Gaspard swung his arm around and swept the flowers off the tombstone. He was surprised by his action. There was no reason for him to react so violently to . . . what? He stared at the name. Laetitia Leblon. He repeated it several times, first silently, then out loud. There was something about the name. What was it? He had to admit to himself that the name had struck him not on account of its familiarity but merely on account of its alliterativeness. Like the rest of the house, the name on the tombstone did not return his look, did not speak to him as an old acquaintance. But how could a place he had never seen before, a place that stirred no memories in him—other than the desperate, obsessive desire to be overwhelmed, against his will, by memories—make him so nauseous when he first saw it?

He looked up. The curtains in one of the windows on the second floor moved: someone stepped away from the window. Was he being watched?

Over the next several weeks Morel prepared elaborate, exquisite meals as per his master's detailed instructions. The stranger always sat at the head of the table, explaining to Gaspard the texture, smell and taste of every dish and instructing him to eat slowly so as to savor every bite.

In early May the stranger informed Gaspard that he was going to Paris for a few days. Gaspard sensed an opportunity—for what he couldn't quite say yet—opening up.

"Will you be fine here on your own?" the stranger asked him.

"I am sure I can find ways to amuse myself," Gaspard said.

The stranger left the following morning around ten. As soon as the carriage disappeared from view Gaspard went into the stranger's bedroom. His blue velvet tailcoat was hung over a chair. Gaspard took off the inconspicuous brown frock coat he was wearing and tried to put on the tailcoat. It was too small for him. He tried to take it off but couldn't. He rang the bell. Morel appeared at the door.

"This tailcoat is too small. It won't come off," Gaspard told him, exasperated. "I don't understand why it suddenly feels so tight."

"But Monsieur Blanc, this is Monsieur Leblon's tailcoat," Morel said.

There was a loud knock on the door downstairs. Gaspard slipped past Morel and ran down the stairs. Standing at the main entrance was a woman in her late sixties. When she saw Gaspard she lifted her hand to her mouth and her eyes filled with tears.

"My dear Gaspard, is it really you?" she exclaimed.

She opened her arms and embraced him.

"Let me look at you. The last time I saw you, you must have been no more than sixteen."

He squinted at her.

"Of course, of course, Madame . . ."

"Renault," she helped him.

Morel served the tea in the sitting room. The phonograph was playing Handel. Madame Renault kept rhythm with her little foot.

"Even as a child you loved music. Your mother always said you had the soul of an artist," she said, unfolding her wrinkled face into a smile. Even her voice sounded wrinkled.

Gaspard sat back and crossed his legs, enjoying her obsequiousness. Suddenly he heard a familiar noise and glanced out the window: a carriage pulled up in front of the main entrance. Moments later the door opened and the stranger walked in. When he saw Madame Renault he smiled.

"I decided to postpone my trip to Paris. I see it was all worth it. What a pleasant surprise!"

"Good afternoon, Monsieur. Gaspard and I were just reminiscing about the old times." Madame Renault informed him.

"The old times?" The stranger looked at Gaspard mockingly.

"He was a quiet boy," Madame Renault blabbered on. "I saw him a few times when he was home from the seminary. He always had a book with him. Sometimes he would disappear for hours, daydreaming."

The stranger sat down and crossed his legs.

"Well, isn't this fascinating? Forgive me, Madame, but Monsieur Leblon never speaks to me so openly about his past. Would you believe it: he's never told me anything about his parents."

He turned to Gaspard.

"What does your father do?"

Gaspard smiled nervously. What does his father do? Who is his father? Does he have a father? He tried to recall his father's face but his mind drew a blank.

"We've grown apart over the last several years," he said quickly.

Madame Renault looked puzzled.

"My dear boy, I thought your father passed away years ago, soon after your mother."

The stranger raised his hands. For a second he remained still. Madame Renault and Gaspard stared at him, wondering what he would do next. He clapped his hands. Again. And again. He applauded for quite a while. Madame Renault looked completely lost. The stranger smiled at her warmly.

"Madame, I am afraid we've been slightly dishonest with you. My dear friend, Monsieur Blanc and I have gotten into the habit of playing a little game with our guests: he pretends to be me, and I pretend to be him. I've told him so many times we can't fool anyone, but he insists."

Shocked, Madame Renault looked at Gaspard.

"You are not Gaspard?!"

The stranger pointed his finger at Gaspard.

"Madame, allow me to introduce to you Monsieur Theodore Blanc."

Madame Renault studied Gaspard's face carefully.

"Incredible!" she finally said. "He looks exactly like his . . . I mean your mother."

At dinner Gaspard watched the stranger carefully: nothing in his gestures, actions, and mannerisms betrayed him. Madame Renault chewed her food slowly, listening with admiration to the stranger's reflections on art, literature and Handel.

"There's nothing better than listening to Handel on a Sunday," the stranger was saying. "I mean, how many times can you reread Balzac? All that robust artistry! I find it simply insufferable."

Gaspard put down his fork. The fois gras was tasteless, the wine stale. He felt his face tightening up, his facial muscles contracting one last time before turning into stone. He ordered himself to focus on the stranger's monologue and slowly raised his hand to his face. The texture of his skin reminded him of a death mask he had once seen in the Ethnological Museum. He tried to move his head to the left to face Madame Renault but he was afraid his face would break down and fall to the floor. One has to be careful with museum artifacts, especially human ones. They break so easily, even the wax ones.

He excused himself from the table. He was not feeling well, he said. He would take a bath. He filled the bath to the brim, got undressed and sat in the water. There was a knock on the door. Morel came into the bathroom, towel in hand. Gaspard's face was white, his lips and fingernails blue. His eyes were burning feverishly. Morel checked the water in the bathtub.

"Monsieur Blanc! The water is freezing!"

"Is it?" Gaspard said.

He touched his right hand with his left one, touched different parts of his body but as hard as he pressed, squeezed, and twisted his skin he felt nothing.

Later that summer the grass down in the valley turned completely yellow. A fiery dust rose from the charred roads.

Gaspard stood, naked, in the middle of his bedroom. He closed the window. Arms falling inertly by his side, shirt sticking to his back, teeth chattering, he looked around as though expecting help. He rushed to the dresser, opening and closing different drawers, until finally he found what he was looking for: a fur coat. He wrapped it around his naked body.

"It's freezing here! Freezing!" he mumbled to himself.

When the stranger and Doctor Gervais opened the door to the bathroom the next morning Gaspard was asleep in the bathtub, covered with furs. Gervais frowned.

"Why is he covered with furs in this heat?"

"How would you characterize the mental state of a man sleeping in the bathtub, wrapped up in furs, on a hot July day?" the stranger asked.

"A few days ago," he went on, "when my servant told him the beams in the shed should be replaced before someone gets hurt, he laughed at him and told him he'd never take advice from someone who is 'not entirely real.' The man is deranged! He believes whatever he wants to believe!"

The stranger left the room. When he came back he was holding a white patient robe with the initials "TB."

"Perhaps it's time for Monsieur Blanc to return to the hospital. He doesn't seem fit to live outside it."

In accordance with the law Gaspard's case had to be put to trial before he was sent back to the psychiatric ward. The judge stared at him in disbelief.

"I believe we all know the defendant."

The prosecutor stood up and looked triumphantly around him.

"Your Honor, new facts have come to light. It is my intention to prove that the defendant is, in fact, guilty of all the crimes he confessed to. I call to the stand Doctor Charcot."

"It is a scientific fact," Charcot began, "that there is a strong correlation between sensitivity to pain and insanity. The discriminative faculty of idiots is curiously low: they hardly distinguish between heat and cold, and their sense of pain is so obtuse that some of the more idiotic seem hardly to know what it is. In their dull lives, such pain as can be excited in them may literally be accepted with a welcome surprise. Please bear with me while I carry out a simple test."

Charcot motioned to one of his assistants to escort Gaspard to the middle of the courtroom. The assistant placed two containers filled with water on Gaspard's either side.

"The water in the left container is boiling hot and that in the other is freezing cold," Charcot explained before submerging Gaspard's hand in one of them.

Gaspard didn't react. Charcot submerged Gaspard's other hand in the other container. He then took out a needle and pricked Gaspard's arm. Again, no reaction.

"When the defendant was first brought to the hospital," Charcot turned to the judge, "I noticed a large scar above his elbow. Monsieur Leblon's servant, Morel, recalled an incident when the defendant accidentally cut himself. Apparently, liking the keenness of the new sensation, he took the next opportunity of repeating the experience but he overdid it.

Monsieur Leblon's testimony was invaluable to my investigation as he was able to recall multiple occasions when the defendant inflicted pain on himself in a vain attempt to restore his sensitivity and, by extension, his sanity."

Charcot rolled up Gaspard's sleeves, exposing multiple scars underneath. The women in the audience looked away.

"By contrast," Charcot continued, "Monsieur Gaspard Leblon exhibits an exceptional sensitivity to very slight variations in taste, sound, light. I shall refrain from conducting a parallel test for fear of subjecting the Duke to unnecessary pain."

Following the trial Gaspard was sent to the psychiatric ward at La Salpêtrière and placed in a cell with another patient, Gorin. During the first several days of their co-habitation Gorin would approach Gaspard, then remember something and cover his mouth with his hand. He would sniff his clothes, raise his arms and smell his armpits, his face twisting in disgust.

"God, it's awful!"

Gaspard didn't say anything for fear of encouraging Gorin to continue the conversation. On the fourth day he made the mistake of engaging in the conversation. As usual Gorin was going on and on about how he smelled like compost and how his hair smelled like rotten eggs.

"Look, I am infested with insects!" Gorin said and to illustrate his point he shoved his greasy hair under Gaspard's nose.

"I don't see anything," Gaspard said.

Gorin withdrew, scratching his head and looking at Gaspard suspiciously.

"Except for the cockroaches," Gaspard added, pleasantly surprised to have his delusion confirmed.

"It's nice to have company. The last time I had someone to talk to was over a year ago. He wasn't the talkative type. What the hell was his name? Blanc! That's it! Kept telling everyone he was a Duke. Duke Leblon. Yes, that was it."

Gaspard looked up.

"What was he in for?" he asked.

"Stealing, murder, you name it."

"What happened to him?"

"*Ran away. I heard he was passing himself off as insane—which, of course, he was—and getting paid for it, right here, at the hospital. He accused everyone else of being an impostor but if there was one thing that kid was good at, it was being someone else. A real actor, that one!*"

Gaspard swallowed.

"*What happened to the real Duke?*"

"*Who knows! There never was such a man. The kid invented him. Enough about him! What are you here for?*"

"*Murder,*" Gaspard said. "*Murders,*" he corrected himself.

"*In that case, I'll have the pleasure of your company for a while,*" Gorin grinned.

Charcot visited the ward every week. In late August he came accompanied by a man in a lavender waistcoat. Gaspard recognized his impostor right away.

"*Have you made any progress with him?*" the stranger asked, studying Gaspard as if he were a curious specimen.

"*His condition is most peculiar. I call it le délire de négation. It starts with sadness, depression, self-absorption, self-loathing, et cetera. In rare cases, like this one, it can escalate to the ultimate negation.*"

"*The ultimate negation?*"

"*The patient denies his own existence,*" Charcot explained.

The stranger asked Charcot if he could give the patient a small gift. Charcot was puzzled by this strange request but consented. The stranger squeezed his arm through the cell door and placed an accounting ledger book on the floor.

"*I imagine he has a lot of time on his hands. He might enjoy writing down some of his thoughts,*" he said.

The two men walked away. Gaspard dragged himself to the door and opened the ledger. A loose sheet of paper was slipped between the pages. The following sentence was handwritten in the middle of the page: "*He is the perfect embodiment of everything I find despicable and pathetic in men of his social class. He will go to any lengths—steal, even kill—to roll on that sofa again . . .*"

Outside the air was warm, the sky unnaturally blue. The stranger stopped in the middle of the street to light a cigarette. A newspaper boy carrying a bundle of posters came running towards him, yelling at the top of his lungs:

"You want to be in the movies? You want to be in the movies?"

In Studies in Hystera (1895) Josef Breuer and Sigmund Freud demonstrated that mental pathology is rooted in normal psychological processes such as daydreaming, for example, which after a certain point deteriorates into "a hallucinatory absence." [XVII] Breuer and Freud saw pathology as a lack of self-presence manifesting as an increasing compartmentalization of consciousness, part of which continues to exist automatically in the real world (usually performing some kind of mechanical action) while another part becomes dissociated. The dissociation of personality starts out as a dissociation from reality, since reality fails to make a strong enough claim on the individual, leaving him free to disengage that surplus energy somewhere else (in unconscious acts, reveries and hallucinations).

14

"Monsieur, you have to leave," someone said. "They are beginning to set up."

Bruno looked up. They? The hotel receptionist pointed at several young men with long hair and artistically unkempt clothes who were measuring the length and width of the hotel lobby. He looked around: he was sitting in the lobby of Hôtel Dauphine. A dozen gaffers, key grips, dolly grips, lighting technicians, best boys, costume assistants and camera assistants were milling about; there was another group of people whose function on the set was not immediately clear. As far as Bruno could tell, their sole occupation was to stand at a respectful distance from the dark figure seated in one of the leather armchairs, a man in his sixties who was rubbing his forehead with one hand and drawing mysterious figures in the air with the other. His body was moving back and forth to a grand symphony only he could hear. Just when it seemed that the symphony was going to explode in a glorious display of mental fireworks, the man froze in his seat. First, he puckered up his small face, then his messy eyebrows touched each other, remolding his face into a frown that was meant to express the creative turmoil and self-sacrifice he was known for, and finally a little beatific smile alighted on his thin, colorless lips. It was a performance worthy of a Kabuki actor.

The man who, Bruno now realized, was none other than the film director, stood up. He was a man of small stature whose awkward incongruity with the excesses of his spirit left some people, especially talented female Production Assistants, nothing short of breathless. He wore a pair of pants a little too short for him, as if to underscore the sublimely ridiculous nature of his physique, and a tastefully crumpled shirt that was a size bigger. The rolled up shirt sleeves, with their suggestion of revolutionary toil, provided one last touch to this general image of unstoppable, creative *élan vital*. The director strolled through the set, barely glancing at the lights, cameras, props or people. Upon completing his inspection of the set, he stood in the middle, left arm akimbo, right arm propping up his face as if he had a terrible toothache.

"This is no good."

He took a few steps, seemed to remember something, and stopped.

"Where is he?"

His assistants anxiously searched the foyer for someone, the film's star perhaps, to no avail. The director noticed Bruno standing by.

"Brad."

Bruno turned around: there was no one behind him. The man was addressing him.

"I beg your pardon?" he said.

"Brad," the director repeated. "You're not in the zone."

The man had clearly confused him with one of the actors. Bruno wasn't sure how to correct him.

"I am sorry you feel that way," he said. The man flashed his teeth at him, though the effect he was going for was slightly diminished by his apparent refusal to use teeth whitener. He walked up to Bruno, stuck his long skinny finger under his nose, and waved it ever so slightly.

"No, no, no. You can't be sorry 'that I feel that way' unless you mean to tell me that you are indeed in the zone but I, for some reason, have not noticed it. Is that the meaning you are trying to convey?"

"You are right. I am not in the zone. But I would very much like to be there. I am having some trouble understanding my character."

"Precisely," the director whispered conspiratorially, as if he had just shared with Bruno a terrible truth that shook the very foundations of our understanding of human nature. He stared at Bruno for a long time. Bruno knew he could not get away without responding in some way.

"What I am trying to say," Bruno continued, "is that my character doesn't seem to be the sort of person who would murder someone out of sheer boredom."

The director turned away from Bruno in a deliberate way, though Bruno didn't realize what the deliberation was about until after the man turned around again and, if that were possible, even more dramatically. His facial muscles had rearranged themselves into one of his award winning, awe-inspiring, ponderously meditative philosophical faces, which he usually accompanied with a deep premonitory voice.

"What is pain?" he began simply.

"Well . . ." Bruno ventured.

The director waved his hand dismissively.

"My character is going through a crisis?" Bruno ventured again, a little less hopefully than the first time.

"Not just any kind of crisis," the director said wearily. "An existential crisis!"

He smacked his lips as if he had just eaten a piece of especially good tiramisu.

At this point Bruno was saved by the film's real star, a handsome man with a revoltingly dreamy face. The director didn't seem to notice that Bruno had stepped aside, replaced by another man. The receptionist came up to Bruno and again asked him to leave because they were going to start processing the extras. He asked her what kind of film they were shooting.

"A detective story, I think," she said, rolling her eyes to convey how little she thought of the genre. "A film adaptation of a play. *The Novel in Space*."

"*The Space of the Novel*," he corrected her.

Bruno found a spot behind one of the gigantic flowerpots in the far corner of the lobby from where he could watch the rehearsal undisturbed. The hotel lobby was quickly transformed into a psychoanalyst's office for the scene in which Private Eye Ford Harder interrogates Doctor Sloan, a psychoanalyst.

"There has been a murder," Harder informed Sloan. "I'm looking for the suspect."

"Who?" Sloan asked.

"I don't know. That's why I'm looking for him."

"What has he done?"

"Murder, presumably."

"And you presume it's him?"

"I wouldn't be looking for him if I didn't."

"But you wouldn't suspect him if you weren't looking for him!"

Sloan seemed pleased with his powers of ratiocination.

"You're quite the sophist, aren't you?" Harder noted. "So, what do you know about this man? Who is he?"

"I don't know. Someone insignificant."

"That tells us something."

"What?"

"Something insignificant. Is he comfortable?"

"With himself?"

"Are there others?"

"There always are. But he is not comfortable with them."

"He lives alone then. Is he dangerous?"

"Is that important?"

"If it's specific enough."

"Danger is not specific."

"Are you saying he's not dangerous?"

"Not in these specific words."

"The plot rarefies."

"It's only because the blood hasn't coagulated yet."

"So there's blood then?"

"It comes with the corpse. Are you looking for one of those as well?"

"Don't get cute with me. Have you got one?"

Doctor Sloan furrowed his brows.

"I forget: why are you looking for him?"

"He's a suspect in a murder case."

"That would make him suspicious, wouldn't it?"

"You're quick, aren't you? What do you think his motive might be?"

"The perfect crime."

"A worthy ideal. Arrogant yet cliché."

"Don't underestimate the power of clichés."

"To do so would be arrogant, wouldn't it? What is 'the perfect crime', Doctor?" Harder asked.

"Do you believe in self-fulfilling prophecies, Mister Harder?" Sloan grinned. "You should. You collected all the clues. You analyzed them. You solved your own death in advance. There is nothing left for you to do but die!"

"Cut! Cut! Cut!" the director yelled.

Bruno came out from behind the flowerpot. He noticed a policeman standing by the hotel entrance, talking on his cell phone. Bruno walked up to him.

"I want to turn myself in."

The policeman glanced at him and continued talking on the phone. Bruno didn't move. The policeman put his hand on the phone and looked around.

"Why are the extras middling about here?" he asked no one in particular. "Did they process you already?" he asked Bruno, studying his face and hair.

"No, there hasn't been a trial yet."

The policeman said to the person on the other line "I'll call you back," and looked at Bruno more carefully.

"Who's been doing your hair and make up? Sarah? Jennifer? Kim? God, this is tight."

The policeman unbuttoned his uniform and took it off. Bruno realized now that the policeman was an actor.

He walked up the stairs to the impostor's apartment on the fourth floor of the hotel. The door was open and a tray with cleaning supplies was parked by the entrance. He peeked inside: the room was absolutely clean. The maid smiled at him and walked down the hall to the next dirty room. He didn't know what he was looking for; he only knew he had to expose the man as an impostor and confess to the authorities that no one else but he, Bruno, had murdered the real X. He would point them to the evidence in his own bedroom, inside his pillow, and they would have no choice but to acknowledge that Bruno was a murderer but, more importantly, a sane one. He had physical evidence he had committed the crime, but what about motive? Did he have one? How would he ever manage to convince anyone of his guilt without a believable motive?

He left the hotel and strolled down to the small park at the bottom of the street. He chose a bench in the sun and sat down. Another man was sitting on the bench, looking rather enthused about life. His face was radiant, almost ecstatic, as he nodded approvingly at the Sunday people passing by and waved 'hello' to them. There was something proprietary in his look, as though he owned the park. He leaned back, crossed his legs and began whistling, occasionally casting a glance at Bruno. Bruno was not actively ignoring the man, simply not registering his presence.

The man slapped his knee ardently and got up. He stretched in a demonstrative manner as a way of getting Bruno's attention. Bruno closed his eyes, enjoying the warm sunlight on his face. The man circled around the bench a few times, staring at Bruno with mounting resentment. Finally, he stopped and cleared his throat.

"Beautiful weather, isn't it?" he observed.

Bruno opened his eyes.

"On a day like this, you just want to . . ." the man exclaimed. "Oh, I don't know. . . ."

The man waved his hand, signifying nothing in particular. Bruno stared in the distance. The man was not discouraged, yet.

"Nice little park we've got here. Very nice."

The man nodded a few times as though agreeing with himself. Bruno shook his left hand and listened to his watch.

Tick-tack. Tick-tack.

"It's not going to last," the man announced. "On Thursday it will be in the twenties but starting on Friday temperatures will start falling and there's a slight chance we'll see some rain."

Tick-tack. Tick-tack.

"Nice watch you've got there," the man said.

Bruno put the watch back in his pocket.

"My mother is coming to visit me on Friday. I hope Friday will be sunny, like today. I missed the weather forecast. Did you listen to the weather forecast?"

Bruno glanced briefly at the man.

"No," he said.

The man was pleased he had finally gotten Bruno's attention. He moved closer to the bench.

"So you don't normally listen to the weather forecast?"

Bruno looked down at his hands.

"You don't normally listen to the weather forecast?" the man insisted.

"No."

"You just don't care that much about the weather."

Bruno lifted up one foot. His shoelaces had come undone again.

"It's all the same to you. You just can't be bothered with it."

Bruno yawned.

"I like the weather." The man thrust his chest out. "I like it, and I like talking about it."

Bruno uncrossed his legs.

"Well?" the man said provocatively.

Bruno stood up. The man pushed him back down.

"Come on! Make an effort!" the man said.

Bruno stared at the man's hairy hands pressed against his chest.

"The weather. Today. Yesterday. Tomorrow. Next week. Next year. Pick a time. Like it. Hate it. Describe it. Comment on it. A chance of rain. A slight chance of showers. A five percent chance of precipitation in the morning."

The man walked around the bench. Bruno watched him without the slightest curiosity. The man took a long piece of string out of his pocket. Then he bent down and tied Bruno's right foot to the bench. He moved to the other side of the bench and did the other foot as well.

"Put your hands behind your back," he said gently.

Bruno did. The man tied Bruno's hands behind his back. Bruno tried to move his fingers to check how tight the knot was. It was tight enough, for a while at least.

"Now, let's start from the beginning," the man said pleasantly. "I am going to go back over there and then I am going to walk up to the bench. Are you paying attention?"

The man walked away but suddenly stopped, turned around, and walked back to the bench. He bent over Bruno, bringing his sweaty face right against Bruno's.

"Listen here. I worry about you. I sit here, I look at you, and I just can't stop myself from getting worried about you. I see you sitting here, unsure of what you are looking for, afraid to hope, yet secretly hoping. Well, you don't need to hope any more."

The man smiled magnanimously. He gave Bruno a reassuring pat on the back before walking away. Seconds later he walked back toward the bench and sat down next to Bruno.

"Isn't it a lovely day?" he said.

Bruno did not respond. The man lit a cigarette. He smoked silently, blowing smoke rings and puncturing them with his finger. When he finished his cigarette he casually pressed the butt against Bruno's hand. Bruno was too surprised to scream. The man smiled at him.

"So, what's it going to be?" he asked pleasantly.

Clearly, one had to do something about the man.

So *one* did.

There comes a point in a person's life when he learns, at first with resentment, which later gives way to relief, to refer to himself as 'one'. Bruno Leblon's experience of that crisis is faithfully recorded in the annals of the PICI (the Psychiatric Institute for the Criminally Insane). The following is an excerpt from Bruno's personal account of this universal linguistic-ontological crisis, which is experienced by the average person some time in secondary school.

At the end of one of those long entries recounting some embarrassing adolescent experience or other, I remember pausing for a second before committing to paper the following trite observation: "There comes a point in *one's* life when *one* is simply forced to acknowledge that *I* am absolutely free." I was absolutely free thanks to *'one's* pleasing elusiveness. Whenever I was forced to consider my actions, especially those that others condemned as abominable, 'one' would graciously ride into the sunset and take on the burden of responsibility, spreading it as thinly as possible until it vanished in 'one's comforting impersonality. 'One' was guilty of this or responsible for that, but 'I', homunculus-like, was always in the clear, politely excusing myself from the proverbial dinner table just in time. Oily and slippery like a fish, 'I' would slide off the scales of justice, occasionally shedding one or two of my own, though never enough to tip off the scales in favor of this or that pun, mixed metaphor or what have you. In the span of a few words expressing an observation whose utter triviality I know none of you would contest, a titillating abyss had suddenly opened between 'me', the fifteen-year old pimpled philosophizer, and 'him' of whom I spoke, the 'one' who had reached a point in *his* life when *he* was made fully aware of his absolute freedom. The point, ladies and gentlemen, is precisely that 'he'—not I—had made this discovery. 'He' was standing on the sidelines, as it were, watching the game distractedly since he already knew how it would end, while I was bumbling around, drooling and grinning, doggedly identifying, comparing, contrasting, or analyzing motives, chalking them up to discreetly repressed appetizing little traumas, and extrapolating to future behaviors.

I am not sure how long I have been sitting here, he thought, deliberating with myself, he continued thinking and reminding himself that 'he' was doing it. He sat there a lot nicer than me, holding his chin up. God, I thought. And he did too. Why can't you just. Just be, he continued. I nodded. And withdrew, as politely as I couldn't. I had to go stretch my legs. I closed the door behind me. He continued sitting there, drowning pronouns in his whiskey glass, and forcing himself to delete every reference to me. He sat there. First he did it because it was so easy to write it down. But after a while he felt a sort of restlessness, perhaps even resentment that he should be sitting there just because, let's face it, that was a sentence whose coordinates on the keyboard were so familiar. Abruptly raising his right hand, he pushed his left hand away from the familiar configuration of letters. But even as he was doing it, he sat there. He sat there. There he sat, getting more and more comfortable and resenting it. He was hot, his mouth was hot, his tongue was tingly and wet. I briefly considered getting up from where he was sitting there, and smashing everything he owned. But the thought of gloating over my ferociousness made him tired. He looked back at me with a blank face. And since there was only one chair, there was nothing left for me to do but sit in *his* chair.

He did not object. *He* must have known they would come looking for *me*.

POSTSCRIPT

"A special form of misery had begun to oppress him of late. There was nothing poignant, nothing acute about it; but there was a feeling of permanence, of eternity about it; it brought a foretaste of hopeless years of this cold, leaden misery, a foretaste of an eternity in a square yard of space."

Jacques leaned back in his chair and put another cigarette in his mouth without lighting it. Raskolnikov shuffled a few steps forward and raised his right hand dramatically.

"We always imagine eternity as something beyond our conception, something vast!" he said. "But why must it be vast? What if it's one little room, like a bathhouse in the country, black and grimy, with spiders in every corner? What if that's all eternity is?"

Jacques yawned for what seemed to him an eternity despite the lack of spiders to confirm it. The cigarette dropped from his mouth into his lap. He fiddled with it for a while, unsure if lighting it would make any of this any better. Raskolnikov was silent. Jacques ran his finger down the page.

"Long, long ago his present anguish had its first beginnings," he said. "It had waxed and gathered strength, it had matured and concentrated, until it had taken the form of a fearful, frenzied and fantastic question, which tortured his heart and mind, clamoring insistently for an answer."

Raskolnikov held his disheveled head between his hands and shook it tentatively a couple of times.

"I wanted to find out whether I was a louse like everybody else or a man, whether I can step over barriers or not," he whispered portentously, or so he must have imagined.

Jacques could not deny he was impressed by the youth's power to project a whisper across a five hundred-seat hall. Unfortunately, that was the only thing the hall whisperer had going for him. Jacques raised his hand and waved it apathetically, a gesture that was, alas, completely lost on the Raskolnikov wannabe, who now stepped closer to the edge of the stage and looked down at what he must have imagined was the Neva flowing lethargically at his feet. He then granted Jacques another one of his signature portentous whispers.

"As I stood above the Neva this morning at dawn I knew I was a villain."

"Thank you, that will be all for now," Jacques said.

The failing Raskolnikov looked embarrassed. Apparently, he was having difficulty recognizing the exact provenance of Jacques's last sentence, which he took to be a line from Dostoevsky's novel. He hovered, handsome and chiseled like a Greek statue, on the edge of the stage, anxiously searching his brain but failing to make the right connection between the devious mnemonic device he imagined Jacques to be using and the passage from the novel he was expected to recall using Jacques's prompt. When everything else failed—as it certainly did—all he could do was deliver automatically the next random line from the novel to pop in his head.

"Yes, all is in a man's hands and he lets it all slip from cowardice: that's an axiom!" he said. "But I am talking too much. It's because I chatter that I do nothing. Or perhaps, perhaps . . ."

The Raskolnikov candidate furrowed his thick brows, which, Jacques suspected, he had spent an entire morning grooming in what he believed to be Russian 19TH century fashion.

"Perhaps it is because you do nothing that you chatter," Jacques mumbled under his nose. He checked the rest of the names on the audition list. There were four more this afternoon. The young man walked back on stage. Jacques rolled his eyes.

"What is it now?"

The unsuitable Raskolnikov sighed heavily and wrung his hands. Jacques had never imagined he would one day witness an ordinary action performed in such a stylized way that it warranted an equally conspicuous literary description but there was simply no other way to describe the particular twisting movement the Raskolnikov candidate's unsuitable hands executed at this very moment.

"If I could just take another minute of your time. The thing is, I've spent months preparing for this role. It's a work in progress and I know I still have a lot to learn but there are several lines I believe I've nailed down perfectly, even better than the real Raskolnikov would have said them. Of course, I am aware there never was a 'real Raskolnikov'. However, I do know that one of the most popular tourist attractions in St. Petersburg is following Raskolnikov's 'real' murder route."

He froze, shocked by his own garrulousness. Jacques's face was stone.

"I just meant to say that I would not forgive myself if I didn't take this opportunity to deliver my best lines."

Jacques raised his hand, determined not to allow such nonsense, but the unacceptable Raskolnikov's obliviousness to anything around him once he was 'in the zone'—in the Raskolnikov zone that is—was no match for Jacques's notorious tactlessness.

"Why does my action strike them as so horrible? Is it because it was a crime? What is meant by crime? My conscience is at rest. Of course, the letter of the law was broken and blood was shed. Well, then, go ahead and punish me for the letter of the law . . . and that's that!"

"Indeed it is!" Jacques yelled.

Thornton, who was unfortunate enough to be producing the play and to be sitting behind Jacques, leaned forward and placed his hand on Jacques's shoulder.

"Are you alright?"

"I want him out of here," Jacques said through his teeth.

"Why are you so tense? Personally, I find him quite amusing."

Thornton turned to the young man on the stage.

"A very spirited performance! We'll give you a call next week."

The ill-suited Raskolnikov's face lit up and he finally withdrew, light-headed, carried on the wings of false hopes and dramatic cliches.

Jacques closed his eyes. When he opened them Raskolnikov #16 was already on stage.

"Whenever you are ready," Jacques said skeptically, slumping into his chair.

"Good God!" #16 cried out.

Jacques sat up and looked around.

"What?"

"Can it be, can it be that I shall really take an axe, that I shall strike her on the head, split her skull open . . . that I shall tread in the sticky warm blood, break the lock, steal and tremble; hide, all spattered in blood . . . Good God, can it be?"

#16 needed a few seconds to come off of the frenetic high he had worked himself into.

"I was summoned . . . by a notice," he said sadly.

But it was not the fact that #16 evoked the wrong kind of feeling altogether in the police office scene that detracted from his already disappointing performance. Misreading a scene and overacting were not the worst things a stage director had to expect from an actor. There was something far worse than that, something so unbearable that many a stage director had fallen pray to embarrassing rhetorical language to describe the predicament of witnessing an amateur take a studiedly casual approach to dramatically complex, intense scenes in order to prove that he is well versed in the modern minimalistic approach to acting, which dictates that for a scene to produce the most dramatic effect possible one has to strip it of any drama altogether and deliver one's lines super-casually, with a touch of over-familiarity, in a slightly confessional tone of voice. #16 slipped his hands in his pockets and strolled across the stage.

"A gloomy sensation of agonizing, everlasting solitude and remoteness, assumed conscious form in his soul," he muttered to himself. He delivered the lines in the falsely guttural voice of a beatnik who is not at all self-conscious about being on stage, no sir, not at all, and accompanied them with the broad gestures of a cunning Italian who amuses his foreign friends by enacting— ironically—their stereotype of the average Italian as a bit actor in an operetta.

"It was neither the meanness of his sentimental effusions before Ilya Petrovitch," #16 continued, "nor the meanness of the latter's triumph over him that had caused this sudden revulsion in his heart."

At this point #16 had the courage to take a (badly) calculated risk to impress on Jacques and Thornton how comfortable he felt with experimental, interactive approaches to drama. He stepped down from the stage and sauntered down the isle all the way to where Jacques was sitting. He sat down in the seat right in front of Jacques's, turned around half-way, rested his arm on the back of his seat, and delivered the rest of his lines as if he were sharing some tête-à-tête time with an old friend.

"Oh, what had he to do now with his own baseness, with all these petty vanities, officers, German women, debts, police-offices? If he had been sentenced to be burned at that moment, he would not have stirred, would hardly have heard the sentence to the end."

At this point Jacques was supposed to give #16 the next prompt. He leaned forward and carefully removed #16's hand from the back of the seat, as if he was removing the slime off of okra.

"A new overwhelming sensation was gaining more and more mastery over him every moment," Jacques said. "An immeasurable, almost physical, repulsion for everything surrounding him, an obstinate, malignant feeling of hatred."

Jacques's face was now so close to #16's that he could smell the odorless cocktail of sedatives #16 had taken earlier to calm his nerves.

"Everyone he met seemed loathsome to him," Jacques went on. "He loathed their faces, their movements, their gestures. If anyone had addressed him at that moment he felt he might have spat at him or bitten him."

It was around this point that Thornton thought it best to cancel the rest of the auditions and escort Jacques to the bar across the street.

"That was quite the performance back there," Thornton said into his glass of bourbon.

"His or mine?" Jacques grinned.

"Perhaps you should play Raskolnikov yourself," Thornton suggested.

"You know how I feel about actors."

"I do, and I am afraid they do too," Thornton said, still talking into his bourbon.

Jacques signaled to the waiter to bring them another round.

"Perhaps we are looking for Raskolnikov in the wrong place," he said.

★★★

The Head of the Psychiatric Hospital for the Criminally Insane, Monsieur Dumont, pointed to the chair across from him. Jacques sat down.

"Thank you very much for agreeing to see me," he began. "I realize it's not every day you have appointments with people from the culture sector."

Dumont raised an eyebrow.

"The 'culture sector'?"

"You know, people working in the arts and such."

Dumont closed his eyes. His lips were moving, as though he was counting.

"I see," he said without opening his eyes.

"I am sorry, what did you say?" Jacques asked, moving his chair closer to the desk.

Dumont opened his eyes and stared at him.

"I didn't say anything. I was counting."

"Counting what?"

"I was counting to ten," Dumont said curtly. "Usually ten works for me but lately I find I need to count to twenty. But in your case even twenty proved insufficient. Quite, quite insufficient, I am afraid. Or should I rather say 'rather' insufficient? I always get these two confused."

"I do too," Jacques hastened to say, afraid that he might have gotten off on the wrong foot with the man on whose benevolence *Crime and Punishment* now depended.

"Surely representatives of 'the culture sector' are immune to such foolish mistakes," Dumont said sharply.

"I have the feeling you think I offended you."

"You are very perceptive," Dumont said. "I suppose like all your fellow representatives of the 'culture sector'."

Dumont closed his eyes and started moving his lips again. Jacques realized he had to swallow his pride unless he was agreeable to swallowing something else.

"Monsieur Dumont, if there is any way I could reduce the counting time you require to continue this conversation . . ."

Dumont's lips stopped moving.

"Monsieur Schrödinger—a strange name for a Frenchman, n'est pas?—if you keep interrupting me and forcing me to start counting from the beginning I am afraid you will use up the little time allotted to you for this meeting."

Jacques apologized and asked Dumont to continue. Dumont's lips started moving again. This time, however, he didn't close his eyes. He looked Jacques up and down, as though trying to decide if he was even worth the counting. Afraid that he might provoke another counting countdown Jacques waited, using the time to do some counting of his own, though he did it purely recreationally, without any of the vengeful determination that had inspired Dumont's counting. Finally, when Jacques had counted to thirty-six, Dumont crossed his legs and smiled pleasantly.

"I will be honest with you. I find your condescending attitude infuriating, although I am willing to excuse it on this occasion since, as you yourself admitted, you are absolutely ignorant of the day-to-day life in a correctional facility of this kind."

"My condescending attitude?"

"Monsieur, you will be surprised to know—though you really shouldn't be!—that the 'culture sector' as you call it extends well beyond the confines of the theatre stage. Do you assume, Monsieur, that just because our lifestyle here happens to be slightly more . . . regimented . . . we don't feed our souls as well as our bodies, indeed we spoil the former to the neglect of the latter, what with the appalling quality of the food in the prison cafeteria and the constant comings and goings of cooks with questionable credentials. We encourage our tenants . . . our prisoners, to pursue a variety of creative endeavors, not only with a view to distracting themselves from the despicable acts for which they are serving time but mostly because . . . 'man only plays when in the full meaning of the word he is a man, and he is only completely a man when he plays.'"

Jacques stared at Dumont, who appeared deeply satisfied with himself.

"Are you surprised to hear a man such as myself quote Schiller? It might interest you to know that for two years in a row Schiller has topped the list of literary favorites among our tena . . . prisoners. Indeed, just a month ago we had a 'Schiller weekend' filled with readings and theatrical performances."

"This is precisely what I wanted to talk to you about," Jacques said. "As I mentioned in my email this Spring I am directing a play, an adaptation of *Crime and Punishment*. We have already cast all the parts but we've had terrible luck finding ourselves a Raskolnikov. We've seen dozens of talented actors, including some very well established ones, but no one has come even close."

Dumont pulled on his moustache (but not ironically).

"Let me guess: you think they all failed because they were not real criminals."

"When you put it this way it sounds absurd . . . but yes, that's exactly it."

"So you've come down here hoping to catch yourself a real criminal."

"Well, fortunately, for us, you've already taken care of the *catching* part," Jacques grinned. "I am more interested in *identifying* the most suitable criminal . . . actor . . . tenant . . . for the part."

Dumont pulled out the top desk drawer, flipped through several folders, picked one and slid it over the table to Jacques.

"Let's make one thing clear: first and second-degree murderers are off the table."

"That's disappointing," Jacques frowned. "I was really hoping to work with someone who fits the Raskolnikov profile as closely as possible."

"First and second-degree murderers are not necessarily the most hardened criminals. You would be surprised—though you shouldn't be!—to find some of the most wretched human beings among small time crooks and other bit players. Take a look for yourself."

Jacques pulled the folder towards him.

"These are photographs of prisoners serving a sentence in the second sector of our facility," Dumont explained. "Small time crooks, embezzlers, et cetera. The first sector, reserved for first and second-degree murderers, is housed in a separate facility outside town. On a side note, I could also provide some personal recommendations based on each prisoner's individual performance history."

"Performance history?"

"Their participation in various volunteer theatre groups here at our facility. Incidentally, some of them are quite experienced in experimental theatre if this is what you are going for."

Jacques removed some of photographs from the folder and began arranging them on the desk in front of him. Dumont closed his eyes and rocked back and forth in his chair.

"Incidentally," he remarked, "did you know that Nabokov intensely disliked Dostoevsky?"

Jacques looked up from the photographs. Dumont had slipped into an irreversible literary mode. Apparently it could not be helped.

"He says in one interview: 'I dislike intensely *The Karamazov Brothers* and the ghastly *Crime and Punishment* rigmarole.'" If I remember correctly he goes on to say something exactly like this: 'No, I do not object to soul-searching and self-revelation, but in those books the soul, and the sins, and the sentimentality, and the journalese, hardly warrant the tedious and muddled search.' See anything you like?"

Jacques pointed to one of the photographs in the top row.

"You have a good eye, Monsieur Schrödinger. This one has considerable experience playing the antagonist."

Jacques picked up the photograph and inspected it closely.

"Nothing special, right?" Dumont grinned. "That's precisely what makes him the perfect antagonist, don't you think?"

Jacques flipped the photograph. The name and the date the man was admitted to the Institute were written on the back: Bruno Leblon, March 25, 2013.

"What is he here for?" Jacques asked.

"Now that *is* the question, isn't it?" Dumont said with a cryptic smile.

NOTES

[I] Robert Macnish, *The Philosophy of Sleep*. 3rd ed. (Glasgow: W. R. M'Phun, 1830), 44, 47–48. Welcome Library Rare Books Collection.

[II] Kiekegaard, Søren. "Sickness unto Death." *The Essential Kierkegaard*. Eds. Howard V. Hong and Edna H. Hong (Princeton, NJ: Princeton UP, 1995), 350–373. 353 and 356.

[III] Quoted in Michel 71. Michel, Pierre. *Lucidité, désespoir, et écriture*. Société Octave Mirbeau. Presses de l'Université d'Angers: Angers, 2001.

[IV] Comte-Sponville, André. *Vivre: Traité du désespoir et de la béautide*. (Paris : Presses Universitaires de France : 1988), 291–292.

[V] Ibid 285–86.

[VI] Ibid 279, 285.

[VII] Rothman, William, ed. (2005) *Cavell on Film* (Albany, NY: SUNY Press), 131.

[VIII] Stanley Cavell, *The World Viewed* (Cambridge, MA: Harvard UP, 1979), 128.

[IX] Cited in Jonathan Auerbach, "Caught in the Act: Self-consciousness and Self-rehearsal in Early Cinema." *Le Cinématographe, nouvelle technologie du XXe siècle / The Cinema, A New Technology for the 20TH century*, ed. Andre Gaudreault, Catherine Russell, and Pierre Veronneau (Cinéma: Editions Payot Lausanne, 2004), 94.

[X] Ian Jeffrey, *Photography: A Concise History* (New York: Oxford UP, 1981), 10. On the idea of photography as nature's spontaneous reproduction, see Mary Warner Marien, *Photography and Its Critics: A Cultural History, 1839-1900* (Cambridge: Cambridge UP, 1997), 1–21.

[XI] Albert Londe, *La Photographie Moderne* (Cripto 1986 [1888]).

[XII] In "Photography and Fictionality" (*Mediascape*, Winter 2013) Jens Schröter challenges a common assumption among philosophers and photography scholars, what Roger Scruton calls "photography's fictional incompetence." Following Peirce's concept of the index as a sign that signifies by means of causality, the photographic image is essentially understood as a trace of the real objects and processes which were in front of the camera at the moment of exposure. This connection to an actual 'this' which has existed in the past seems to severely limit the possibilities for fictionality in the photographic image, if not to exclude this possibility altogether. In his 1983 essay "Photography and Representation" Scruton writes: "Of course I may take a photograph of a draped nude and call it Venus, but insofar as this can be understood as an exercise in fiction, it should not be thought of as a photographic representation of Venus but rather as the photograph of a representation of Venus. In other words, the process of fictional representation occurs not in the photograph but in the subject: it is the subject which represents Venus; the photograph does no more than disseminate its visual character to other eyes." Setting aside Scruton's problematic equation of "the scene photographed" with "the photograph of the scene," Schröter recognizes that in order to rebut Scruton's argument it is necessary to demonstrate that "understanding a photograph as a photograph means more and/or something different than understanding that it points causally, indexically to a scene." The most significant challenge to Scruton's claim is that put forward by McIver Lopes, who acknowledges that "considering a photograph as a photograph means considering the object"—that is, "considering a photograph only with regard to its formal structure . . . means *not* considering it as a photograph"—but then reminds us that "considering a photograph as a photograph also means taking account of the difference between the photographed object and the object itself, a difference which can reveal to us aspects of the object that we would not be able to perceive in a direct encounter with the object." Because of the irreducible difference between the photographed object and the object itself "no photograph of a fictional scene can guarantee that the scene will be understood as fictional," which suggests, conversely, that no photograph can guarantee that it will be understood as a trace or document (this, Schröter remarks, is evident both in the fact that photographs used in journalism or science require interpretation and in the phenomenon of 'docufiction', i.e. fictional pseudo-documentaries).

What does this mean for photography's alleged "fictional incompetence"? First, what does 'fictional' mean? Schröter derives the notion of "fiction" from film theory, quoting Edward Branigan's account of "fiction," itself derived from Hartley Slater's definition proposed in 1987. Branigan relates fiction to "a specific cognitive process in which, step by step, an initially un-determined reference is augmented." This points to a fundamental problem in the fictional reading of photographs and other static images: "Fictionality typically surfaces in narrative form (including narrative poetry, drama and film); it is not generally employed to define poetry, sculpture or music, and in painting is restricted to specifically narrative representations" (Fludernik qtd. in Schröter). In this context, then, *fiction* presupposes a *process of narration*, which "allows us, step by step, to form, confirm, or reject assumptions about the referential status of the objects presented." Inasmuch as a still image—a photograph—is not extended temporally it is, supposedly, incapable of narrating and, therefore, "fictionally incompetent."

Schröter proposes a way out of this dilemma by reminding us that the question of fictional competence involves a consideration not only of photography as a medium, but also of its signifying processes. Media specific analyses define a medium negatively by defining what definitely cannot be done with it (e.g. a photograph is not suitable for receiving radio programs), which leaves the kinds of semiotic processes that can be produced with a given medium *undetermined*. In some cases, e.g. in the case of staged photography—Cindy Sherman's *Untitled Film Stills*—the possible semioses can *contradict* the limitation thought to be deducible from the medium's specific qualities. Indeed, argues Schröter, inasmuch as staged photography foregrounds *this tension between medium and semiosis*, it constitutes a better example for an aesthetic of photography than the type of photography that merely displays its indexical relationship to the world.

Bruno would object, however, that all photography—not only staged photography—exhibits the tension between medium and sign, i.e. straight photography—photography that displays its indexical relationship to the world—also possesses narrative, and thus fictional, competence. Barthes already hinted at this when he drew a distinction between the photograph's punctum (the indexical aspect of the photograph) and its studium (the horizon of cultural, historical, philosophical and social meanings we glean from any photograph). Narrativity does not necessarily involve the unfolding of an event over a succession of images (cinema); rather, it appears in any form that functions through the organization of the visible into the saybale (to use Jacques Ranciere's terms). Photography's wealth of incidental details demands a reading that involves the translation of the involuntary, the incidental, the wealth of details recorded mechanically, into language. As David Campany puts it in *Art and Photography*, "there are strong parallels between photography's emphasis on incidental details and the involuntary memory fragments that are the raw material of psychoanalysis. It is a matter of putting the parts together and inserting them into language" (21). The transformation of the visible into the sayable, of presence into language, does not require a special act of interpretation: *the photograph's indexicality, in fact, guarantees it*. This is why for Barthes, "indexicality could be more powerful, subversive even, than any creativity or artiness of construction. The photograph's forte was its authorless, *mechanical quality that turns the existing world into a sign itself*, not a sign of the creative ego. In this sense its power resides in the very traits that make it independent of art, independent of authorship" (23).

To reiterate, "fictional competence" is understood as "narrational competence," where 'fiction' and 'narration' presuppose "specific cognitive process in which, step by step, an initially undetermined reference is augmented." The indeterminacy of the reference is a necessary condition for "fictional competence." This idea is not entirely new. Kracauer attributed the "redemptive potential" of cinema precisely to the indeterminacy of the cinematic reference. In *Theory of Film: The Redemption of Physical Reality* Siegfried he argued that film has "affinities with such aspects of the natural world as 'unstaged reality,' 'chance,' 'the for-tuitous,' 'the indeterminate,' 'the flow of life' and 'endlessness'" (173). The fundamental quality that camera-reality shares with physical reality, the essential quality that embodies and guarantees cinema's redeeming potential, is *indeterminacy*. Indeterminacy pertains to the ontology of the photographic image, referring to the perceptual inexhaustibility or illegibility of the image irreducible to signification or verbal summary. Thanks to the homology between the indeterminate, transient, and undramatic nature of the Lebenswelt and the equally indeterminate nature of the film image (298), film can *redeem* the Lebenswelt from its repression by the objectifying discourses of modern science.

From this follow some paradoxical consequences about fictional competence. An image possesses "fictional competence"—it can tell a story—only if its initial reference is un-determined, which triggers the cognitive process of "augmenting" the reference and evaluating its referential status. Conversely, the more determined the initial reference, the more fictionally incompetent the image: by this logic *the staged photograph has the lowest degree of fictional competence.*

XIII J. C. Lavater, *Physiognomy, or the Corresponding Analogy between the Conformation of the Features and the Ruling Passions of the Soul* (London: T. Tegg, 1775), 301. Welcome Library Rare Books Collection.

XIV Benjamin Rush. M.D., *Medical Inquiries and Observations upon the Diseases of the Mind* (New York: Hafner Publishing Company, 1962) (1812), 310, 301. Welcome Library Collection.

XV Jean Etienne Dominique Esquirol, *Mental Maladies: A Treatise on Insanity* (New York and London: Hafner Publishing Company, 1965) (1845), 21, 23, 28. Welcome Library Collection.

XVI Max Nordau, *Degeneration* (London: Heinemann, 1920) (1892), 47–49, 50, 51. Welcome Library Collection.

XVII Josef Breuer and Sigmund Freud, "The Case of Fraulein Anna O.," *1900: A Fin de siècle Reader*, ed. Mike Jay and Michael Neve (London: Penguin Books, 1999), 142, 141–144.

ACKNOWLEDGEMENTS

I am thankful for the support and help of my family, my friends in Berlin and Toronto, and my fellow writers in the Fiction Workshops taught by Victoria Gosling of The Reader Berlin.